THE DEAD YEARS

THE DEAD YEARS

Jeffrey B. Burton

SEVERN
HOUSE

First world edition published in Great Britain and the USA in 2024
by Severn House, an imprint of Canongate Books Ltd,
14 High Street, Edinburgh EH1 1TE.

Trade paperback edition first published in Great Britain and the USA in 2024
by Severn House, an imprint of Canongate Books Ltd.

severnhouse.com

British Library Cataloguing-in-Publication Data
A CIP catalogue record for this title is available from the British Library.

ISBN-13: 978-1-4483-1241-2 (cased)
ISBN-13: 978-1-4483-1459-1 (trade paper)
ISBN-13: 978-1-4483-1240-5 (e-book)

Typeset by Palimpsest Book Production Ltd.,
Falkirk, Stirlingshire, Scotland.

Praise for Jeffrey B. Burton

About the author

Novels in **Jeffrey B. Burton**'s critically-acclaimed Mace Reid K-9 mystery series include *The Finders*, *The Keepers*, and *The Lost*. His Agent Drew Cady thrillers include *The Chessman*, *The Lynchpin*, and *The Eulogist*. Jeff lives in St. Paul, Minnesota, with his wife, Cindy, an irate Pomeranian named Lucy, and a happy galoot of a Beagle named Milo.

https://jeffreybburton.com/index.html

For my father, Bruce W. Burton –
You are so missed

ACKNOWLEDGEMENTS

First, super-sized kudos to the team at Severn House – from Assistant Editor Extraordinaire Tina Pietron to Copy Editor Penelope Isaac to Acting Editorial Director Rachel Slatter to Senior Brand Manager Martin Brown. Second, a special shout-out to Jem Butcher (of Jem Butcher Design) for the terrific cover art. You are all gifted, talented beyond belief, and an absolute joy to work with. Also, my wife, Cindy, who moonlights as my photographer, Beta Reader, and biggest fan. Finally, my father, Bruce W. Burton, who has been my sounding board and editor going back to my short story days. Dad passed away unexpectedly last year, but, being the workaholic he's always been, not before he finished editing the first draft of *The Dead Years*. Dad thought it was my best work yet . . . who am I to disagree?

You think dogs will not be in heaven? I tell you, they will be there long before any of us.

Robert Louis Stevenson

PART ONE
The Talent

The greatest pleasure of a dog is that you may make a fool of yourself with him, and not only will he not scold you, but he will make a fool of himself, too.

Samuel Butler

ONE

*I*t was the same dream.

The same damned dream I've been having for nearly six years now, ever since I was a junior in high school, ever since I was seventeen years old.

Ever since my parents died.

I'm in the car with them, sitting in the backseat – though somehow I'm belted into the center spot where, with just four of us in the family, I'd never sat before. In the dream it's as though I'm five or six instead of an adolescent. I'm staring straight ahead, through the car's windshield, as if I were at a drive-in theater, and watching as the freezing sleet slaps down upon the hood of the vehicle. I watch as we come into a curve, as Dad struggles with the steering wheel, as Mom clings to the Jesus handle above her side window.

I watch as we slide across several lanes of traffic as though we're on an ice-skating rink.

I watch as blinding headlights bear down upon us.

Then I wake in a cold sweat, my hands trembling, and Alice is on my chest, licking at my face as though I were a Popsicle, and then there's a second commotion. My cell phone is vibrating on the bedside table.

'Hello,' I managed to mumble, more unconscious than awake.

'Get out of bed, dead-butt.'

'I worked last night.'

'I heard you come in at ten,' my sister replied. 'I bet you were up all night with that VR headset of yours.'

She did have a point. 'What time is it?'

'It's time for you to get your ass out of bed, let the dogs tinkle, and jump in the pickup,' Crystal said. 'I'm texting you an address and you need to get there yesterday.'

'An asphalt trail leads off the back alley and winds through the woods until it hits Parkview Park.'

'Parks and rec went all out naming that one, huh?' I said. 'Parkview Park?'

The Chicago Police Department officer ignored my quip. 'We need the dogs in the woods. The guy's not been seen in five days. His ex-wife told us he runs the trail first thing in the morning and right before he eats at night, said she could set her watch by that.'

'You think he cut through the woods?' I asked, wondering if an avid jogger would risk an ankle injury on unequal terrain.

The officer shrugged. 'We're just checking all boxes because no one knows where the hell the guy went.'

Assignment received, my bloodhound, Alice, and my springer spaniel, Rex, and I began cutting through the home's backyard when the officer called to me: 'Hey.'

I turned back.

'Are you related to Detective Pratt?'

I nodded. 'She's my sister.'

Once past the backyard, we headed down the alley in search of the intersecting blacktop that wound its way through acres of woodland and underbrush on its journey to Parkview Park.

I knew why the officer had asked me if I was related to my detective sibling. My name's Cory Pratt, I go by Cor, and I'm the CEO and president, treasurer and secretary, sole proprietor and all-around gopher at the COR Canine Training Academy – using *academy* instead of school reels in the clientele – and run classes throughout more than a few of the Windy City's suburbs. Wherever I can fill a warehouse or gymnasium or other facility – I've done barns – to host a series of obedience classes for new pet owners and their puppies, I'll be there. And if you are in need of private lessons for your new best friend, just give me a call . . . at least through the end of the year.

In January, I'm heading back to school. Community college – Harper Community College. I'm not sure where my focus will lie – maybe IT, maybe computer science – but at least Harper's campus is in Palatine, a mere fifteen minutes from Casa-de-Pratt in Buffalo Grove.

I read somewhere that less than fifty percent of businesses succeed past their first five years, and, at age twenty-three, it looks like I'll be joining that statistic. In my case, though, I'm the one pulling the plug. Don't get me wrong – I love dogs, deeply, it's in my DNA, my bone marrow. My father was a veterinarian and the proud owner of Pratt Pet Clinic, also in Buffalo Grove, where I'd been doing odd jobs – cleaning cages, wiping down exam rooms, mowing the clinic's lawn if I promised not to let Mom know – since I was eight. Dad told my eight-year-old self he was grooming me so I could someday take over the family business, but Crystal spilled the beans a couple years later, informing me that by the time she hit fourteen she'd started rebelling against always having to babysit her *snot-nosed brat* of a kid brother, and my parents found themselves in need of an alternate place to stash me.

Dad's the one who got me into training canines at age ten, starting with our brood at home and then reaching out to work with friends' and neighbors' pets. It was a blast and, eventually, Dad started offering the occasional obedience class, which often took place afterhours in the clinic's parking lot. At first, Dad did most of the talking – introductions to the differing exercises – as I roamed amongst the attendees offering up tips and tricks and best practices as well as awarding treats whenever a puppy successfully performed a task. But a few years before the night that changed my life forever, Dad began wandering amongst the pupils, tendering the occasional snack for good behavior, while allowing me to lead the training sessions.

Turned out my father was grooming me for something after all.

Cheap help trumped nepotism and Dad had Mom – a certified public accountant – doing both the clinic's bookkeeping and taxes. Crystal was the only one who went unscathed. She was too busy getting A's in every class as she never let any of us forget.

Anyway, COR Canine Training Academy wasn't going bankrupt or anything like that. We were almost twenty-five grand *in the black* last year and very likely to hit that lofty mark again this year. Yup, I'm a regular Rockefeller. If training dogs was all there were to it, I'd be happy as hell, but the endless Charlie Hustle involved – booking facilities, hauling gear all over Chicago in Dad's decades-old Chevy Silverado, working the phones, doing the paperwork, dealing with deadbeats, rinse, repeat – triggered a young-life crisis.

A few years back Crystal nudged me into taking on a crazy little side gig. She's also lived up to her word and, with her connections, has promoted the hell out of it. I work with search-and-rescue dogs. More specifically, I specialize in human remains detection; that is,

I train dogs to hunt for the dead. I train HRD dogs or, heck, let's stop beating around the bush, I train cadaver dogs. My pack and I help law enforcement – CPD, other local PDs, various sheriff departments – hunt for any lost souls that have gone missing and are presumed dead, much like what Alice and Rex and I will be doing in the woods surrounding Parkview Park today.

My sister-tormentor – Detective Crystal Pratt is an investigator in the Violent Crimes Section inside the Area 3 Detective Division. She'd caught wind of a missing person's case in which HRD dogs were required and tossed the job my way. Some poor sap named Tim Gorski had been missing for either three work days or five full days, since no one, not even his mother, ex-wife – but why would she? – or neighbors had seen hide nor hair of him since he'd left work last Friday. Colleagues at Gorski's job had gotten concerned as he'd not scheduled time off and hadn't been returning their calls or texts or emails. Evidently, Gorski's boss had gotten in contact with Gorski's mother who, in fact, did have an extra key to his home. Gorski's boss then met the mother at her son's brick bungalow in South Edgebrook, a neighborhood on Chicago's Northwest Side, only to find said bungalow empty. However, Gorski's well-worn Honda Civic, the man's only vehicle, sat idly in his single-car garage.

Gorski's mother reported she'd last spoken to her son on Thursday evening, six days ago, and that nothing was mentioned about Gorski taking any trips in his immediate future. Rather they chatted about how crazy-busy his work had become. Ma Gorski also swore her son detested public transportation, would rather drive his Civic in downtown Chicago rush hour than jump on a train or bus. Evidently, she'd gotten panicky when she spotted his car sitting in the garage.

The police were called, a report was filed, Crystal heard they might need cadaver dogs to search the wooded area near Gorski's property, gave me the heads-up and texted me the address in South Edgebrook, and now me and Alice and Rex were hiking a winding stretch of asphalt that eventually dead-ends at the neighborhood park. It was quarter past one in the afternoon. I had an obedience class in Archer Heights at five – plenty of time to rip apart this little stretch of woodland. I figured it'd be a quick exercise in futility, another false alarm, like most of the searches we're called in to perform, and wondered if this Tim Gorski fellow had a drinking problem. If so, perhaps he was tying one on, up in the thousand-and-one barrooms of Milwaukee.

So imagine my surprise when noses and tails popped up, then the dogs converged as one, Alice ahead by a whisker, as they darted off the blacktop and down into the underbrush. I trotted along after them, needing to keep my team in sight less they get too far ahead and disappear into the thicket. I stepped off the trail, cut diagonally down a minor incline, and hustled around shrubs and fallen branches. With Halloween a week away, the ground was a carpet of fallen leaves. It took me all of ten seconds to catch up, and there they were. The two sat as though sharing a park bench, staring down at their discovery, each patting gently on the terra firma with a front paw.

I followed their line of vision to the forest floor, flinched, and took a step backward. The blood was a river of black ink on the leaves and muck. Lots of it, as though a butcher decided to *screw the slaughterhouse* and gut porky out here in the woods instead.

I glanced back toward the asphalt trail, realized I couldn't spot the blacktop from this crevasse, this dimple in the terrain, which meant any passersby out for a casual stroll would not have been able to witness whatever butchery had occurred. One thing I knew for certain, considering the amount of blood-loss: whomever this was done to did not leave the woods surrounding Parkview Park – or anyplace else ever again – of their own volition.

The dogs watched as I scanned the immediate area. There was a part in the sea of red, green, yellow and orange leaves, heading west, deeper into the thickets, along with a smear of dirt and dark blood on the forest floor. You didn't have to be Einstein to see what had occurred. Something or someone had been dragged from the crime scene. And I put the odds on it being an errant hog at slightly below zero.

I looked at my dogs and said, 'Go.'

'You at the guy's house, Cor?' Crystal asked upon answering her cell phone.

'A few steps beyond that,' I said. 'The pups found Gorski.'

'Which means he's dead?'

'Yeah. I don't know if he got mugged or something, but there's a patch of blood about twenty yards off the park trail.' I heard activity on the other end of the line and figured Crystal was flipping open the pocket notebook she kept with her at all times. 'And I'm talking a shit-ton of blood, much more than a nosebleed.'

'So Gorski got stabbed to death?'

'He had to have been killed by the trail, but – and this is weird – the guy then got dragged another hundred yards and parked under a pine tree.'

I was down on my knees, twenty-something feet off to the side, and staring at the body my dogs had sniffed out. Even at this distance, I caught wind of decomposing human flesh – an odor you never forget. Though temps had gotten down into the mid-thirties at night, the days remained sunny and pushed sixty. Now I'm no medical examiner, but I'd lay money the poor guy met his fate closer to the five-day-ago mark than three. Gorski was dressed in sweatpants and a sweatshirt. One of his running shoes was missing, likely slipped off somewhere along the hundred-yard trek to the pine tree. Fortunately, all I could make of Gorski's face was a colorless cheek peeking out from under a stretched hood.

'His hoodie is all yanked out of shape,' I said. 'I think the killer used it to drag him here.' Then I followed his sweatshirt down to an exposed and pallid wrist. 'Jesus, Crys, don't expect the most appetizing of scenes.'

'You've notified the officer at Gorski's house, right?'

'Yeah, he got all excited,' I said. 'He's calling it in and grabbing his partner. I'm meeting them at the trail in five but figured I'd let you know what's coming your way.'

TWO

'Gorski was a voice-over actor,' Crystal said as I worked the griddle, flipping pancakes. Several days had passed. It was Saturday morning, and we'd both met on the main level for breakfast. 'The guy did a bunch of radio and TV commercials, promo videos for tradeshows, documentaries, and was working on an audiobook when he didn't show up at the studio.'

I looked up. 'Anything I'd know him from?'

'A commercial for Subaru, and those penguin spots for Miller Lite.'

'The penguin ads?'

Crystal nodded.

'Those are great.' A CGI penguin buys beer for everyone in a bar, but when the waitress hands him the bill, he pats at his pockets for his wallet with his flippers or fins or whatever and then gets a startled look on his face. It ends with the narrator saying, 'Perhaps you left it in your other tuxedo.' The next spot has the penguin buying the beer with a credit card, but then he's unable to sign his name with his flippers or fins. The most recent commercial finds the penguin fumbling about trying to pay his bar tab by making an ATM work. 'I love those ads.'

'Somehow I knew you would,' Crystal said as I set the plates down and waved Rex away from the table.

When our parents passed away, life insurance and the sale of Dad's veterinary clinic allowed us to pay off the two-story we'd both grown up in. Crystal moved back home – she'd completed her bachelor's degree in Criminal Justice at the University of Illinois and was well into her second year as a police officer – so I could finish high school in Buffalo Grove as opposed to attending some school in Minneapolis, where Mom's parents hailed from, or, worse yet, someplace in Sioux Falls, South Dakota, where Dad's parents lived.

Shortly after Crystal arrived back home, she took ownership of the top floor, which was fine by me as I'd already migrated to the basement – Cor's little bachelor pad, Dad had called it – once she'd left for UIC. I think I've been upstairs all of three times in the past year, mostly to help Crystal lug furniture about in her never-ending quest to remodel her old bedroom.

Whenever our schedules allow, such as today, we'll meet in the middle to share a meal.

I spurted a half-cup of syrup on to my pancakes. 'Anyone pissed off at Gorski?'

'His colleagues say he was a nice guy, well-liked, loved his work – first one there, last to leave; brought in donuts all the time,' Crystal said. 'The audiobook people feel terrible. They couldn't have known what happened to him, but some of the messages on his answering machine weren't very nice. The producer called him a *thimblewit* and threatened to sue his ass if he didn't show up.'

'Probably can't do much with an audiobook without the narrator guy.'

I've told you about my training academy. Now let me tell you about my partners in crime. Alice is my six-year-old bloodhound. With black and tan fur, she's eighty pounds of equal parts affection and protectiveness. I named her Alice for my mother's middle name, which comes from a great-aunt my mom had whom I never met; she lived out on the west coast and passed away not long after my parents died. Rex, my four-year-old springer spaniel, is named after my father's middle name, which I don't believe was based on any relative, dead or alive.

Alice and Rex or Rex and Alice – no matter how you slice it, they sound like an old-fashioned couple from the 1950s.

Alice saved my life. Or perhaps I should say she reeled me back into the land of the living. After our parents' funeral – Dad died at the scene, Mom in the ambulance on the way to the hospital – I barely left my lower-level hideaway. Already a skinny runt at seventeen, I shed more weight. I didn't eat, responded in single syllables to any requests from Crystal or my grandparents, and slept maybe all of an hour a night.

Guilt tends to do that to you.

Then, one morning, the door to my basement mausoleum opened and in squirmed this eight-week-old bloodhound puppy. She squiggled up to my bed and began licking at a hand that hung over the side. Crystal stood in the doorframe. I looked at her with annoyance and said, 'What's this bullshit?'

'Rocko's getting up in age,' Crystal replied, referring to our fourteen-year-old Australian shepherd who'd recently lost his eyesight. 'This place has always been alive and hopping with our fur babies . . . Mom and Dad may be gone, but we're not about to give that up.'

I pretty much hated Crystal for saying that; however, as the days passed slowly – as I intentionally ignored the yet-to-be-named bloodhound puppy – a strange thing occurred. Though I'd not adopted Alice, she'd fully adopted me. The basement became her hangout, coming in to check on me every five minutes her daily routine. She'd sleep on the carpet near the bed, and – one day – she went to the sliding glass door and whined. Crystal had been working with her on bathroom etiquette, but as I lay on my bed, ignoring her – ignoring life – I heard her whimper . . . and I knew what my neglect had made the poor kid do.

I walked over to the sliding glass door, saw the wet spot on the carpeting, knelt down, and said, 'That one's on me, little girl.' I shook her paw for the first time. 'And I'm sorry.'

After that, I began feeding Alice, taking her outside to do her business, taking her for walks, petting her as she sat on my lap, and, eventually, training her on basic commands.

Since then, we've been as thick as thieves.

Alice is a brilliant sniffer dog; I've never met one better. Certain canine breeds, like bloodhounds, have three hundred million scent receptors in their nasal cavity, whereas mere humans have only five million, and this massive amount of scent receptors allows them to decipher thousands of different odors. And, *voilà*, sniffer dogs are able to discover survivors after a natural disaster, or locate illicit drugs, or find explosive materials . . . or lead a dog handler like myself to human remains.

You've got to be quick around Alice, able to zig and zag, lest you get nailed full-on with a wet, slobbering kiss, the kind only bloodhounds can provide.

I picked up Rex a few months after Rocko had gotten so old he could barely move, and he finally just lay on the kitchen floor. Me and Crystal brought Rocko out to the backyard – his kingdom – and sat by him in the sun a long hour before bringing him to my father's old clinic to have him put down. Rocko had let us know it was time weeks earlier, but neither Crystal nor I were ready. We loved the Rock, and we saw his death as yet another link to Mom and Dad severed. As I sat there in the afternoon sun, patting Rocko's forehead and telling him how he'd always been a good boy – always – I wished for the millionth time that our best friends could have life-spans at least as long as horses.

But Rex is a good boy, too, as long as you don't mess with his knotted sock. When the knotted sock comes into play, I call him T-Rex. He's chocolate with white, has floppy ears, of course, and a moderately long coat. Rex is no slacker, either – the little guy's forty-five pounds of continual motion. And, though he's not quite at Alice's level in the human remains detection department, he has his moments, and the three of us can cover a chunk of ground in no time flat.

Yes, Alice is my A student. Rex, on the other hand, gets mostly B's and C's, much like my high school GPA before Mom and Dad passed away, before my grades cratered, before I slinked through graduation by the hair of my chinny chin chin.

But whatever Rex lacks in gray matter, he triples in enthusiasm.

I finished chewing on a pancake and said, 'Maybe Gorski put up some kind of fight and the mugger went apeshit on him?'

'Gorski wasn't mugged.'

I stared at Crystal and waited.

'There are shoe prints in the dirt on the other side of the trail where we believe the perp waited in ambush. And there's a deep toe print from where the perp pushed off and lunged at Gorski.'

'You got shoe print people, right?'

Crystal shrugged. 'Probably tennis shoes, probably men's size ten.' She looked at me and continued, 'The perp jabbed Gorski with some kind of military-grade fixed blade, right in the abdomen, knocking Gorski's air out so he couldn't scream, and then used the knife handle and his own momentum to steer Gorski off the trail and down into that little gully behind the trees where no one could spot them.' Crystal pushed her half-eaten plate of pancakes aside. 'You were right, Cory. It was there he cut Gorski's throat; more specifically his jugular vein as well as his larynx, which is his vocal box, or his voice box, with that Rambo knife of his.'

I pushed my empty plate to the side, too. 'No blood on the actual trail to indicate the perp got pissed off there because Gorski had no money on him.'

Crystal nodded. 'Gorski's wallet had been left on his dresser back at the house. Apparently he never took it with him when he jogged the nearby trail.' She added, 'There couldn't have been a more perfect place for an ambush, especially if your prey is someone who runs that pathway twice a day. The kill-spot had to take some planning or advance recon, same with the spot where he dragged Gorski's body. You know, under the pine tree.'

'Yeah, what mugger's going to drag a body the length of a football field?' I thought for a second, and then asked, 'If it wasn't a robbery, what the hell was it?'

'Maybe a thrill killing, maybe something else.'

'Why'd your perp drag him all that way?'

Crystal shrugged again. 'I don't think he wanted Gorski found anytime soon.'

'Who'd kill a voice-over guy that always brought donuts?'

Crystal shrugged a final time.

OK . . . yup . . . my sister's a cop. A police officer by her twenty-first birthday and a homicide detective before she's even turned thirty.

I couldn't be more proud of her.

Crystal's always been a go-getter, an A-student whose report cards my parents could juxtapose against my B-minus GPA. Once upon a time, I was jealous, but her go-getter-ness has landed me and my HRD dog side-gig many an opportunity with the Chicago Police Department. I'm one of CPD's go-to guys should some poor soul go missing.

I should probably pay Crystal a commission, and don't think she hasn't brought this up.

Crystal is nearly five-eleven to my nearly six feet in height, but any pair of her high heels makes that point null and void. My sister has an athlete's build, whereas I tend to maintain a wiry, stringbean-like physique. Don't worry, though, I'm not in Ichabod Crane territory. I've got old Ichabod beat by a pound or two. My sister and I both have the same dark brown hair; though Crystal keeps hers shoulder-length, with alternating styles, while mine is close-cropped.

Crystal loves her work as an investigator inside the Area 3 Detective Division, especially since her partner, a backstabber of a man named Mike Heppner, has been effectively neutered. We'd have called a guy like Heppner a poopy-diaper throughout our initial years of elementary school; by junior high, we'd have dubbed him an asshole and been done with it; but, with the grace and wisdom attained in senior high, he'd be known as a dick.

Crystal's promotion to detective had ruffled Heppner's feathers, leaving my sister with a partner who'd been openly condescending, vindictive, and actively rooting for her failure.

Not the most carefree of work environments.

But – and I could have warned Heppner – Crystal doesn't take a lot of shit. Believe me, I've chucked a fair amount her way. I wasn't the only one who lost their parents six years ago. Crystal did, too – she was only twenty-three at the time, the same age I am now – and in mourning herself, yet she had to deal with a broke and busted sibling while stepping into a quasi-parental role. Yes, I could have warned Heppner not to push her, but I doubt he would have listened.

Crystal didn't go running to the captain or lieutenant or whatever. No, she'd pushed back. Hard. And, as bullies have done since time immemorial, Mike Heppner backed the hell off.

'He's still a snake, though,' Crystal summed it up over beers the other night, 'and I need to watch him all the more.'

I sat while Crystal rinsed the dishes – hey, I made breakfast – and placed them in the dishwasher. Even though the food had been put away, Rex edged back into the kitchen and stared up at me. Alice watched from across the room just in case Rex's pleading eyes sent me running for the treat bin. But for now, I wasn't about to make a move. It was Saturday morning; I was relaxed, unperturbed, stuffed full of pancakes, and it took several seconds to realize my cell phone was vibrating on the kitchen table.

'Hello,' I said into my iPhone and listened for a spell. 'Really?' I stood up and listened some more. 'Yeah, dirt's no problem. Text me the address and we'll head out now,' I said, ending the call.

Crystal caught my eye. 'What's up?'

'Another missing person.'

THREE

'He is wife says he spends all his free time out here,' the police officer said as he led the way.

Nothing as I parked outside the Park Ridge address texted me by CPD – an olive-colored farmhouse on a dead-end street – primed me for what the homeowners had done with their backyard. As Crystal, who'd tagged along for the ride, and Alice and Rex and I trailed the officer around the side of the house and through the back gate, I thought we'd accidentally wandered into the Garfield Park Conservatory.

I do not have a green thumb. Plants and flowers gifted to me tend not to have lengthy lifespans and, if they could, would probably sue under Article 3 of the Geneva Convention for mistreatment. Their backyard was a solid acre of multi-tiered garden beds with landscaping blocks of orange and red separating endless levels of flora and shrubbery, plants and vegetation – wave after wave of perennials. My mother would be in her element here, able to point at the various sections and mumble terms like *wild quinine* or *garden phlox*, *oakleaf hydrangea* or *butterfly weed*.

The officer continued his briefing. 'His wife got home from visiting her parents in Scottsdale last night. Her husband was supposed to pick her up at O'Hare, but he didn't show or answer his phone, so she grabbed a cab instead.'

We passed a wheelbarrow loaded with pruners and hand trowels, a few pairs of gloves, a metal bow rake, and one of those cultivators used to loosen topsoil. Next in line lay a pile of burlap bags followed by several stacks of cones, which would be used to slip over plants or bushes. Leaning against the first tier of blocks were a dozen bags of black mulch. Whatever master gardener lived at this address must have winterization in mind. I could practically hear my mother preaching the virtues of cleaning out weeds and dead leaves, diseased or bug-infested plants, as well as cutting back on perennials before the first snow flies.

As for me, I get worn out just looking at gardening tools.

'She said she wasn't happy with him, figured he was in his studio or out farting around back here, so she went straight to bed.' The cop added, 'But when she woke at two in the morning and he wasn't there, she went looking for him.'

Though I'd run Alice and Rex along the bottom tier of garden beds to see if they alerted to any scent, the real reason our presence had been requested lay tucked away at the furthest edge of the property, hidden behind a line of trees as though it were an afterthought, certainly not part and parcel of the botanical garden they had going with the multi-level plots. The real reason Alice and Rex and I were here was due to a fifteen-by-fifteen compost heap with both a shovel and a garden spade sticking upright in the soil on the far corner.

'Her husband wasn't in his office or nodding off on a couch as I guess he sometimes does. Even though both cars were in the garage, he was nowhere to be found. That's when she called 911.'

I remembered what I'd been told on the phone and said, 'The back door was unlocked, right?'

'Yeah, the sliding glass door on the lower level had been left unlocked and, what scared his wife even more was that her husband's tools and those shovels,' the officer said, motioning toward the compost heap, 'were left outside. She says he's got OCD and puts every last tool, including the wheelbarrow, away in the shed whenever he's done for the day.' I noted the toolshed, also sheltered by the line of trees, was a stone's throw from the compost heap. 'She said a speck of rust on any of his tools will drive him nuts.'

Somewhere around the time Alice and Rex dismissed the compost heap as a burial lot for the missing homeowner, Crystal disappeared. I figured she'd ducked inside to chat with the police officers or any detectives at the scene, possibly even speak with the frightened spouse. I had been walking the dogs along each of the tiered garden beds. Several of these plots were a complete waste of time; that is, unless the potential killer relished clawing away at a tangle of roots with a pickaxe for half a day before burying the homeowner in the loosened soil. We were walking the top tier nearest the house when I spotted Crystal rushing up the sandstone steps from the lower yard. Something was up. I left the dogs to complete their work and cut across a string of block wall caps to meet her.

'Cor, it turns out Casey Oselka is a documentary filmmaker.' Oselka was the name of the missing homeowner, husband, and master gardener the dogs were currently searching for in his tiered garden plots. Crystal then added, 'And he's had Tim Gorski narrate at least three of his documentaries.'

'You're kidding?'

'I did a Google search and then surfed IMDb. They did several projects together, probably more, but I stopped searching once I made the connection. Oselka produced and directed, and he used Gorski to narrate.'

I weighed that a second. 'This cop I know once told me she doesn't believe in coincidences.'

'I still don't.'

'Then maybe this turns out to solve itself. Oselka killed Gorski for whatever reason – personal or professional – and now he's on the lam.'

Alice and Rex joined us at the top of the steps. I had no idea where in hell Casey Oselka was, but I knew the guy wasn't buried anywhere in his own backyard. I was about to expand on my thesis, but a thick-set woman in black jeans and a light red sweater hustled across the deck, a look of concern across her features.

'Did you find anything?' The woman I took as Mrs Oselka called out as she headed our way.

'No ma'am,' I said. 'We didn't find a thing.'

She looked to be in her early fifties, her eyes were red – there'd been tears – and she choked back a sob. 'I've called half a dozen hospitals, the nearest ones. It wouldn't make sense to take an ambulance fifty miles away.'

'Yeah,' Crystal agreed. 'Smart move.'

We stood in awkward silence a beat as Mrs Oselka stared down at Alice and Rex. Then she said, 'Would your dogs like a treat?'

'These two goofballs?' I said, figuring it'd be a nice distraction for the poor woman. 'They'd love a treat.'

The kitchen had that gourmet thing going, hanging pots and pans, a double-oven, eight burners on the island – someone did some serious cooking here. If the backyard was Mr Oselka's domain, I suspected the kitchen belonged to his wife. She currently riffled a hand into a stoneware cookie jar.

'Our son has a dachshund named Freddie, so we keep some snacks on hand for whenever he comes to town.' I recognized the Greenies Mrs Oselka pulled from the jar. They were dental treats, but my dogs would snarf them down all the same. Alice and Rex are the opposite of finicky eaters.

'Where does your son live?' Crystal asked, keeping the conversation light and breezy.

'Los Angeles,' Mrs Oselka replied, handing Greenies to each of the pups. 'My son does a ton of work for trade shows, putting booths together. It can be really involved, like sets for a Broadway musical. But he loves it.'

'Did he get that from you and your husband?'

'Sort of. He'd help us set up backgrounds for our shoots, and he's got my husband's eye for—' Mrs Oselka choked up again and took a second. 'Well, you've seen what he's done with the backyard.'

Crystal went on to ask innocuous questions about filming

documentaries. Evidently, we were standing at ground zero of Oselka Productions, Inc., the couple's filmmaking company. Her husband had a small office upstairs where, between phone calls, he labored over scripts. They also had a soundproofed studio on the lower level, which contained their audiovisual equipment as well as a green screen backdrop for when they did interviews. Per Mrs Oselka, she was her husband's girl Friday, working as his personal secretary, accountant, editor, and makeup artist, as well as a dozen other administrative tasks.

'I noticed you've got an ADT security sign out front.' Crystal segued into a less innocuous topic.

Mrs Oselka cringed. 'A house down the block was under foreclosure a decade back. No one was living there at the time, so Casey grabbed the sign and stuck it in our yard.'

I had to smile. I'd wondered how many homeowners have signs but no security system.

'So there's no ADT, no cameras set up?'

Mrs Oselka shook her head. 'I work here most of the time, and when Casey's not on a shoot, he works here, too.'

At that moment, the detective assigned to the case, a tall African American and the man Crystal had chatted with as she searched the Internet, stepped up from the lower level with a cell phone glued to his ear, spotted us, and stepped into the living room, talking in hushed tones. He'd been triple-checking all rooms and closets.

I glanced over at my dogs. Both had been sitting on the tile in the kitchen's entryway, well behaved, of course, and any sign of their Greenies long gone. But now Alice's nose was in the air as she stared toward the stairwell detective hushed-tones had just stepped out from.

Alice was air scenting, and a second later Rex followed suit.

'Seriously?' I said, and then realized I'd said it out loud.

'What?' Mrs Oselka asked.

Alice stood and stepped toward the stairwell, then stopped and glanced my way. Rex stood and stared my way from his spot on the kitchen floor.

Mrs Oselka had followed my gaze to the dogs. 'What are they doing?'

One of the benefits of my job, thank God, is that I never have to deal with family members. I was at a loss for how best to respond to the concerned spouse, so I settled in on a white lie. 'This time of year, field mice start looking for ways to come inside – they might have caught a whiff.'

She looked confused. 'We've never had a problem.'

'Do you mind if I run them downstairs?'

I saw the look of apprehension return to her face, but she replied, 'Be my guest.'

I mouthed, 'Go' and my dogs took off down the staircase, Alice in the lead, Rex in hot pursuit. Crystal followed me as I stepped into the stairwell.

'That mouse thing was BS, right?' Crystal whispered as we headed down to the Oselkas' lower level.

I nodded.

'She ripped this place apart in the middle of the night. The responding officers checked the house, so did that detective.' Crystal added, 'Where the hell could he be?'

We hit the carpet at the bottom of the staircase, definitely out of earshot. 'I don't know if they have a crawlspace.' I looked up and shook my head. 'You can't stuff a two-hundred-pound guy in the ceiling tiles.'

I peeked into the recording studio – soundboard station, several cameras on tripods, the infamous green screen, a Christmas tree in one corner – as Alice and Rex jogged down the hall and took a left, and then onward into the utility room. Crystal and I watched as they strode past the furnace, water heater, washing machine and dryer, and on to the far end of the room which appeared to serve as a storage area. Cardboard boxes were stacked on metal shelves, nearly to the ceiling. Project names – likely containing materials associated with the ghosts of documentaries past – were etched on the front of each box in black magic marker.

But Alice and Rex sat in front of a single box tucked between the metal shelving and the far wall. The box was maybe four feet tall and labeled *Christmas tree*, also in black marker. Alice and Rex looked our way; both patted at the concrete floor beneath them with a front paw.

'It's not quite Halloween yet,' I said, 'but he's got a Christmas tree in his studio room.'

'Yeah, I saw it. No decorations.'

I couldn't smell anything and held out hope as I used my

pocketknife to slice free the packing tape on all four sides of the storage box. So much packing tape made it seem as though the Oselkas were storing the artificial tree for a millennium instead of a single year. When I finally freed the top flaps, I stared at Crystal a long second, and then flipped open the box.

I now realized why the gardening tools had been left out in the backyard. Mrs Oselka's husband never got the opportunity to place them back in his shed.

The figure inside was a blur, likely due to the yards and yards of Saran Wrap he'd been cloaked in. With his neck at an impossible angle, the man's face stared straight upward, as though he were expecting us.

Though it was a bit like looking through ice, and though I'd never met Casey Oselka before in my life . . . I was sure he'd seen better days.

FOUR

'Becca's the only person I've ever really loved,' actor Derek Ambler whispered slowly, a single tear sliding down his face and dripping on to his lap. Ambler, whose non-stage name – his real name – was Steven Henderson, they'd already covered that topic, was anchored to his family room armchair by strips of duct tape about his wrists, abdomen, and ankles.

They were finally getting to the crux of the matter . . . to Ambler's kernel of truth.

And the man sitting on the ottoman before Ambler *lived* for kernels of truth.

Ultimately, it was what these *encounters* were all about.

The man cherished *breakthroughs*.

But it hadn't always been that way.

Not at first.

Years back, after he had graduated from the University of Chicago, he'd flown back home, if you could call it that, to spend the summer months at his father's lake house. He'd double-majored in Criminal

Justice and History, graduated Summa Cum Laude, and had been accepted into the University of Chicago's School of Law. But he wasn't certain if he wanted to follow in his father's legal footsteps – if anything, he was heading in the opposite direction – and, on the surface, was spending the summer finalizing his decision.

Below the surface, however, something entirely different consumed his time.

In fact, there was that occasion his father had shown up unexpectedly at the lake house and caught him digging through his box of memories – the only thing he'd hung on to after his mother's death, after his years at the boarding school, and asked, 'What's all this about?'

'Just trying to Facebook with some old friends, but I need the correct spelling of their last names,' he had responded.

Truth was, he wasn't on Facebook, and what he actually searched for in the box was a yellowing slip of paper that made not a whit of sense for him to have hung on to – paperwork from his driver's education course back in the summer of his fifteenth year. He found it near the bottom of the carton and, sure enough, it contained the name of the driver training instructor who had taken both him and another student driver out on the streets, highways and byways for the driving portion of the program. The instructor's name was Bill Colson and, in a faded note in the margin, he'd written 'Science Teacher'. Bill Colson was not only a driving instructor, but a science teacher at a local high school. The sheet also contained a barely legible home address penciled in the margin from all those years ago.

While as a student driver, his fifteen-year-old self hadn't come to a complete rest at a stop sign. Instead, he'd offended the powers that be with a rolling stop, causing Instructor Colson to slam on the special set of brakes from his perch in the passenger seat, bringing the vehicle to a halt on an industrial boulevard that curved around a handful of warehouses and industrial plants. At that point, Colson proceeded to rip him a new one regarding traffic laws concerning rolling stops, how they were tantamount to running a red light. His fifteen-year-old self had nodded along with the instructor's critique, yet wondered why Instructor Colson had left them exposed, blocking the street, which seemed a far worse offense than rolling past a stop sign at one mile an hour. Sure enough, an eighteen-wheeler rounded the corner and headed their direction at fifty miles an hour. An instant later, the Peterbilt's air horn announced its presence with a heart-stopping blast.

'Get us out of here!' Colson screamed, his eyes wide as saucers, lifting his foot off the passenger's side brake. 'Get us out of here!'

As his fifteen-year-old self goosed the gas pedal and dodged the truck by cutting right on to a residential street, Colson continued his rant, barking derogatory sentences about his lack of driving capabilities. Then Colson had him pull into a church parking lot and switch drivers with the other kid who'd been sitting in back, awaiting his turn at bat, witnessing what had occurred as well as Colson's subsequent outburst.

'Why did you stop us in traffic?' he'd asked Colson as he put the car in park.

'You did a rolling stop,' the instructor replied. 'You're lucky I don't flunk you.'

He spent the rest of the session buckled in the backseat, eyes scorching holes in the back of Instructor Colson's head.

So instead of granting serious contemplation – or any contemplation at all – to attending law school in the fall, his college-graduate-aged self spent a chunk of June and half of July following full-time high-school science teacher and part-time driving instructor Bill Colson.

He found the small rambler in which Colson lived, came to realize the man lived alone – discovered he'd been divorced some years earlier – and found out the man still spent a chunk of his summertime as a driving instructor. He knew which weekdays Colson worked, Monday through Wednesday and Friday, as well as what time Colson returned home at night – around six p.m., often with a bag of fast food or bucket of chicken.

On the night he reacquainted himself with his old driving instructor – a Wednesday evening – he'd already made himself a known presence in Colson's neighborhood, what with his daily bouncing of a basketball down the sidewalk past Colson's rambler while sporting a red baseball cap and hoop earrings, mirrored sunglasses, fake skull tattoos on his forearms, shorts and a too-tight T-shirt, Nike tennis shoes, as well as a small backpack with a green Powerade sticking out of a side pocket.

Just another dipshit neighbor kid on his way to the park to shoot some hoops with his equally dipshit friends.

He often paused to bounce the ball at the foot of Colson's driveway, a couple times bouncing it up to Colson's garage door, lingering and looking, to see if there were any neighborhood busybodies or anyone else around who might give a damn.

There wasn't.

At two o'clock that Wednesday, he bounced the ball up to Colson's front door, dribbling while repeatedly ringing the doorbell and knocking. He even pretended to be talking to someone through the screen door, even giving a thumbs-up through the front window as he bounced past – just a friend or relative stopping by to say hi. On his way back from the park, at four o'clock, he scanned around, spotted no one, and again bounced the ball up Colson's driveway, but this time he slid around the redwood fence at the side of the rambler, where Colson's trash and recycle bins lay, opened the unlocked gate to Colson's backyard, entered, and hovered in the bushes off to the side and out of sight, waiting and watching for any red flags. An hour later, he slipped on to the backyard deck and edged up to the side of Colson's sliding glass door. He hadn't heard the air-conditioning unit in play and the curtains were shut on the sliding glass, likely keeping the sun from beating down inside the rambler. The temperature was in the mid-eighties, and he pictured Colson as the kind of guy who'd save on the electric bill until temps got well into the nineties.

Hidden inside his backpack, underneath a couple of towels and a pair of leather gloves, was a small canister of mace, a Swiss Army knife, and a ballpeen hammer. While awaiting his old driving instructor's arrival, he sliced open several inches of screen with the main blade of his Swiss Army knife. He also used the blade to flip the lock on the screen door as well as slide it open. He figured Colson would open the sliding glass door in order to allow the evening breeze to help cool off the house. That's when he'd take him, and he didn't want to *Three Stooges* it with a screen door between the two of them.

And that's exactly how it went down.

Driving instructor and science teacher Bill Colson took a full blast of pepper spray as he slid open the glass door, yet still managed to put up a good fight against the intruder. It took several swipes of the ballpeen hammer to knock Colson to the floor. In a fit of panic – fortunately, even his college-graduate-aged self had the ability to think on his feet – he lifted some antiquated green couch Colson must have inherited from a long-dead relative and dropped it over the driving instructor's torso, pinning the instructor to the floor as he then dropped his full body weight on to the sofa.

'Take whatever you want,' Colson screeched, peering up at him between blinking eyes, struggling to catch his breath, blood from a gash in the side of his head flowing on to the beige carpet.

He shook his head at Colson and took his time reminding his old driving instructor of a particular bout of unpleasantness on an industrial boulevard seven years earlier.

Colson squinted up at him a long second, his eyes red and moist, appeared to remember the incident, and said, 'You've got to be shitting me.'

His college-graduate-aged self flashed back on how events had unfolded the afternoon Colson slammed the brakes on the student driver vehicle. His ire rose, became uncontainable, and he slashed at Colson's cheek with the main blade of the Swiss Army knife – letting the driving instructor know his role as a subservient teenager had long since passed its expiration date.

More blood flowed on to the beige carpeting as Colson began to hyperventilate.

'All you had to do was be a decent human being, slap my wrist about the stop sign – fine, no worries – but then acknowledge the incident with the oncoming truck was on you,' he said to Colson. 'But you just didn't have it in you to do that . . . did you?'

He wanted to chat more, but Colson bucked at the sofa that pinned him to the floor, a prize bull at a rodeo, and when it became evident that was going nowhere, Colson began screaming for help. The sliding glass door remained open, leaving him no choice but to stab at the side of Colson's neck with the Swiss Army knife until the screaming stopped.

It had been messy.

There'd been no crux of the matter for Colson.

There'd been no kernel of truth.

All that would come in time . . . as he honed his craft.

He tidied up the scene as best he could, placed the tools into the bottom of his backpack, buried them with towels, and waited until dusk to bounce the basketball down Colson's driveway, on to the sidewalk, down the street, and back to the Walmart where he'd left his car.

Later that night, after changing clothes and getting rid of everything he'd brought or worn to Colson's house, the realization struck him like a bolt of lightning. His decision had been made. And his father would be so proud.

He'd be attending law school in the fall.

The man sat on the ottoman and studied the actor who'd portrayed him in the Netflix true crime docuseries. Ambler's face was bruised and swollen, mostly from the blow that allowed him entrance into the actor's home. And though he already knew the answer from his deep dive into all things Derek Ambler, he said, 'Who the hell is Becca?'

'My sister.' Ambler slurred his words; perhaps his jaw was broken.

'Your sister?'

'It's not like that,' Ambler replied, another tear dropping on to his lap.

Halloween had made it all so ridiculously easy. He'd parked two blocks over from the actor's brick townhouse on Maple Avenue in Blue Island. It was eight o'clock, the skies were dark, an end-of-October chill hung in the air, and the herds of trick-or-treaters had been thinning out. He wore a rubber Frankenstein mask – classic Karloff – that made his face a sheen of sweat as he wound his way down Maple, up the driveway, and then the cement walkway and steps to Ambler's front door, where he rang the bell.

Ambler opened the door. He sported a cheap pair of vampire's teeth and black cape and gelled-back hair – always the performer – and clutched an oversized bowl with barely a dozen bite-size candy bars at the bottom. He stared in confusion at the monster before him, a person too tall to be of trick-or-treating age.

'My girls will be here in a second,' he told Ambler, glanced about, and held up a hand as though waving to some kids a door or two down. 'They ran into some goblins they know from school.'

Ambler popped his teeth out and tossed them at a table near the door. 'Would you like a candy bar?'

'I shouldn't,' he said, taking a step forward, bending his knees, blocking the entryway from any passersby, 'but why not?'

He sprang forward, delivering a solid uppercut to Ambler's chin.

A split-second later he was inside, the front door shut and locked. An instant after that, the outside lights flicked off.

That had been three hours ago. Since then, there'd been a fair amount of pleading and sniveling as Ambler gradually worked his way toward *acceptance*. The initial breakthrough came when he'd realized the fates of his fellow documentarians – Tim Gorski and Casey Oselka – could no longer be laid at the feet of arbitrary big city violence. Ambler had only read of Oselka's death in the *Chicago Tribune* that very morning. The police kept mum on most of the gory details, not providing the news media much to play with beyond that of a home invasion taking a fatal turn.

'It was just a part I auditioned for and got. I cleared maybe five grand for a month of work,' Ambler had insisted when he'd thought *insisting* would make a difference. 'We shot that thing two years ago . . . two years.'

The man on the ottoman nodded at Ambler's point. 'I've fallen behind in my streaming.'

But the thespian's actual breaking point came when the man he'd once portrayed ran a hand over the remaining candy bars in the Halloween bowl and asked, 'When does Erik's shift at the bar end?'

Though tightly bound to the armchair, Ambler's shoulders trembled once, twice, and then his head dropped. He sat there motionless, saying nothing. Erik was Ambler's roommate in the Blue Island townhome – his partner, or perhaps lover would be more accurate – and Erik's shift ended at midnight, which meant the bartender would be home no later than one o'clock in the morning. And, it hit Ambler like a ton of bricks; if this intruder, this psychopath, were still here at that time . . . Erik would die as well.

The man on the ottoman let that linger in the air as he worked his way through the bite-size Snickers bars. After all, they were his favorite. Once he finished the final Snickers, he could tell it was time. They were ready for the crux of the matter, the kernel of truth . . . for Derek Ambler's kernel of truth.

'Tell me about Becca,' he asked. 'Tell me about your sister.'

And Derek Ambler did; only Derek Ambler – bit-part star of stage and the small screen, once the lead character in an unexceptional documentary about the Dead Night Killer – was long gone. Derek Ambler had checked out. The bound man reverted back to his true self, back to Steven Henderson, or rather the Steven Henderson of his formative years.

And his story was typical, like the script of some been-there/done-that made-for-TV movie. The man on the ottoman stifled a yawn. Young Steven knew he was different from a very early age, he'd never been comfortable in his own skin – yada yada – and by seventh grade he knew he was gay. Young Steven's parents had already known, he could tell by the whispers, the hushed murmurs he caught bits and pieces of whenever he was in a nearby room or passed by in the hallway.

Bits and pieces like 'What'll the relatives think?' and 'Where did we go wrong?' and 'How could this happen to us?'

But Young Steven's story perked up when big sister Becca entered the fray. One day both he and Becca – she was a year older – were playing cribbage in the family room when the whispers and hushed murmurs drifted in from the nearby kitchen, loud enough for the siblings to digest what was being said. Young Steven's face turned red. He spun about to face his sister . . . only Becca was no longer sitting across the cribbage board from him.

Then he heard her voice coming from the kitchen; not a murmur or whisper, but loud and clear. 'He's your son,' she told their parents in no uncertain terms. 'Love him . . . love your son.'

As the man on the ottoman listened, it occurred to him that even though Ambler cared about his partner, and he certainly didn't want any harm to come to him, Erik the Bartender was not Derek Ambler's crux of the matter. Erik was not Ambler's kernel of truth. The man on the ottoman got the sense that the bloom had come off the rose, and had he not decided to pay Ambler a visit, Erik the Bartender's days in their relationship were numbered.

Becca was Ambler's kernel of truth.

And she had been since that day long ago when she left a game of cribbage to tend to some important business in the kitchen.

Ambler then talked of a bully – junior high schools come well-equipped with them – named Jim Pettis, an eighth grader who went out of his way to make seventh grader Steven's life a living hell. One day at lunch, Pettis and his gang of toadies had Young Steven pinned against a display case right outside the cafeteria. Pettis said, 'Eat this, faggot,' and shoved a slice of pizza down Young Steven's shirt to waves of mirth and merriment when, out of nowhere, Becca stepped between the two boys and popped Pettis in the nose as hard as she could. Pettis dropped to the tiled floor, tried to rise, but Becca stepped hard on his stomach with her tennis shoe.

Now that was fine and dandy and certainly appreciated – *thanks, big sis!* – but what made that particular lunch hour memorable, what made it the stuff of legend was what happened next – a loud and lengthy farting sound followed by the release of Pettis's bladder.

Everyone standing near the bully was stunned, in shock, but a second later Becca went in for the kill, shouting to students as they passed by, 'Pettis peed his pants! It's Peed Pants Pettis!'

Even some of Pettis's sycophants snickered at that one.

And *Peed Pants Pettis* stuck with Pettis well into senior high.

Ambler finished reminiscing about his big sister and looked up at his uninvited guest.

'Wow, what a great story,' the man on the ottoman said, and he meant it. 'I wish I could have been there when Peed Pants Pettis got his comeuppance.'

Ambler nodded slowly, his eyes glossy.

'How 'bout we take a few moments, Derek, OK? Just close your eyes and think back, and treasure the memory of your sister . . . bigger than life itself outside the cafeteria that day.'

Ambler nodded again and closed his eyes.

'Picture her standing there – Becca, your personal guardian angel – slaying the monster as only she could do. There's no better *remembrance* in the world than that, is there, Derek?'

The man on the ottoman was relieved Erik the Bartender would be the one finding Derek Ambler . . . and not his sister.

He gave Ambler a few more seconds to think of Becca.

FIVE

If you've got dogs, more than likely you're an early riser, whether it's a repeated nudge from a wet nose to an exposed arm or, more alarming, if one of the friskier of the hounds dive-bombs the bed. Yes, I'm talking about you, Rex. With my hyper-enthusiastic springer spaniel, every morning is Pearl Harbor Day. With Rex in the mix, I needn't waste money on an alarm clock. After Rex's sneak attack, I'll sleepwalk the two dogs outside so they can take care of their morning business. Then, with eyelids fixed at half-mast, I'll set up the canine buffet, fill a couple of water dishes, and, by the time the breakfast rush is over, my eyelids are at full-mast and, screw it, I'm up for the day.

It was almost seven, the sun on the rise, and I was running the two goofballs around the backyard while Crystal got ready for work. Two can't shower at the same time in our house without the water pressure plummeting to squirt-gun level or, worse yet, there's cold water for the poor sap – usually me – who steps into the shower stall immediately after the first one has finished bathing. I suspect today's canine workout was more for me than Alice and Rex, in order to make up for all the Halloween candy I'd wolfed down the night before.

We had a fair amount of trick-or-treaters. Of course, I overbought all of my favorite candy bars and, unfortunately, my sweet tooth took control and, when all was said and done, I'd eaten more candy than probably a dozen of the doorbell-ringing buggers combined.

Of course, since dogs can't eat chocolate, I make this sacrifice for them.

Even a holiday like Halloween makes me a little melancholy; it makes me think of Mom and Dad, and how things might have been were they still around.

I've told you about Alice and Rex, and what I do for a living. I've also told you about my detective sister. But now it's time I tell you something about myself . . . something even Crystal doesn't know.

Mom and Dad died on a Saturday evening. The accident took place a little before nine o'clock. I got the call at ten.

I'd made good money off the obedience classes I taught at my father's veterinary clinic, at least better ka-ching than any of my seventeen-year-old contemporaries. Saturday evening had traditionally been date night for Mom and Dad so I'd purchased two tickets for some romantic comedy on Fandango and presented the movie tickets as a gift to them earlier in the week, as a way to say 'thank you' for all they've done for me with the dog-training stuff.

Dad's eyes lit up. Mom was happy, too – after all, it was a rom-com, her favorite genre.

But my gesture was far from altruistic. I had an ulterior motive.

It was mid-March of my junior year of high school, and I'd been seeing Megan Caple since the second week in January. Megan made me feel all giddy and goofy and mushy inside and, improbably, she found me *cute* and liked me back. Love songs suddenly made sense, poetry gave me warm fuzzies, and I walked around school with a big, dopey smile plastered across my mug.

I was in love.

It ended that night.

I'd known Megan since kindergarten, since we were rug rats, but hadn't said boo to her until we'd wound up in the same bible study class at church. But on that particular Saturday, bible study was the furthest thing from my mind.

First and foremost, in my mind, was how much I wanted my parents out of the house that evening.

Hence the free movie tickets, hence the egging them on to enjoy a restaurant date afterward, hence the subterfuge about how I was going over to Megan's house for dinner with her parents when, in fact, Megan would be coming over to our house.

I may have overplayed my hand as Mom contacted Megan's mother under the guise of asking what I should bring to their house for dessert that night, and soon my entire house of cards came tumbling down around my ears.

'Nothing was going to happen,' I protested when confronted, though I'd spent the past week most definitely hoping *something big* would happen.

'You shouldn't have lied to us,' Mom said as Dad stood by her side.

I shrugged. I wasn't sorry. 'Now you've got Meg's parents thinking I'm some kind of pervert.'

'They don't think you're a pervert,' Dad said. 'They know the two of you hatched this together.'

'I just wanted to be with Meg alone, without everyone buzzing about like flies,' I said. 'Now it's turned to shit.'

After a long silence, Dad said, 'Come to the mall with us, go to the movie.'

I shook my head, still pissed off. 'You guys go.'

'Come on,' Mom said. 'We'll have fun. It'll be like old times.'

I didn't want to have a thing to do with either of them. 'Just fucking leave already.'

Dad stepped forward. 'You better watch your mouth, kiddo – I don't care if you are angry.' He looked like he had more to say on the matter, but his eyes softened, and he added, 'We'll have a *talk* when we get home.'

But we never got a chance to have that *talk*.

Because my parents never came home.

Before you start in with *accidents happen* and *it wasn't your fault* in order to make me feel better . . . I'm not done yet.

It gets worse.

And you'll see why I've never shared this with Crystal.

It had been a forty-degree March day. The sun was shining overhead, the snow melting, but, as Chicagoans will tell you about living next to Lake Michigan, the weather can turn on a dime. And it turned on a dime later that afternoon. It was probably during the opening credits to Mom and Dad's movie when the freezing rain began to pour. It was probably halfway through their rom-com – probably the part where boy loses girl – when the frigid winds swept in off the Great Lake and temperatures shot down to zero.

Around this time, I let Rocko go outside to take care of his business and watched as he slipped and slid all over the patio as he made his trek in from the backyard.

Holy shit, I thought, and went upstairs to check the front of the house. The Silverado sat on the far side of the driveway, its windows a dense glaze of ice. Our driveway was a skating rink. I returned inside and clicked on the evening news. The weather led the coverage and, due to the ice storm, all of Chicago was under a winter storm warning.

I started tapping a text message to send to both of my parents' cell phones, telling them to bag dinner – they normally ate a leisurely meal at the Applebee's inside the mall – and come straight home as soon as the movie ended. I wrote in the text message how the *storm of the century* had arrived, and that they should take the back roads home.

But then I remembered how shitty the day had gone, and I thought *screw them . . . I hope they do crash.*

I deleted the message without sending, and then went into the kitchen to toss a frozen pizza in the oven.

I never saw my parents alive again.

That's my story.

And now you know who I am.

And why you shouldn't root for me.

I leaned against the chain-link fence, caught my breath, and watched as Alice and Rex sniffed about the yard. It was going to be long day. I had an obedience class in Englewood at ten o'clock, then another class in Humboldt Park at two, and then back to Englewood for a six o'clock training. I was lost in thought over the dozen things I'd need to toss in the back of my Silverado before heading out when I heard Crystal.

'Cory,' she called from the frame of the sliding glass door on the upper deck, pulling me back into the here and now.

It wasn't Crystal's *I'm heading out now* voice; rather, it carried a certain *get here immediately* resonance, and I jogged up the cedar steps of the deck, Alice and Rex hot on my heels. 'What's going on?'

'Todd Surratt just called.'

'Who the hell is Todd Surratt?'

'He's the special agent in charge of the Chicago Division of the Federal Bureau of Investigation.'

I stared at Crystal in confusion. The head of the Chicago Division of the FBI wouldn't call this early in the morning to shoot the breeze or exchange recipes with a CPD detective. 'What happened?'

'He knows I'm working the Tim Gorski case, and he knows about Gorski's connection to Casey Oselka in Park Ridge.'

'Why would the FBI care about those cases?'

Crystal shrugged. 'He said flip on the news – any channel – and we'd find out what he's talking about . . . and that we both need to come see him as soon as possible.'

'He wants *me* to come?'

'Both of us.'

We stepped through the kitchen, into the family room. Crystal grabbed the remote and flipped on WGN-TV. We both listened as the morning news anchor spoke over a video of what appeared a squad of flashing lights outside some brick residence somewhere – a shot that must have been filmed earlier as it was pitch black outside.

'. . . where our WGN-TV news crew arrived shortly after the police had been summoned to the Maple Avenue townhome of actor Derek Ambler, whom WGN can confirm is the most-recent victim of the serial killer known as the Dead Night Killer, a killer who stalked Chicago suburbs and nearby towns less than a decade ago before disappearing – as though into the ether – until now. A 911 call was made to the Blue Island Police Department by Derek Ambler's roommate, Erik Grant, who made the grisly discovery upon returning home from his shift at the Raven's Place bar and nightclub at 12:50 a.m.'

At the word 'actor', Crystal and I exchanged a glance. The City of Blue Island lies adjacent to Chicago, fifteen or so miles south of the Loop. I knew Blue Island well as I've trained dogs there on multiple occasions.

The morning news anchor continued.

'For those just joining WGN-TV, this station, as well as numerous other news outlets, both local and national, received an email timestamped 12:26 a.m. from the iPhone belonging to actor Derek Ambler, whom we now know portrayed the Dead Night Killer in a Netflix documentary released in the middle of last year. The email contains photographs of Derek Ambler's lifeless body. WGN-TV will not air these explicit images, not even blurring over the deceased's face, for the same reason WGN doesn't name mass-casualty shooters, as not to glorify or play into the killer's agenda or to spur on copycats.'

I got a creepy feeling of what was coming; sadly it was answered in the anchor's next sentence.

'Information in the text of the email sent to WGN-TV ties Derek Ambler's murder to the recent homicides of two other individuals associated with the Netflix documentary – Casey Oselka, who directed the docudrama, and Tim Gorski, who narrated the piece. The body of Tim Gorski was found last week, stabbed to death in the woods off a South Edgebrook park. Casey Oselka was discovered three days ago, strangled in his Park Ridge home. Appearing on your screen is an enlarged image of the email that was sent to WGN-TV early this morning.'

I grabbed the remote and clicked pause to keep the station from cutting away from the email. Alice leapt on to the couch and faced the television, as though to read along with us, while Rex slithered about our ankles.

My blood ran cold.

> *Subject: A Belated Critique of 'On the Trail of the Dead Night Killer'*
>
> *Dear Friends in the Media,*
> *Please accept my deepest apologies for having been remiss in not sharing earlier my take on last year's Netflix offering, 'On the Trail of the Dead Night Killer'.*
> *Fear not, I've met with Tim Gorski and Casey Oselka, and, as of this evening, Derek Ambler (please note enclosed images), in order to share my two cents with each of them individually.*
> *Quite intimately, of course.*
> *Feedback is often best on a face-to-face basis, wouldn't you agree?*
> *Again, please accept my most heartfelt of apologies for such a lapse.*
> *Be seeing you . . .*
> *T.D.N.K.*

PART TWO
The Killing Wound

Dogs are better than human beings because they know but do not tell.

Emily Dickinson

SIX

Six Weeks Ago

'Always lock your doors at night before you go to sleep,' the narrator embellished in a mock-dread voice, more akin to telling dark and twisted tales around a campfire than chronicling a documentary series. 'Never forget to lock your doors and windows because, in the wee, wee hours of the night, when you're off in sleepy-leepy land, the Dead Night Killer comes a-checking. He'll try the front door first. If the front door's locked, the Dead Night Killer will try the back door, a side entrance, and, finally, the sliding glass door.'

He turned up the volume and headed into the kitchen. It had been a long and vexing day. Work itself had been tedium personified, six hours of conference calls and pushing papers around his desk with little to show for it, but, of course, there had been that other matter – *that goddamned other matter* – and he needed to unwind in front of some mind-numbing BS on TV. He set the plastic bag of Chinese food on the kitchen counter. He would have killed for shrimp dumplings and a plate of short ribs with honey sauce from MingHin's, but the Kung Pao Chicken from Panda Express would get him home quicker and have to suffice.

'Occasionally, in the summer months, the Dead Night Killer will check a window or two,' the narrator continued from the man's Samsung in the family room. 'And if he finds an open window, he will come inside to *check on you* . . . and you will find yourself eyeball to eyeball with an *unforgiving creature* that does a great deal more than go *bump* in the night.'

The man reached into the fridge for a bottle of carbonated water, took a detour, and returned with a bottle of Stella Artois. It had been that kind of day. He went back to the TV room, set his beer, white cartons of Kung Pao and fried rice, and a fork on the table next to his usual spot on the sofa. Then he pawed at the remote again, cranked up the volume even more, dropped the clicker on a cushion, and headed upstairs to the master bedroom to change out of dress clothes as Kung Pao stains wouldn't complement his Van Heusen dress shirt or Italian silk tie.

'I cannot tell you exactly what occurs when the Dead Night Killer gets inside, boys and girls, because it's *unspeakable*. What occurs when he gets inside your house is simply unspeakable,' the program continued as the man shed his suit jacket, pants, tie and dress shirt. He tossed on a pair of possibly clean sweatpants off the closet floor, jogged down the steps, plopped down on the couch, and tore into his two cartons of Chinese cuisine.

Though he'd stumbled across this true-crime Netflix docuseries a few times over the past year, and had heard colleagues talking about it at work, he'd finally gotten around to streaming the initial three episodes last night when it became apparent that sleep was, once again, not in the cards. The overall series was titled *On the Trail of* and wasn't dissimilar from old true-crime favorites, such as *Unsolved Mysteries* and *Forensic Files*. The series' first install-ment was a nearly seventy-minute documentary on Elizabeth Short, who had been posthumously nicknamed the 'Black Dahlia' by the media due to her reported fondness for wearing sheer black dresses. Short had been murdered – carved in two, drained of blood, each corner of her mouth sliced to her ears – in LA in January of 1947. Although the episode recounted how LAPD had looked into over 150 suspects and filtered through sixty confessions during the inves-tigation, none of it led to anyone being arrested or charged. The docuseries spent the final fifteen minutes walking the audience through some of the more recent theories; however, no one can say for certain who killed Elizabeth Short.

Episode one was titled, of course, 'On the Trail of the Black Dahlia'.

Episode two was titled, 'On the Trail of Jimmy Hoffa' and, quite frankly, outside of being an interesting recap on the life and untimely disappearance of James Riddle Hoffa, it did nothing to change the narrative that the mafia had been behind Hoffa's murder on July 30 of 1975. The documentary was a rehash of all that came before. The man found it a yawner. He had heard the story, seen the movie, and, fortunately, the episode, including the credits, was barely fifty minutes in length.

More interesting had been episode three, which he completed

before drifting off to sleep a little before 3:00 a.m. This episode of the Netflix docuseries was titled 'On the Trail of the Tylenol Murders' – a heartwarming tale of drug tampering and poison that occurred in the Chicago metropolitan area in the early 1980s. Tylenol bottles containing capsules laced with potassium cyanide had, evidently, been reverse shoplifted; that is, left in various stores for unwitting customers to purchase.

The poisoning caused the deaths of seven people, several more if you tacked on the subsequent waves of copycat crimes.

The documentary pointed out that, though no one was ever charged with or convicted of the poisonings, the murders led to major reforms in the packaging of over-the-counter substances. Great, the man thought, that's why I damn near pop an aneurysm twisting open a salad dressing lid in order to peel off the seal.

'So remember to double-check your doors and windows at night,' the spooky-voiced narration continued. 'And don't ever forget, as you'll not like what happens when the Dead Night Killer comes a-calling . . . not one little bit.'

Between sips of Stella, the man shoveled in forkfuls of Kung Pao Chicken and rice. Like the Tylenol murders, episode four was a Chicago story – what is it about Chicago? – and he distinctly recalled the string of unsolved homicides from back during the early years of his career. Hard not to as it had captured the imagination of the press – *if it bleeds, it leads* – which ran with this fear-provoking anecdote about locking your doors at night. The narrative took on a life of its own and served to scare the bejesus out of school children, the elderly, or – quite frankly – anyone who followed the story.

Unfortunately, like most unsolved mysteries, there'd been no closure. The killer has not been seen nor heard from in nearly seven years, and the docuseries posited that the Dead Night Killer had either passed away or was doing time in prison, having been arrested for a differing crime.

Not bothering to crank the volume this time, the man brought his empty cartons to the bin in the kitchen, dropped his fork in the sink, grabbed another bottle of Stella, and returned to his perch on the sofa. The first three episodes were fine and dandy if you were a true-crime aficionado – a hardcore fan – or perhaps lock-downed during some kind of lengthy pandemic, but the segment on the Dead

Night Killer, the one he'd been most interested in viewing, was strictly a hit-and-miss affair.

The hits included a timeline of the killer's active years, the names and backgrounds of his victims as well as the locations and dates of their murders, so even the most uninformed would learn about the Windy City's equivalent of Jack the Ripper. Next on the list of hits was an attractive female profiler from the Chicago field office of the Federal Bureau of Investigation who identified a series of likely characteristics – *male; likely Caucasian; between the ages of 20 and 48; has carryover effects – unresolved trust, relationship issues – due to an emotionally or physically abusive parent during his formative years, or an absentee or emotionally distant father during such years.*

Men can also have *daddy issues*, the man thought, but the profiler's description of the Dead Night Killer could – to be blunt – fit a third of the male population of Illinois.

The documentary's list of misses included an overblown musical score that would fit better in a penny arcade. It served to drown out commentary in several of the more interesting scenes. Another miscue was how surreal the actors appeared in the reenactment scenes. It seemed as though the booking agents sent only the weakest links from failed off-Broadway productions. The performers gestured madly as though they were in a silent movie.

As for the biggest oddity of all, the actor portraying the Dead Night Killer took home the grand prize. He pranced about darkened rooms and hallways as though he were Bela Lugosi or perhaps Nosferatu from that ancient German film. And every time he glanced at an intended victim, his eyes bulged in a manner that'd turn the most alien of bug-eyed monsters green with envy.

Since the case was still active, albeit cold, there wasn't much the episode could provide to advance the plotline. Though there was a modus operandi in which the Dead Night Killer, after a night of psychological terror, dispatched his victims, Chicago PD and the FBI kept that factoid tightly under wraps. Instead, what leaked to the press, and was belabored in the documentary, was how the victims appeared viciously beaten and bruised – antemortem bruising, before death. Another leak, also knocked about in episode four, was the cause of death listed generically as sharp force trauma, which indicated some manner, form or shape of the victims having been stabbed to death.

Any specifics were verboten.

The man grabbed his third and final beer of the evening when they brought in a balding Chicago police detective who, outside of nodding his head to facts already of public record, took several minutes to say that, because the case was still *technically* open, he couldn't say anything. The cop stretched *No Comment* out long enough to secure his spot in the Netflix documentary and acquire his fifteen minutes of fame.

After the docudrama ended, the man rinsed the beer bottles in the sink and then placed the dead soldiers in his recycle bin. He figured the campiness of the reenactment scenes had to be intentional. Perhaps the director had subversion in mind; perhaps he wanted to create some kind of satire based on the excessive nature of the homicides or the notoriety of the case. Whatever the docudrama hoped to accomplish, it fell flat.

The man headed up to bed.

The beer helped him nod off but he was back up an hour later. He retrieved his briefcase from his home office, sat in bed, and paged through a handful of work documents. He then tapped at his iPhone and noted that, yet again, half his upcoming day would be eaten up by meetings and conference calls.

Finally, he hit the lights, lay back, and stared at the ceiling, lost in thought. He'd suffered from insomnia for years, learned to live with it – sleeplessness actually helped him accomplish a tremendous amount of work – and, truth be told, he'd long since made peace with skating by on four hours a night.

Four was all he'd ever needed.

At two o'clock in the morning, after a protracted bout of tossing and turning, the man got up, took the steps back down to the TV room, clicked on Netflix, and brought up 'On the Trail of the Dead Night Killer'. He fast-forwarded through two-thirds of the episode, stopping when he reached the reenactment of the dead UPS driver and his equally deceased son – certainly one way to address unresolved daddy issues.

He had lost interest in the show by that point, had actually been more concerned with peeling the label off his beer bottle, but thought he'd spotted something and wanted to verify the docudrama actually *went there*.

Sure enough, there was the main actor strutting about in the shadows as though he were Nosferatu, dragging the dead son down the hallway, and leaving the young man's body at the feet of his chair-bound father. And when he had finished with the father, the actor stood staring at what he'd accomplished. The camera lingered on the actor's back as he admired his work, and then the musical arrangement kicked back in, building and building to a crescendo as the actor played master maestro, his arms bouncing in the air as though conducting an orchestra in honor of the blood-splattered scene before him.

When the music reached its climax, the actor dropped his arms and began kicking at the body of the dead son as the scene faded to black.

The man pressed pause and sat down, his usual spot on the couch, of course, and stared at the frozen screen . . . and doubted there'd be any more shut-eye tonight.

Poetic license was one thing, but this was theater of the absurd.

Just one of many things the documentary had gotten wrong, or done intentionally to spice up the ratings. That, and perpetuating the fanciful myth of a killer trudging about darkened yards in the middle of the night, checking doors and windows in the unlikely event that he might gain entry.

How fucking stupid was that?

It'd be like begging to get caught . . .

The man continued staring at the frozen screen.

. . . He'd never begged to get caught.

SEVEN

He didn't get migraines often, but when he did – Katy, bar the door.

His head throbbed, both sides, the pain permeating downward to his jawline. He looked at the *Wall Street Journal* on his desk, but didn't read it. Instead, a couple of fingers lightly massaged his temples. He'd already popped two tablets of ibuprofen, two hundred milligrams each, to no effect, and he considered popping two more.

A doctor had once instructed him, amongst other things, to avoid alcohol and caffeine. He'd chuckled in the MD's face. No, that wouldn't be happening. He'd not be giving up his evening glass of single malt scotch. His cases of Macallan would not be orphaned without a fight. And he'd be double-damned if he gave up his morning's dark roast.

At his age, the pleasures got to be fewer and fewer.

'Rye bread toast, lightly buttered.'

He glanced up from the *Journal*. 'I don't deserve you.'

'No, you don't.' His executive admin crossed the pale gray carpeting, set the plate of toast on the mahogany desk next to his newspaper, and picked up the bottle of Advil. 'Have you taken any more?'

He began to shake his head but ceased before the act of shaking it would add to his discomfort and said, 'No.'

She shook two more tablets on to her palm and then dropped them on his plate. 'Best not take these until you're done with the toast, save on your stomach lining.'

He reached for a slice, took a bite. Somehow the act of chewing egged on the migraine. He noticed his admin remained standing by the corner of his desk. 'What?'

'Roland Jund called.'

'It's not even eight o'clock.'

'The voicemail logged him calling at five o'clock this morning,' she replied. 'He says it's urgent, and that he needs to speak with you as soon as you're in.'

'Of course,' he said, and sighed as his admin worked her way back to the outer office.

He gummed the rye toast and thought of Roland Jund – a barrel chest of a man who was one part master administrator, another part insightful sage, and a final part pompous ass. Like rock beats scissors, pompous ass crowded out the man's *nobler* qualities. Jund wore on him, and he wondered – like how those with chronic pain can predict bad weather per achy joints or arthritis – if today's migraine was a harbinger of Roland Jund appearing on his morning calendar.

As though in answer to his query there came a light knocking on his open door, and in the frame stood the man himself.

'Good morning, Roland,' he said, waved Jund over, thought

screw it, and popped the two ibuprofen tablets into his mouth and reached for his coffee.

Jund nodded in return, crossed the room, and settled his two hundred and something pounds into the guest armchair opposite him. 'Have you heard about Chicago?'

'No.'

'Do you remember the serial killer from a few years back called the Dead Night Killer?'

'Yes.'

Jund stared at him a long moment. 'He's back.'

The director of the Federal Bureau of Investigation turned his attention toward the line of windows in his corner office of the J. Edgar Hoover Building . . . and wondered how soon before he could take more Advil.

EIGHT

'Would you mind repeating that louder so the entire room can hear?' Detective Mike Heppner, Crystal's much-beloved partner, cut me off midsentence.

With the morning rush hour in play, it'd been a miracle we made the FBI's Chicago field office on West Roosevelt Road in under an hour. I barely got buckled in, with Alice secured on my lap – if they summons me, they get my dog as well – before Crystal blasted us out of the sleepy suburb of Buffalo Grove in that Honda HR-V of hers as though she were piloting the *Millennium Falcon*. I clung to the Jesus handle above the side window, but Alice didn't mind.

Alice liked going fast.

And as Crystal shattered speed limits and other traffic laws, she worked her speaker phone to contact Detective Heppner and inform him that his presence – they were both working the Tim Gorski case – was requested at the FBI field office as soon as possible. I also worked my cell phone, a whirling dervish as I tapped through my contact list to find a fellow dog handler willing to cover my morning obedience class in Englewood. Fortunately, I wrapped that up as Crystal swung the HR-V into a parking ramp and pulled into the nearest open spot.

An agent awaited us in the lobby. He handed out visitor lanyards and escorted us up to a large, windowless conference room on the eighth floor, dark blue carpeting with multiple tables set in a rectangular figure. All chairs were occupied, it was standing room only. A man I took to be Todd Surratt, the special agent in charge of the FBI's Chicago Division, was the only person inside the rectangle. He was dressed in a dark gray suit, crisp white shirt and red tie, leaning back against a table, arms folded across his chest, and looking every inch a G-man. With his square-jaw and hawk-nose, screaming red, white and blue, Surratt could appear in recruitment posters.

Surratt nodded at us as we took a spot against the wall next to Detective Heppner, who made a Hollywood production out of checking his watch – nonverbally tut-tutting our tardiness – though I suspected Heppner himself had only arrived minutes earlier.

And now Heppner was heckling me as I attempted to answer Surratt's query.

'Sure can,' I replied. The detective had backed off hassling Crystal, but, evidently, I was up for grabs. Heppner figured he'd throw me off my game, get me stuttering and stammering and double-checking my fly in a room full of hardened CPD officers and federal investigators. And, if Heppner got exceedingly lucky, I'd pee my pants and maybe spurt a half-cup of barf on to my shirt. But what Heppner didn't realize was how a large part of my canine-training job included public speaking. And I'd been doing it for over a decade, since I was a kid in the parking lot of my father's veterinary clinic, all the while competing with a crossbreed chorus of howls, yelps, yaps, and assorted other barks and whines.

When put that way, I'd been heckled by better than Mike Heppner.

'Can everyone hear me?' I asked in the same tone I'd been speaking at before.

I stared at the person farthest from me, a man in a black three-piece and a royal-blue tie at a corner table – one of the prosecutors from the Cook County State's Attorney's Office per Surratt's rushed introductions – who, in turn, nodded his head, as did most of the others in the room.

Surratt's ad hoc morning task force included detectives working the Gorski case, Crystal and Heppner, and the detectives on the Oselka case, as well as the investigators most recently assigned the Derek Ambler murder. There were a handful of Chicago police lieutenants and captains tossed into the mix, as well as what appeared to be half the prosecutors from the State's Attorney's Office, not to mention the double-digit number of federal agents who reported to SAC Surratt.

I continued, 'Agent Surratt's question was *how far off the park trail had Tim Gorski been taken?*' I glanced around the room. 'The poor guy was killed about twenty yards off the trail, but had then been dragged another hundred yards.' Alice sat upright between Crystal and me, and I patted the top of her head in acknowledgement. 'My dogs found Gorski's remains shoved under a pine tree.'

Surratt followed up. 'So he wasn't visible?'

I shook my head. 'It was a pretty dense and secluded spot; I had to walk the police in. I would not have spotted him if I were out for a casual stroll.' I thought for a second. 'If I got near the pine tree, I'd have caught a whiff of something bad, but that was quite a bit off the beaten path.'

'So the unsub wanted the body hidden?'

Unsub stands for unknown subject; I love FBI lingual.

I nodded. 'Absolutely.'

'Why?' Surratt queried the room, though I suspect he'd already formed an opinion.

'To buy him some time,' said the African American detective I'd met at Casey Oselka's home in Park Ridge. Evidently, he'd made the meeting in time to score one of the coveted conference room chairs. 'So he could kill the other two victims without either of them becoming aware or getting forewarned. In fact, the medical examiner puts Oselka's death on the same day Gorski's body was found. This means the documentary director never knew his long-time narrator had been killed.'

'And then our unsub hid Oselka's body in a Christmas tree box in Oselka's furnace room and . . .' Surratt grabbed a stack of papers off the tabletop next to him and scanned the top sheet, '. . . then rolled the poor man's body in cling wrap.'

'Oselka died of asphyxia; he was strangled,' the detective working the Park Ridge case continued. 'Once the killer got inside the house, he strangled Oselka with a thin piece of rope. Oselka's wife was out of town, so our guy took his own sweet time tinkering about their home. He found Saran Wrap in the kitchen and likely figured it'd help hold back the stench of decomposition, at least for a little while. Then Christmas came early in the Oselka household as the killer set up the artificial tree in their basement studio, and he then jammed Oselka's body into the tree box he'd emptied out. He did this brutally, fracturing Oselka's cervical vertebrae in the process.' The detective looked my way. 'If not for the dogs, we might still be scratching our ass and wondering where the hell Oselka had disappeared off to.'

The room digested this in silence.

Then Surratt said, 'Derek Ambler had been aware of Gorski's death. His partner mentioned he and Ambler had discussed it as Ambler had worked with Gorski on the Netflix documentary. Ambler's partner also mentioned Ambler learned of Oselka's death yesterday morning.' Surratt placed his notes back on the tabletop. 'So why did Ambler stay in his house? Why didn't he flee for the hills?'

The man I figured was a prosecutor from the State's Attorney's Office raised his hand and said, 'The entertainment industry is too intertwined, with so many projects occurring at any given instant for Ambler, or even the detectives,' he nodded toward the CPD tables, 'to connect the dots. Tim Gorski narrated most of Oselka's documentaries, but he also did a ton of other voice-over work in commercials and trade-show promos and audio books. Derek Ambler had only worked with Gorski and Oselka once before, on the Dead Night Killer documentary, and that was two years ago.'

The woman next to him, likely another Cook County prosecutor, added, 'It'd be like a temp worker hearing about the deaths of a couple of colleagues from fifteen projects ago. They wouldn't run for the door unless the police alerted them a link existed.'

'True,' Detective Heppner piped in. 'Very true.'

What a brilliant contribution from Crystal's sleuth partner. What a brilliant mind.

I peeked down at Alice. She was now sitting at Crystal's feet, but her muzzle turned toward the sound of each speaker as though she were following the conversation, even if English was her second language. Perhaps someday I'll find the words to explain how much my bloodhound has taught me, and not just her Zen-like ritual of circling three times before lying down for a nap.

Crystal took the ball from Heppner and ran with it. 'I think Cory and the dogs gummed up our guy's timeline.'

All eyes turned to her, and Surratt prompted, 'Care to expand?'

'Who wants to drag a body the length of a football field and then curl it up under a pine tree if you don't have to?' Crystal looked at the table of detectives working the Casey Oselka case. 'Who wants to cover a man in Saran Wrap and fracture his neck stuffing him inside a Christmas tree box? You would only do such things to put off their discovery for as long as possible, right? Otherwise, leave Gorski on the side of the trail; leave Oselka in his entryway, or wherever he was strangled.' She glanced down at Alice. 'I think your unsub was hoping Derek Ambler would be the first one found, followed by the other two. That progression would have made a bigger splash.'

'But he's already made a *big splash*,' Surratt said, pointing at the television mounted on the conference room wall. The sound was muted, but CNN was still covering the story.

'Don't get me wrong – I'm sure he's not complaining, and the email and photos from Ambler's phone were a master touch,' Crystal also pointed at the TV screen, 'but I think he'd have preferred it vice versa. We find Derek Ambler who's been done in with the Dead Night Killer's modus operandi – you know, the killing wound – and after we're clear on what we're up against, it builds to a crescendo as we discover more of his victims, as we find Gorski and Oselka.' Crystal added, 'We're in quicksand before we even know what hit us.'

Agent Surratt shrugged. 'Could well be, but let's focus on *what hit us*. I know this dropped in the middle of the night, but has anyone already seen the documentary, "On the Trail of the Dead Night Killer"?'

Several hands shot up, including a middle-aged woman in a black pantsuit and pink scarf at one of the FBI tables, the guy I took to be one of the prosecutors from the State's Attorney's Office, and a bald guy at one of the CPD tables.

'OK then, the rest of you have a homework assignment. Stream the documentary if you've got Netflix. We can send you a link to the video in case you don't,' Surratt said. 'Now, it appears we have a couple celebrities in the house. This case predates my tenure in Chicago,' Surratt looked toward the woman in the pink scarf who had raised her hand, 'but Loris Renn was the profiler on the original task force, back when the case was active. And Loris was actually interviewed in the documentary.' There were a couple of cheers and some clapping, but Surratt silenced the room with a sharp glance. He then looked at the bald guy from the cop table. 'Detective John Hempstead of Violent Crimes in Area 1 also worked the case, and he, too, was interviewed for the documentary.' There were no catcalls or applause for Hempstead and Surratt continued, 'Loris is going to take the next several minutes to get everyone up to speed on the initial investigation. She's going to walk us through the unsub's active years as well as when he fell off the radar. You'll each be getting a packet containing—'

A light tapping on the conference room door interrupted the special agent in charge. The door opened and there stood the agent who'd escorted us from the lobby to the conference room. 'Sorry to interrupt, sir,' he said, locking eyes with SAC Surratt. 'Director Westbrook is on the phone and would like to speak with you right away.'

NINE

The moniker 'Dead Night Killer' was lame, not only because it was inaccurate – he never skulked down midnight lanes checking doors and windows in order to get inside and club slumbering homeowners to death – but also because it sounded like one of those straight-to-video horror flicks he'd seen as a kid. The nickname lacked the over-the-top testosterone of a Jack the Ripper, Night Stalker, or Boston Strangler. It also lacked the provocativeness of the Zodiac Killer, Gray Man, or Son of Sam. And it most undoubtedly lacked the down-and-dirty *ick* factor of John Wayne Gacy's Killer Clown or Patrick Kearney's Trash Bag Killer.

However, the man imagined the moniker held a certain lyrical ring to it, and the news media had swallowed the bogus narrative hook, line and sinker. To say it'd struck a nerve was to put it mildly. Even the good citizens of Dead Skunk, Nebraska, were now double-checking their doors and windows before shuffling off to beddy-bye.

Not since Andrew Cunanan had gone on his rampage, which included the shooting death of Gianni Versace, had the masses been so fearful and/or titillated by a killer who'd captured the headlines. He'd even read an article on how police dispatchers were becoming overwhelmed with post-twilight reports of unknown figures lurking about anxious callers' yards or driveways, which – more often than not – turned out to be neighbor kids at play, dates being picked up or dropped off, a chiaroscuro of trees and bushes, or, even more likely, nothing at all.

Dear old Dad would be so proud.

Yup, dear old Dad, stellar human being that he was, once you got beyond the abandonment of his wife and son a week after his boy turned six in order to marry his mistress and start anew – a new home, new kids, a new family. Out with the old, in with the new. However, to keep things honest, dear old Dad never skimped on the child support. No siree Bob, his father would stand for none of that . . . dear old Dad paid the *blood money* on the first day of each and every month.

Though he'd not seen his father in ages, dear old Dad was there for him, right after his mother's funeral, when he was fifteen years old. He even got to stay at his father's lake home that summer, watched over by a series of sitters while Father determined which boarding school – several states away, of course – would be the best to groom him into the man he was meant to be. Once at boarding school, he never traveled home on weekends – the offer to come visit his old man had never once been on the table – and, by age sixteen, he was spending summer sessions at the school and holidays with a classmate's family, sleeping on a spare bed or pullout sofa.

Nor did his father come to visit him at the boarding school, not even once, but who could blame dear old Dad – nope, Dad had his *real family* to attend to.

The man shook his head as though to dislodge old memories and continued on his run in the brisk air of a sunny November afternoon. He wore a knit cap, covering his ears and stretched down to his brow, wide sunglasses, new sweatpants and sweatshirt, a wind-breaker, tube socks, and a costly pair of running shoes. He had a gym towel wrapped loosely about his neck to serve as either a scarf or sweat mop. Underneath the towel he'd clipped a Covid mask, ready to slip over his face in case shit got real, in case he spotted an opportunity.

Though he could certainly shed a pound or two, he was in excellent shape, and whenever he went jogging, he wondered why anyone in their right mind would run for pleasure. He'd endorse biking or swimming or pumping iron or – here's a novel idea – perhaps a little more discipline on the food intake side.

The man kept himself busy as he jogged the walkway, pondering the meaning of ancient rock and roll lyrics and classic lines of poetry, anything to take his mind off the burning in his lungs. *Sleep but lies, I dreamt her mine* echoed throughout his mind, and he struggled to remember the rest – *listen to a heart, let it tell a tale, listen to a heart, colors red and pale.* The man found himself reliving a pleasant memory, as the author of those lines of verse had been one of his *recipients*. The author of those line of verse had, in his final moments, found his crux of the matter . . . the poet had discovered his kernel of truth.

The man had been gym-hopping, trying to find a fitness club that best suited his needs, and happened to be working out at a gym in Bridgeport when he first became aware of the oversized baboon. He'd been doing chest flies and left his station to see if a gym member required first aid as the incessant bellowing sounded as though some unfortunate fellow had caught his tit in a rowing machine. Turned out no member had been flung off a treadmill or dropped a kettlebell on their big toe. Rather, some musclehead had the leg press set for maximum weight and grunted obnoxiously throughout each and every rep, letting the fitness gods know he was one of them.

After his third visit to the Bridgeport gym – accompanied by his third helping of the attention-seeking baboon's growls of exertion – he followed the gym member home.

You see, the weightlifter had made the grade; he'd found himself a top spot on the Dead Night Killer's *list of recipients*.

And as the weightlifter sat at his kitchen chair and worked his way toward his kernel of truth early that moonless morning, after the remains of his equally baboon-like son had been laid on the floor before him, he'd discovered the weightlifter spent whatever remaining free time he had penning poetry. And though the man was no scholar of verse, he thought the weightlifter's poem wasn't half bad.

Sleep but lies, I dreamt her mine was a constant refrain in the weightlifter's rhyme about the loss of a first love.

'Wow – huge irony,' he'd said after the weightlifter had finished expressing his poem in a muted monotone, right before he brought the night's events to an abrupt conclusion. 'I wouldn't be here if I'd known you'd written something as beautiful as that.'

Unfortunately, not all of his *recipients* were as talented as the musclebound poet. There was the banker who'd cut him off in traffic and, amid the horns and brakes and swerves of a near-collision, had thrust a middle finger from out the driver-side window of his black BMW as he sped away.

Turned out the banker's crux of the matter was that he secretly fancied himself an opera singer. He'd even allowed the man to spend his final moments singing from *Don Giovanni*. And though the banker's voice was adequate, it lacked the required stamina to sing at that Luciano Pavarotti level . . . completely understandable, though, considering the circumstances.

The kernel of truth for most of his other recipients was nowhere near as grandiose as the weightlifter and the banker, but he imagined that was just part of life.

The nurse who'd left him shivering in a patient gown in the clinic waiting room for forty-five minutes, and didn't have it in her to apologize for wasting his time, turned out to be a closeted chef, and he'd permitted her several final forkfuls of the garlic shrimp linguine she'd made earlier in the evening for dinner. After bringing their session to a swift completion, he'd tried the linguine and, not to speak ill of the dead, but he'd had better.

The kernel of truth for the quarrelsome clerk he'd had to hunt down in order to check out of a convenience store regarded the young man's days in track and field. Evidently, no other athlete at his or any of the nearby high schools had come close to touching him in the hundred-meter dash, and he'd gone on to compete at the state tournament. Though he'd placed at state, and received a partial scholarship at a second-rate college, his glory days had truly been his high-school years. The man had made sure to congratulate the clerk on his athletic prowess, and left him to reflect on races run and races won as he ushered the young man across his final finish line.

And the kernel of truth for the retiree who'd butted ahead of him in line to pay at the gas station – and ignored his meager squawk of protest – had been one of pride in leading his team of IT professionals in the development of applications utilized in healthcare. Though barely able to keep his eyelids open as the retiree recited his curriculum vitae, prattling on and on about his illustrious accomplishments, the man made sure to thank the sexagenarian for his years of service in the medical industry right before – well – right before one thing led to another.

The night with the retiree had been . . . *regrettable*.

That rumination passed through his mind, and he sprinted all-out until he reached the bus stop shelter at the corner of Fourteenth Avenue. At the shelter he paused, hands on hips, to catch his breath. Even though he ran not for fun, anything but, it was his third time circling the immediate locale. He ran to get the lie of the land, to commit to memory the streets and alleyways, roads and parkways, as well as any of the neighboring homes surrounding Detective John Hempstead's redbrick two-story in the densely suburban village of Broadview, Illinois, some twelve miles west of downtown Chicago.

John Hempstead was the detective featured in the Netflix documentary – the cop who basked in his video spotlight by taking forever and a day to say nothing of importance.

Detective John Hempstead had made the cut.

Detective Hempstead sat alone at the top of his list of recipients.

TEN

Τhe killer's father ladled another cup of water over the heated rocks to create steam and humidify the air, and then sat back down on the old cedar bench that had lined the rear wall of his sauna since he'd bought the lake house property a quarter century ago. He'd cranked the room temperature to 190 degrees Fahrenheit, about as hot as the aged sauna could achieve. If he could crank the temperature higher, he would gladly do so, in some muddled attempt at burning off the day's stressful events.

The father was shrouded in a sheen of perspiration. It felt good.

It helped him focus on a day that required nothing but focus. He'd been in the sauna an hour; even his bath towel was drenched. He'd toyed with grabbing another as his wife, Sheila, had enough towels stacked in a nearby closet to service a cruise ship. But he didn't need to dirty another one as he'd shortly be shutting down the sauna room and returning upstairs to shower.

It had been a smart decision to leave the office a few minutes early and drive to the lake house, even though it'd taken extra time in the jammed rush-hour traffic. He needed the solitude. He was in no condition to be around his wife or youngest daughter, Jessica, who, as a junior in high school, still lived at home.

Quite frankly, he was in no condition to be around anyone.

Good Christ – nothing had prepared him for this nightmare. Nothing. Not his eight years in the United States Marine Corps; not his stint at Yale Law, where he'd both headed up the *Yale Law Journal* and graduated number one in his class; not his early years in practice – contentious as they'd been, or his partnership at the firm that bore his surname in its letterhead, and not any of the extraordinary honors and opportunities that came later.

He'd married his high-school sweetheart the week before reporting to boot camp. With 20/20 hindsight, he prayed for a do-over – instead of marriage, he would just give Janine a peck on the cheek, a pat on the back, say goodbye, and wish her well as he leapt atop his father's old Harley-Davidson and rode off to basic training.

But Janine had been a stunner back in the day, and he'd been horny, and they'd both been kids . . . and marriage seemed like a good idea at the time.

At that young an age he'd known nothing of bipolar disorders, and even less regarding the debilitating depression such a disorder could trigger. During his four years of active service, he'd been away much of the time. When he was home, he figured Janine's mood swings were situation-based and common amongst newlyweds who were separated for chunks of time. Later, during his years of IRR, Individual Ready Reserve, back when he was attending Yale and he and Janine lived together in the same household, it became painfully obvious something was wrong with her, and that his lovely bride suffered from mental health issues.

The home front turned into a bigger minefield than he'd seen in his years of active duty – he lived on pins and needles, crept about the place as though on eggshells – but he'd made a commitment to Janine which he intended to keep, a wedding vow, and so he soldiered on, throwing himself into his studies. Eventually, Janine perked up when the test indicated she was pregnant. The ultrasound indicated a boy and, for the briefest of periods, it was as though they were back in high school again, happy and content as they painted the spare bedroom bright blue.

But it didn't last long, and Janine spent her final trimester in tears, eating like a bird, and rarely leaving her bed.

The day his son arrived, he was so elated he went old school, handing out cigars to visitors, hospital staff and, in some cases, gowned patients who'd roamed out into the corridor. He had a son to shower with love and affection, a boy to mentor, to teach how to toss and catch a ball.

Life would get better.

But the years slipped slowly past, and life didn't get better. Far from it. He'd demanded Janine seek counseling, which she did, but none of the medications prescribed worked as their reams of literature had indicated, or helped in the long-term; or, obviously, had any efficacy at all whenever Janine got locked into one of her darker moods and refused to take her daily pills.

Life became hellish.

Worse yet, something was seriously wrong with his son. Not physically; more upstairs. The father found it all but impossible to connect or bond with his little boy. Sure, responsibilities at work and his deteriorating relationship with Janine kept him away long hours; he'd not been around much, and there'd been no tee-ball or little league or Cub Scouts or pee-wee soccer or friends to invite over for birthday parties. There was nothing. His son had no interests or friends, and whenever he tried getting the boy involved in some new type of activity, any type of activity, there'd be hushed whispers from the master bedroom, and eventually Janine would saunter out from her lair long enough to put the kibosh on his latest suggestion.

Though not in the traditional manner of clinginess or being overly passive or continually seeking approval, his son was a momma's boy, for sure . . . but there was something else. It was hard to put your finger on, but the kid's personal interactions were off-key. He had a smile that meant anything but delight, a grin to send chills down your spine.

The father met Sheila when his son was almost six. She was single, having been recently divorced. Something sparked between the two of them almost instantly, and he realized he had a fleeting shot at happiness after all and, God forgive him, he leapt at the opportunity.

He gave Janine the house, the furnishings, the cars – everything to get out. And he paid a hefty amount in monthly child support. It took discipline; the father couldn't deny the pangs of guilt in those early days of his second marriage, but he'd been able to compartmentalize the previous chapter of his life – stuffing his mentally ill ex-wife and a most-peculiar son inside a drawer, a drawer he opened less and less frequently as the years passed by.

He'd been given the do-over he'd long prayed for. And when he listened to the voice message Janine's mother left nearly a decade after the divorce, he could tell something bad had occurred, something Janine's mother didn't want to share with his answering machine. He called her back immediately. In his heart of hearts, he'd believed Janine had committed suicide, but, as it turned out, she'd passed away in her sleep – no illicit drugs had been found in her system, no blades to the wrist, no pills popped.

His poor, mixed-up ex-wife had died a peaceful death.

But now the father had three young children with Sheila – normal children and a normal wife – to think of, and he'd be damned if he'd drop his *oddity* of a firstborn son into the mix.

But he was the boy's father, and he did everything in his power to help his son in the few years he had left before emancipation and adulthood. He got his son into a leading boarding school, paid for that, as well as the boy's college. He'd even been genuinely happy when his son informed him he'd be attending law school. The two had celebrated the news with their first and only steak dinner together.

But part of what made the father a masterful attorney was his ability to read people. And, though his firstborn had developed into a handsome and presentable young man . . . there was still that certain something *very off* about him.

ELEVEN

Special Agent Loris Renn stood in her open doorway. 'What are you doing here, Mac?'

'You shouldn't open the door without knowing who's out here?'

'I've got a doorbell camera and a nine millimeter.'

'A doorbell camera,' David Macaulay replied. 'I've got to get me one of those.'

'What are you doing here, Mac?' Renn repeated and glanced at her watch. 'It's getting late and I'm surprised you still remember where I live.'

'You were interviewed in that documentary,' Macaulay said, glancing in both directions. 'I don't think you should be staying here at home.'

'You and Surratt both,' Renn said. 'But I'll tell you what I told him. Our guy hit the trifecta – the director, the actor, and the narrator. He's sitting back and sucking up the limelight. He's done, at least for now.'

'But what if he's not?'

'Look, the asshole didn't MO Gorski or Oselka, and he went out of his way to hide their bodies so it could splatter all over the news once he killed the actor,' she replied. 'I'll start worrying when the key grip or assistant cameraman gets whacked.'

'I'm sure you're right, Loris, but what if—'

'Why do you even give a shit, Mac?' Renn cut him off mid-sentence. 'You and I – I thought we had something . . . right on up until you ghosted me.'

Macaulay glanced at the tan stucco on the side of the house and nodded.

'You didn't return my calls or texts, not a one.' Renn added, 'You made me feel like some crappy one-night stand.'

Macaulay nodded again and said, 'You weren't a one-night stand.'

'I don't get you, Mac.' She reached for the door handle. 'And I don't have time for this crap.'

'Remember that musical you dragged me to?'

Renn stared at him in disbelief. *'On Your Feet!'*

'That was our last date, right? For a guy who hates musicals, I had a great time,' he said. 'But the next day I got a call from a doctor – an oncologist I'd never spoken to before – and he requested I come in as soon as possible to discuss my *biopsy results.'*

Renn let go of the door. Her eyes softened. 'I heard about that, maybe a year later.'

Macaulay shuffled his feet on the front stoop. 'We had a lot of fun, Loris, but remember – we'd only been seeing each other a few weeks at the time.' He shook his head and continued, 'The diagnosis hit me hard . . . and I wasn't going to have you switch from dragging me to musicals to carting my ass to chemo.' Macaulay shrugged and looked at Renn. 'I wasn't going to do that to either of us.'

'But you're all good now, right?' Agent Renn said. She'd invited Macaulay inside for a cup of coffee. The two sat on wooden stools at her kitchen island, stirring cream and sugar into their light roasts.

'I am footloose and cancer-free.'

Renn smirked. 'I must admit, when I first heard the news about your condition, I may not have had the most *Christian* of thoughts.'

'I can't imagine you did.'

'Have you given up smoking?'

'That particular slice of heaven was the first thing that went by the wayside,' he said. 'But if it ever comes out of remission, I'll be buying a pack of Marlboros so fast your head will spin.'

Renn set her spoon down on the side of her saucer. 'You really should have told me.'

'It was a most *surreal* period of time. I went radio-silent on the *Big C* right up until I had to request a medical leave from work.'

They sat in stillness a minute, and then Macaulay reached inside a suit pocket and placed a handful of folded sheets on the granite countertop. 'Unlike those of us who toil for a living, I imagine you *federales* have some kind of safe house spa where you can go to hide out.'

'Yeah, right. They send us to a five-star resort.'

'If not,' he said, pointing at the sheets on the countertop, 'I get spammed with these monthly promotions or ads or whatever from my credit card companies. I normally don't read them but, as it turns out, they offer some absurdly good discounts at certain hotels.'

'I'm not using your credit card to get a hotel.'

Macaulay laughed out loud. 'Oh hell no, you're not, Loris. I don't trust you feds with our tax dollars, much less my credit cards. I just printed these off to show you what Visa and Discover had to offer.'

Renn pushed a handful of hair behind her ear and picked up the printouts.

'I'm sure you'd get reimbursed,' Macaulay said. 'They'd probably even spring for the minibar. I think you should give some serious thought to holing up somewhere and not telling a soul where you're at.'

Renn glanced through the different pages. 'But I've got that pesky day job thing going – they actually expect me to show up.'

'OK,' Macaulay said, putting his cup down. 'So . . . whenever you leave work, drive around the Loop for an hour. That'll throw anyone off.'

'It's been years, but once upon a time I got trained in evasive driving.'

'*Evasive driving* – how cool is that?' Macaulay said. 'I should have been a fibbie.' He paused a long second, and then he added, 'Promise me you'll give this some serious thought.'

TWELVE

N ever had I felt more safe to be surrounded by my two pups.

After dinner, I nuked a bag of popcorn, poured myself a supersized glass of cherry Coke, grabbed the remote control from where it hid under a pillow, surfed to Netflix, settled back on the couch, and watched 'On the Trail of the Dead Night Killer'.

Initially, since the attacks occurred in the dead of night, the press referred to him as the *Dead of Night Killer*. However, as victims began to stack up, they truncated it to the *Dead Night Killer*.

And the moniker stuck.

About a third of the way into the documentary, I hit pause and verified all outside lights were turned on, that the front, deck and basement doors were locked and chained, the window blinds were shut, and all curtains pulled tightly together. About two-thirds of the way through the program, I double-checked the locks and flipped on a bunch of interior lights, many in rooms that weren't even in use.

It didn't help that they'd made the documentary more ghost story than docudrama. To make matters worse, whenever narrator Tim Gorski went all creepy and spine-tingly with his periodic rendition of: 'Never forget to lock your doors and windows because in the wee, wee hours of the night, when you're off in sleepy-leepy land, the Dead Night Killer comes a-checking,' all I could picture was Gorski's ashen cheek peeking out from under a stretched hoodie as he lay underneath a pine tree in the woodland near Parkview Park. And when Gorski waxed on about how, if the Dead Night Killer finds an open door or window, 'He will come inside to check on you . . . and you will find yourself eyeball to eyeball with an unforgiving creature that does a great deal more than go bump in the night,' my mind's eye would conjure up the blur of Casey Oselka's face, shrouded in cling wrap, and staring straight up at me from inside the Christmas tree box.

Derek Ambler pranced about the docudrama's reenactment scenes like a poor man's Robert De Niro – skulking about the shadows, seething and hulking over his victims. If anything triggered the Dead Night Killer, causing him to come out of retirement, it might well have been Ambler's portrayal. In one recreation scene – though his back was to the camera – it was filmed in a manner suggesting the killer was directing a symphony over the deceased bodies of his recent victims. It was certainly provocative, but my first reaction was one of confusion. Where's the orchestration coming from? Did the guy bring a boombox along?

If I'd watched the documentary a month ago, it'd have been a bit cheesy and forgettable, but in light of today's news . . . it was bone-chilling.

When the program ended and I'd switched the channel to ESPN, Rex strode up from downstairs, a knotted sock in his teeth. Even though I'm twenty-three and a few odd months, one is never too old for a game of tug-of-war.

I was up for the challenge.

'Really, Rex?' I said. 'You want a piece of me?' I stood and stepped behind the couch. 'You want a shot at the title, huh?' I sat, dug my heels into the carpeting, and reached out my hands. 'Bring it, Rex – step into the octagon.'

My dog lunged forward. I latched on to one end of the knotted sock and the contest began. The sock stretched taut as my springer spaniel and I tugged each other back and forth. 'You think you got what it takes, Rex?' I egged him on as he growled and pulled in reverse. 'In your dreams, my friend,' I said. 'In your dreams.'

Ten minutes later, I held the knotted sock above my head as if it were an Olympic medal. Though victorious, I was sucking air, but my pooch was ready for round two. 'No, Rex. No two out of three – I won fair and square.'

If Rex ever packs on a few more pounds, it'll be me begging for the best two out of three. I handed him his sock and he headed back downstairs, to return his favorite toy to his khaki green doggie bed from where it must never be touched by anyone except him.

Crystal had yet to straggle home from work. I could guess what case she was slaving over and, no matter how late she returned home, she'd certainly be on time for Surratt's task force meeting tomorrow morning, the first one in the conference room no doubt, but unless they needed me and my dogs for an additional search, my role with the task force had come to an unceremonious conclusion. However, as Agent Loris Renn passed the background packets around the conference room after her briefing, I'd managed to hang on to mine.

Once Surratt left the conference room for an unscheduled call with the director of the FBI, the Grand Poobah, Agent Renn's presentation had been short and sweet, providing a ten-minute overview of case events that had come before, instructing us to both watch the Netflix documentary as well as read through her packet of information, which she informed us was the extended play version of her briefing, and come back in the morning, *sans moi*, with any and all questions.

Maybe it was the caffeine buzz from the cherry Coke, maybe it was the nature of the documentary I'd just viewed, but sliding into bed and dozing off to *sleepy-leepy land* was the last thing I had in mind. I set Renn's packet on the kitchen table, filled a glass with ice, added filtered water, sat down in a chair, opened the packet, took out the file, and began to read.

First came a listing of the known victims based on the Dead Night Killer's modus operandi, which included a late-night subduing and securing of his victims to either a kitchen or office chair, whichever was sturdiest. What followed next involved an amount of antemortem bruising – the discoloration of the skin prior to death – indicating his prey didn't die anytime soon. Finally, the killing strike – the Dead Night Killer's *coup de grâce* – of which the final section in Agent Renn's file contained medical examiner notes as well as an unappetizing series of autopsy diagrams and photographs.

All in all, there were eight known victims; however, Agent Renn cautioned the conference room of investigators and prosecutors this was a lowball number, as the serial killer had to have *evolved* toward his *preferred* methodology over a period of time, and that he'd most certainly killed before settling on this particular MO. When asked if she could estimate how many additional victims had been involved, Agent Renn shrugged and said, 'At least one, more likely three or four.'

Our '*evolved* toward his *preferred* methodology' unsub began his killing spree on a May night nine years back, when the body of a nurse – an RN named Leann Hubbard – who worked at a clinic in Western Springs had been discovered in her nearby Hinsdale condominium, duct-taped to a dining-room chair, head lolled forward, considerable blood had trickled down on to her clothes, forever staining her light blue scrubs.

Nurse Hubbard's sink had been stacked high with mixing bowls clouded with water, rinsed-off pots and pans, an assortment of measuring cups and ladles – I think she fancied cooking – as well as her dinner plate and utensils. After dinner, she'd had a lengthy phone conversation with her sister regarding the next day's book club meeting. Hubbard was known to live in her nursing scrubs, often wearing them right up until she changed into pajamas for bed. As Hubbard had remained clad in scrubs, investigators placed the time of the initial assault between nine and eleven that evening. The ME went on to place Hubbard's time of death between two and six o'clock the following morning.

The poor woman had spent several dark hours alone with her killer.

Hubbard's sister found her the next evening when she stopped by to pick her up for their book club meeting. No one answered repeated knocks on the front door, or repeated calls to Hubbard's landline or cell phone, so the sister dug through a pocket in her purse and found the spare key Hubbard had given her several years earlier.

When the police arrived on the scene, they had to call an ambulance for Hubbard's sister, who was experiencing heart palpitations.

Due to the intensity of Hubbard's assault and homicide, the detectives figured the killer was someone close to home, someone Hubbard had to have known and let into her condo – a crime of passion – and they questioned neighbors and family, colleagues and friends, even dragging in an ex-husband from more than a decade past. They gave up the ex-husband line of inquiry after the Dead Night Killer struck again in September of that same year. With the connection made, the police figured Hubbard's killer had either come in through the sliding glass door of her ground-floor patio or, even more alarming, had broken into her condominium earlier in the day and hid as Hubbard went about her cooking and nightly routine. Hubbard's sliding glass door had been locked when the police arrived, and her sister swore she'd not touched a thing, but how hard would it be for Hubbard's killer to lock the sliding door and then exit through the front entry, allowing the door to lock as it swung shut.

Unfortunately, there were no fingerprints or footprints, hair fibers, saliva or other DNA left at the murder scene. The investigators believed the man wore gloves, and possibly a mask and hairnet. There was no security tape or video of any stranger loitering about the complex, so – along with the unsub's seven other killings – Hubbard's homicide remained unsolved.

After reading through every sentence in the Leann Hubbard case, I flipped through the pages on the additional victims. I didn't have it in me to fine-tooth-comb the files on all of these lost souls, but I wanted to review the duo homicides depicted in Oselka's Netflix documentary – the night a father and son had both been murdered.

Peter Wells, age forty-two, drove a package-delivery truck for UPS and lived – and died – with his twenty-one-year-old son, Mark Wells, in a three-bedroom, two-bathroom, single family ranch home in the Bridgeport neighborhood of Chicago. The elder Wells was found duct-taped to a chair in the kitchen. Son Mark, evidently killed in his bed, had his body dragged from his room and presented as some kind of perverse offering to Father Wells, who, like Leann Hubbard had before him, spent several hours with his killer before being murdered himself.

Father and son Wells depended on a closed garage door as the primary deterrent during daytime hours. Girlfriends of the two men, as well as Father Wells's ex-wife, a handful of siblings, and a couple neighbors/friends had been provided with the four-digit code in case they needed to raise the garage door and, once inside the garage, they could gain access to the ranch-style home via a left-unlocked entry door. The police found the side garage door had been jimmied open, likely with one of those seven-inch pry bars you could pick up at any hardware shop. The killer then jerry-rigged the door so it shut and locked, and you couldn't tell the doorframe had been clawed at unless you were practically standing in front of it. The detectives also suspected the killer got inside during the afternoon and hid in the Wellses' unfinished basement until the household had gone to sleep for the night.

What the documentary pointed out – and the medical examiner's notes confirmed – was that father and son Wells were both large men. Peter Wells was six foot one and two hundred and twenty pounds. Young Mark Wells stood at six foot three and weighed two hundred and forty pounds. Both were heavy-duty weightlifters who never missed a day at the gym, often working out both mornings and evenings. The Wells were the kind of bodybuilders that had muscles on their muscles.

It's what the two lived for.

Certainly not the type of men that have 'victim' tattooed across their foreheads.

The last few sheets I scanned detailed the Dead Night Killer's final target, from nearly seven years ago, before the killer fell off the edge of the earth. He'd beaten this poor guy so badly I shuffled the corresponding autopsy photos to the bottom of the stack without looking at them. The coroner determined the man was dead from blunt-force trauma before the Dead Night Killer followed through with his signature *coup de grâce*, as though it were an afterthought.

The victim, a widower named Rick Schabacker, sixty-two, had

taken early retirement from some IT job out east and moved back to Chicago to be near his kids and grandchildren. Schabacker had purchased an executive townhome in Clarendon Hills, but the closing date got bumped back a month. Schabacker didn't want to put his kids out with storing all of his household furniture, so he scored a month-to-month lease on a one-bedroom apartment, also in Clarendon Hills. The retiree used the apartment essentially to stack his furniture and boxed belongings until he could close on the townhouse. Schabacker had a couple pair of jeans and some T-shirts in a closet and slept on a mattress on the bedroom floor.

The police figured the killer slipped in behind Schabacker as the retiree opened the security door to gain entrance to his apartment building. The killer likely gave Schabacker a head start toward his individual unit so as not to feel threatened – possibly hanging back in the stairwell – but then rushed Schabacker as he unlocked and opened the door to his temporary abode. Schabacker was discovered strapped to a wooden armchair in the apartment's kitchen; however, Schabacker is the only victim of the Dead Night Killer whose mouth had been stuffed with a washcloth prior to several strips of duct tape being wound about his head, covering his lips, likely done to keep Schabacker's screams from alerting those in neighboring units.

It broke the killer's MO. None of his other victims had expired while being beaten to a pulp. How much pent-up rage would the killer have had for some random retired guy who'd recently moved in from out of state?

It made no sense.

Why was Rick Schabacker treated differently than all of the other victims?

Was the killer once again *evolving* toward a *differing* methodology?

I got up to use the restroom. Rex was sound asleep, snoring on the couch, so I clicked off ESPN. When I returned to the kitchen, Alice sat on the floor, staring my way. I grabbed a beer from the fridge, hoping the alcohol might defuse the caffeine from the cherry Coke, make me drowsy and ripe for sleep. I rewarded Alice for keeping me company by flipping a handful of pretzels her way as though I were dealing cards.

I took a long sip of Rolling Rock and then dived headlong into what the FBI profiler, Special Agent Loris Renn, had to say. My review of her profile went fast; it took all of five minutes. I leaned back in my chair and stared at my bottle of beer. I liked Agent Renn. I'm sure she has a Mensa-level IQ – she seemed extremely bright at the morning briefing – but I'm a bit skeptical when it comes to this whole profiling thing. It's a bit like method acting where, if the profiler can get inside the unsub's mind, they'll be able to cough up information that'll practically lead the authorities to the unsub's doorway. We've all seen it in movies and on TV shows, repeatedly, but, I'm sorry . . . I call bullshit.

I tend to think living life makes us all shrinks, in one manner or another. Just from growing up, I've got the goods on my parents, my friends, and certainly my sister.

Let's say you're the black sheep of the family, or perhaps you've managed to perform some massive screw-up – well, there's probably eight relatives in the queue waiting their turn at the mic to cough up some highly specified, non-PhD version of your profile that'd nail your ass to the wall better than any agent sipping cups of cappuccino and pulling a Stanislavski in some side room at the field office on West Roosevelt.

For example, Agent Renn went with *male*. Yup, I concur. Not that big a stretch considering the raw force involved in over-whelming the intended targets. Agent Renn also went with *Caucasian*. OK, why not? I'm sure the stats are on her side. Renn thought it likely the unsub had gone on to higher education and received a degree or two. I don't know. Maybe. Quite frankly, I'd be more scared of having a carpenter or mechanic or even a plumber pissed off at me than some guy who wrote his dissertation on Sylvia Plath. Agent Renn then put the age of the unsub between *twenty and forty-eight*. I hate to be persnickety, but I'd kick that up a few notches; maybe make him between twenty-six and forty-eight. Doctors say *you're only as sick as your secrets*, so considering the Dead Night Killer's level of *sickness*, as well as his know-how in doing what he does makes him a bit more mature than some dude who's yet to attend his five-year high-school reunion.

Agent Renn went on to discuss the unsub having *trust* and *rela-tionship issues* – I guess being a homicidal maniac tends to derail any budding hints of romance – *due to an emotionally or physically abusive parent during his formative years, or an absentee or emotionally distant father during such years.* Wow, Renn's got that parental thing covered from every conceivable angle.

Here's where my skepticism comes into play. Unlike in the movies, none of this *conjecture* sent authorities scampering to the unsub's door.

And if Agent Renn's profile is incorrect, wouldn't that *ipso facto* – I live for Latin terms I don't really understand – lead authorities further away from his doorway?

I finished off my Rolling Rock, placed the bottle in the sink, sat back down, and shuffled through the pages to the section focusing on the unsub's modus operandi. Although I'd already reviewed how he stalks his prey in order to find out where they live, then cases their homes, figuring out how best to worm his way inside, there's no discernible pattern as to *whom* he stalks. Male, female, young, middle-aged, those qualifying for AARP, gay or straight – it doesn't matter.

He's an equal opportunity killer.

Also understood is how he gets his rocks off subduing his targets, strapping them to a chair, and having some kind of *tête-à-tête* with them into the wee hour of the morning, until he's quenched his thirst . . . and it's then, and only then, that he delivers the killing blow.

Crystal had mentioned *that Rambo knife of his* in reference to Tim Gorski getting stabbed in the abdomen and then having his throat slashed by the side of the park trail. The medical examiners had come to a similar conclusion: that a combat knife – seven inches of carbon steel with a clip point blade, possibly some version of a Ka-Bar – was used in an upward thrust through the anterior belly of the victim's digastric muscle, under their jaw, with the violent trajectory continuing through the palate or roof of the victim's mouth, ascending through their nasal cavity and ethmoid bone, and, ultimately, lodging in the frontal lobe of the victim's brain.

After the killing wound, the Dead Night Killer spends a few seconds wiping clean his blade on the victim's clothing.

And here I'd been thinking I'd be falling asleep sometime soon.

I placed Special Agent Renn's file back into the packet, grabbed a second Rolling Rock, and took a moment to collect my thoughts.

At the forefront: how does a blood-soaked beast like the Dead Night Killer vanish off the face of the earth for the past seven years?

Where did the man go?

What's he been up to?

The documentary posits he may have gone to prison for a differing crime . . . but I'm not so sure about that. I don't picture him hot-wiring cars or knocking over liquor stores.

And I seriously doubt he ran off and joined the circus.

THIRTEEN

The killer's father dropped the bag containing his hamburger and french fries into the kitchen trash bin. He'd picked up the fast food on his drive in – the bag had been sitting out since his arrival hours earlier – but he was not in the least bit hungry. Or, considering the lateness of the hour, the least bit tired. However, he sipped from his cup of 7-Up as he leaned against the railing, staring out over the dark stillness of the lake, hoping the carbonation would settle his stomach.

So far it wasn't working.

The only thing his son brought to the lake house after his mother's passing had been a box full of knickknacks and memories, tied shut with a red ribbon. The box took residence on a shelf in the closet of the guest room at the lake house where the boy stayed that summer. The father had gone through it on the day his son flew off to boarding school. It contained birthday cards from his mother, pictures of the two of them together, uninspired artwork he'd likely done at school, yearbooks from junior high, and – at the very bottom of the box – a slip of paper from the driver's education course his son had recently completed. It was the only item inside his son's box of memories that had not come over from his mother's house.

And the father saw that his son had written the home address of his driving instructor in the sheet's upper margins. That's odd, he thought at the time; they would never give out such personal information. What purpose would his son have had to go searching for the instructor's address? He jotted the instructor's name and address on a Post-it note before returning the original sheet back to his son's box of memories.

Later, when he was alone in his office, he'd Googled the instructor's name as well as his address and, fortunately, received no results in return. He'd dropped the Post-it note inside a lower desk drawer.

Life went on, and he soon forgot about the driving instructor's name and address.

The father had been proud of his time in the United States Marine Corps. He'd not only hung on to the Ka-Bar fighting knife he'd been issued, but went on to collect historic combat knives. His collection included a World War One-era Mark I trench knife as well as several mint-condition models of the Ka-Bar 1219C2 that replaced the Mark I during World War Two, and which the Marines renamed the Ka-Bar USMC Mark 2 Combat Knife and went on to carry during the Korean War, the war in Vietnam, and throughout the global war on terrorism. The father further beefed up his collection with a Fairbairn-Sykes fighting knife, a British commando knife favored by the OSS and SOE. He rounded out the assortment with a mint-condition V-42 Stiletto, utilized by the First Special Service Force – aka The Devil's Brigade – he'd purchased from a fellow aficionado.

The father had initially kept his collection in a glass display case in the corner office of the law firm in which he'd become the managing partner. Whenever potential clients stopped by for a visit, he'd point and provide a brief history of each combat knife, and end his talk with a wink and a smile, saying, 'This display is here to show you how hard our firm will fight for your interests.'

And nine times out of ten, the law firm got their business.

But as he aged and times became more politically correct, he moved his collection, display case and all, to a little-used storage room on the lower level of the lake house and then slapped a padlock on the room's thick and sturdy door, which was likely overkill as the lake house, due to its infrequent use, was already protected with a state-of-the-art home security system.

More years passed, his firstborn graduated law school and remained in Chicago – the father breathed a huge sigh of relief – and one day he was cleaning out his office desk when he came across a Post-it note gathering dust at the bottom of a side drawer. The father stared at the Post-it note a long second before remembering what it was. He tossed the note in the bin with the rest of the obsolete materials he'd fished from his desk, but a second later he retrieved the slip of paper and brought up Google.

He'd remembered receiving no hits on the name of his son's driving instructor from all those years back after his son had first stayed at the lake house, but now it was different. The results poured in, numerous articles about the driving instructor's death, articles about his *unsolved* homicide. The man had been beaten and stabbed to death in his own home, the murder committed the summer after his son had graduated from the University of Chicago . . . the same summer his son spent dallying about the lake house before returning to the University of Chicago's School of Law in time for the fall term.

After that grim discovery, the father made great haste driving to the lake house. He tapped in the security code and ran to the guest room, to the closet where his son kept his box of keepsakes. He rifled through the box, and everything was there, old yearbooks and photographs, just as he'd remembered from years earlier . . . everything except for the sheet of paper from his son's driver's education training.

Something about the instructor having been stabbed to death in his own home sent the father frantically scurrying about the lake house in search of the key to the padlock on the storage room door, the room that he hoped could be opened by no one except himself. He was at a loss for where he'd placed the key, tearing through every drawer and cabinet, when the lightbulb finally went off in his mind and he jogged to the wall-length bookshelf in the den, yanked the hardcover copy of *Oliver Wendell Holmes: A Life in War, Law, and Ideas* off the ledge . . . and there it was, the padlock key, where he'd hidden it years ago.

He rushed down to the storage room, unlocked the padlock, opened the door, and flipped on the overhead lights. There stood his display case, just as he'd remembered it, and he let free a loud sigh of relief. He almost left, but instead stepped forward to appreciate his historic collection of combat knives.

It was then he realized one of the Ka-Bar Mark 2 knives was missing.

That had been seven and a half years ago, back when something terrifying had been occurring in Chicago, back when a serial killer known as the Dead Night Killer had been stealing his way into homes at night and – with the vaguest of generalities provided in the media – stabbing those inside to death.

Just like what had occurred to his son's ill-fated driving instructor.

The father couldn't know for certain . . . nevertheless, he knew.

He clearly couldn't prove a thing . . . nevertheless, he knew.

Just as he knew his son had discovered the key to the storage room and made off with one of the lethal pieces in his collection.

He knew all this just as he knew he'd be ruined – *no, he'd be destroyed* – if his son ever got caught.

The father had done things he'd not been proud of. First, he'd leveraged his connections in order to glean information into the Dead Night Killer investigation, only to learn his fear was not unfounded. The victims had, in fact, been dispatched with some type of combat knife. Next, he'd done other things – *extralegal things* – that even the most naive of jurors would return with the hastiest of guilty verdicts to charges of obstructing justice and being an accessory after the fact.

Janine had to be cackling in glee from the lowermost depths of her grave.

But out of nowhere came the reprieve.

A glorious reprieve of nearly seven long years.

A reprieve he'd considered permanent until he caught up with the day's headlines.

The killer's father drove to the lake house this evening not only for solitude, or to focus his thoughts, but to check on something. He had replaced the padlock with a newer one, a stronger one, and kept the only set of keys in his office at work, a place his son had never been. So after he tapped in the security code, he rushed down to the storage room and . . . damn near had a heart attack.

This time there'd been no games played with padlock keys.

This time the door to the storage room had been shattered open, as though someone had struck at it with a sledge hammer. And the locks he'd added to the display case itself hadn't fared much better as shards of glass littered the floor.

It was both a mess and a message.

The message was chilling. It was terrifying.

A second Ka-Bar M2 had been taken.

FOURTEEN

'My ex told the truth on the installment plan.' Detective John Hempstead grinned as he held court in his basement family room or, more accurately – considering the wall-mounted widescreen, the neon beer signs above a corner wet bar, the pool table and vintage pinball machine – his man cave. He added, 'Each revelation a bit more mind-boggling, more damning than the previous one until, like the frog in that slow-boiling pot of water, your new norm's a foreign construct of bill collectors, alcohol, and, every so often . . . the police.'

I was the laggard of the bunch, having just arrived at Detective Hempstead's Broadview address with a couple of excited dogs in tow. I'd been instructed to park my pickup truck a block over and wait until Crystal gave me the *all clear* before cutting across Hempstead's neighbor's yard in order to be ushered inside Hempstead's back door. A cop with infrared was on the ground near where Hempstead's neighbor stored a canoe, providing Crystal a verbal thumbs-up whenever one of us night-shifters reported for duty.

The difficult part was the backyard lights had been flipped off at both addresses in order to mask the arrival of Hempstead's CPD colleagues as well as me and my dogs, in case the unsub was lurking outside somewhere, casing the joint as we arrived. I could barely make out the shape and shadow of what I assumed to be a canoe but couldn't spot the officer to save my soul. Rex emitted a low growl and Alice headed toward the canoe – they knew someone was there – but a whispered command brought their attention back to me. The Laurel and Hardy of it all included hoisting Alice and Rex – both dogs amused and bemused – over Hempstead's chain-link fence in the near-total darkness of a post-twilight November night.

Up close, Hempstead had a drinker's face, blushed red with enlarged blood vessels, a bald crown and, based upon the snippet of conversation I'd walked in on, a reprobate's heart. He was half a head shorter than me, and I spotted a handful of silver-colored cavity fillers in the tips of several teeth. Dress the homicide detective in a whiskey-stained T-shirt, sprinkle him with tats, and he'd be cast as the perfect carny geek – the sideshow hawker who draws curious crowds into a freak show. Carnival barker or not, Hempstead had a well-traveled face, its warranty long expired, and I suspected the detective was on the cusp of retirement.

Hempstead continued, 'Final straw was *my boy* – or, as it turned out, he was *my brother's boy*. Haven't seen hide nor hair of her since that *big reveal* dropped, none of us have. Anyway, it's been years, but that's how I wound up with the house to myself and not a penny in child support.' He grinned again, winking silver. 'Why are the crazy ones so damned good-looking?'

'Not the first time I've heard that question,' I replied, and all eyes shifted my way.

Detective Crystal Pratt, her partner Mike Heppner, and Hempstead's detective partner, a younger Hispanic man named Jacobo Alba who'd also attended the FBI task force meeting and asked to be called 'Jake', all stood in a half-circle around Detective Hempstead.

'Well, Gramps did warn me when I was young,' Hempstead said, 'the screwing you get ain't worth the screwing you get.'

Heppner chuckled while Crystal took Alice's leash in one hand and said, 'I'll start upstairs if you want to start down here, Cor. Then we can meet on the main level.'

Crystal had hidden under a blanket on the backseat floor as Hempstead pulled his Dodge Charger into the garage after work. Both waited until the garage door shut before exiting the vehicle and shuffling inside the detective's home. Before the sun went down, Hempstead made a big production out of checking his mailbox and then spent another hour in the driveway pretending to winterize his lawn mower just in case there was an audience of one who'd arrived earlier and hidden himself in the cheap seats. As the sun set, Hempstead flipped on several interior lights, so it'd be easy to tell he was at home for the evening.

'Your dogs can find him if he's already hiding in the house, right? Like he did with some of the other victims?' Hempstead asked me after Crystal and Alice headed upstairs. Detective Jake Alba joined them, in case the girls tripped over any lethal surprises.

I nodded. 'They've never lost a game of hide-and-seek.'

'Since I'm the bait, I'd sure hate to have you guys out combing the neighborhood just to have the fucker slip from behind the furnace and shish-kabob my skull.'

'We'll make sure he's not already here before we head outside.' I doubted we'd get that lucky. It'd sure make for a short night if we caught the unsub hiding somewhere inside Hempstead's two-story.

'Even if he's not under the workbench in the garage, I'm gonna keep Loretta close by,' Hempstead said, affectionately patting a shotgun atop his pinball machine.

Detective Hempstead had been CPD's unofficial mouthpiece to the press over these past two days. *The man's essentially a coward*, he'd informed the *Chicago Tribune*. *Of course, it's sexual; it's always sexual with these clowns*, he'd told WGN-TV. *He's clearly a misogynist, a woman-hater* he'd shared with WBBM Newsradio.

It had been Crystal's idea, only this time, remarkably, she'd received a surprising amount of support from partner Heppner. Crystal figured Hempstead may already be in Dutch with the killer for having appeared in the Netflix documentary, so why not have the detective further *rile the guy up* with some choice quotes strategically fed to the media? If the guy got so damned triggered from a docudrama on a streaming service, why not taunt the SOB in press interviews?

Nothing too blatant or over the top – just enough to get the unsub out in the hood, casing Hempstead's Broadview home for any avenues of entry, at the same time the three investigators, as well as me and the pups, were outside looking for him. Meanwhile Detective Hempstead remained inside, ready to introduce any trespasser to Loretta. Along with the set of infrared eyes positioned to monitor both the detective's backyard and side garage door, CPD had three squad cars in play. They were set up far enough away as not to scare off the killer, yet close enough to swoop in whenever instructed or pull over any suspicious vehicles if directed.

I walked Rex through the detective's mostly finished basement – the guest room and main closet, the bathroom and tub, the storage area under his staircase, the laundry room – as Hempstead trailed along, chattering on and on about the distressing effects of turning sixty. Mike Heppner followed Hempstead, hanging on the man's every word and cackling like a hyena.

'When you get to my age, you get about forty square inches added to your scrotum.' Hempstead mentored Crystal's partner on growing old gracefully as my springer spaniel and I checked behind the washer and drying machines. 'If I lie on my belly at night, it's like sleeping on an octopus.'

Heppner said, 'Maybe they got surgery for that.'

The detective's face lit up. 'I could have a doctor remove that extra scrote and use it as a jar opener,' Hempstead said. 'With all that excess, I could even send a few out at Christmas – you know, for family.'

Rex and I left the two detectives grab-assing in the basement and headed up to the main level where we discovered that Crystal, Alice, and Detective Alba had already completed the lion's share of the work.

Ten minutes later, after the detectives verified all mics and earpieces were in perfect working order, Crystal glanced my way and said, 'Are you ready?'

I nodded. 'Let's do this.'

FIFTEEN

I'd been walking Rex around the blocks surrounding Detective Hempstead's two-story for over an hour. It was nearly eleven, and the only suspicious activity we'd encountered was a couple of teenage boys who kept peeking our way and then stepped off the curb, and into the street, rather than pass us on the sidewalk. The answer was an olfactory one. I would have caught the scent of cannabis had the two crossed the street completely. Rex would have caught the scent had they been one town over.

Just a couple of neighborhood potheads getting a final puff in before heading back home to Mommy and Daddy's house.

Crystal and the other detectives joked about calling the squad cars in to pick up the teens, but figured we'd best stick to our main task and give the little delinquents an early Christmas present by letting them go.

Speaking of Crystal, her true calling could have been that of an air traffic controller. She set up the street patterns for the four of us to wander as well as switched up our routes so as to preclude any enquiring eyes wondering why that incredibly handsome young man with the springer spaniel keeps circling Twelfth Avenue.

Porch lights and the occasional streetlamp illuminated our assigned pathway as Rex and I turned left on to Fourteenth Avenue. We'd already hiked many of the avenues, including Thirteenth and Fifteenth, as well as cutting across both Fillmore and Harvard. Feeling sassy, we'd once even stretched our assigned route all the way to Lexington Street.

A few more laps and I'd qualify as a Broadview tour guide.

Since Crystal took Alice along with her, and I had Rex, each of us would appear to any prying eyes as nothing more than a second-shifter or dog lover taking Fido out for an evening sniff and pee before hitting the hay. Detective Alba, however, took on a new persona as he casually strolled Hempstead's neighborhood, smoking a cigarette – just another poor guy whose wife wouldn't allow him to smoke indoors. In fact, right before we slipped out the back of Hempstead's house, Hempstead recommended Alba wear mom jeans to complete the picture.

As for Detective Heppner, well, he was likely occupied taking his ego for a walk.

Being a lowly dog handler on loan to CPD, I kept my droll banter via the fancy mic fitted to my collar to a bare minimum. So, while the CPD investigators were in constant communication with each other, I kept my trap shut, except when Crystal requested a status update. I figured whenever I spoke, any casual observer would assume I was rocking out to tunes from earbuds while taking my dog for a late-night walk, but, in this dim of light, someone would need to be pretty close by to even notice.

My job was simplicity personified. If I spotted anything suspicious, anything at all – or if Rex alerted me to anything suspicious – we'd call in the squad cars. Pretty much the same task held true for the CPD detectives. And Crystal had taken Alice along with her as, well, Alice was easier for my sister to read on account of that genius thing Alice has got going.

Fortunately, I'd caught a weather report earlier in the day – evening temps were expected to drop to the mid-forties – so I wore a V-neck T-shirt under my polo shirt. Rounding out this fashion apparel was my usual pair of jeans and hiking boots, as well as an ancient red windbreaker of my father's that I found in the front closet.

Although I seldom spoke, kept the verbal reindeer games to zilch, it was clear the other detectives were just as bored as I was. Highlights of the evening's forced march included the occasional passing of a car or bus, a resident or two rolling out their garbage or recycle bin for the next day's pickup, and one idiot, Crystal informed me, had his sprinklers turned on.

I figured if tomorrow night passed as uneventfully as tonight was proving to be, they'd scale Crystal's operation way back. Perhaps keep the infrared guy on the lawn and stick an extra officer with Hempstead in case the killer somehow made it inside.

Either way, I was getting my ten thousand steps in.

'Anything new, Cor?' Crystal whispered over my earpiece.

'Just turned on to Fourteenth,' I said, dropping my chin, feeling as though I had to speak into my collar. Then I caught Rex's muzzle swerve left, followed by a low growl. I tracked his gaze. Thirty yards ahead lay the bus stop shelter I'd passed on a previous trek down Fourteenth Avenue, perhaps thirty minutes earlier, only now a lone figure stood inside the dimly lit accommodation, in front of the bench, and checking his watch.

'Easy now, boy,' I said, calming my springer spaniel.

'Was that Rex?' Crystal asked.

'Yeah,' I replied. 'No big deal, just some guy waiting on a bus.'

SIXTEEN

The man recognized the dog handler in the light kicked off by the corner streetlamp the instant the dog handler turned on to Fourteenth Avenue.

There could be no confusion. The dog handler even had Rin Tin Tin on a leash in front of him, and the man knew immediately he'd stumbled into a trap. The dog handler worked with CPD, and there's no way his presence on the streets of Broadview tonight was any coincidence. Which likely meant that guy he'd spotted earlier, the one smoking the cigarette, was with the cops as well.

Though he'd been scouting Detective Hempstead's neighborhood for weeks, he'd noticed the detective had been getting quite a bit of airtime over the past few days. He'd been amused by it and looked forward to bringing up some of the spicier quotes once he'd secured Hempstead to his kitchen chair . . . once they were ready to hold palaver.

Instead, Detective Hempstead's comments to the media had been part of a CPD trap.

Fuck!

The man didn't feel any sense of panic. There'd been no crime. Not yet, anyway. He was blocks away from Hempstead's home. He'd not been caught prowling about the bushes or trespassing in anyone's yard, and, by all appearances, he was just someone waiting on a bus. The man had dressed again in his jogging outfit, his hoodie up with the knit cap down to his brow, gym towel acting as a scarf against the night air. He brought one end of his towel over his mouth and tucked the excess into his hoodie, over his shoulder. His face was virtually shrouded. It was the perfect disguise. There was no way the dog handler could identify him.

Just a pair of eyes and a nose on a cold and dark night.

No, the man didn't feel panic. Rather . . . he felt cheated.

Tonight would likely have been a final recon. However, if the coast appeared clear – all quiet and settled in for the evening – as he worked his way into Detective Hempstead's backyard . . . it may well have happened. But now he'd have to forget about Hempstead; he'd have to let the news-making detective slip through the cracks; he'd have to leave Broadview and not look back.

He had been cheated.

All his efforts wasted.

Or had they?

Just because Hempstead was off the table tonight didn't mean everyone else had to be.

The man heard the dog growl and glanced down at his watch as though pondering why his bus was taking an eternity to arrive. The dog handler nodded and the man tossed up a hand in greeting as the handler and his pup strode past the bus shelter.

The normal inclination would be to head to his car as though he hadn't a care in the world, get behind the wheel, drive home, and then he could cry into his beer.

That would be the normal inclination . . . but his *normal inclination* was to kill.

The man unclipped his Covid mask from his gym towel and slid it over his face.

He was going to kill the dog handler.

SEVENTEEN

I gave bus dude a quick nod and he shot me a wave – guy talk since prehistoric times. He was bundled up against the cold night air. Parka weather was at least a month away, coming sooner than I'd like, but Chicagoans do the thinner layers dance until late December and the frigid temps can no longer be denied. I swore I'd seen a city bus turn down Fourteenth a few minutes earlier, so bus dude might have a bit of a wait on his hands.

Public transportation discriminates against professional dog trainers like me. I'd get tasered by a squad of transit cops if they caught me sneaking any dogs on the L. It's a moot point, though, as you need a PhD in algorithms to figure out the city's bus schedules. Plus I loathe standing about, waiting on a ride.

I glanced into the dark patch of woods that lay beyond the bus shelter. No houses for fifty yards on this stretch of Fourteenth – after all, who'd want a bus stop at the end of their driveway? – but if you cut through this stretch of trees, you'd hit the backyards of some of the finer homes along Thirteenth Avenue.

I told you I could be a tour guide.

Bus dude was decked out in running gear and my mind flashed to Tim Gorski, the voice-over artist who ran the woodland trail by his South Edgebrook home first thing in the morning and before he ate dinner every night.

Then it hit me, a meteor striking earth.

How would a person lying in wait for Tim Gorski be dressed?

Gorski's killer sure as hell wouldn't be wearing a top hat and tails.

I caught a whisper of movement, began to turn, but Rex was on it, whirling about – a tornado in motion – the leash now taut, growling and lunging at the figure that'd sneaked up behind us.

My heart skipped a beat as I clung to Rex's leash. The man stood frozen on the sidewalk, ten feet away, outside of Rex's range, facing me, a right hand behind his back. Unlike me, he didn't appear terrified. I heard Crystal speaking over my earpiece, but couldn't make out what she was saying. My attention riveted on the figure in front of us.

'Can I help you?' I stammered over Rex's snarls, as if I were taking an order at a fast-food franchise.

Crystal spoke again in the background, asking me questions but getting no response. My focus glued to the motionless stranger. We stared at each other what seemed an eternity. I could only see a strip below his brow – his eyes – like peering at a medieval knight through his visor. The hair on the back of my neck stood at attention as his right hand began to sway out from behind his torso, revealing a blade the size of Navy Pier.

'It's him,' I said, pulling the leash, reeling Rex back toward me. 'It's him, Crys.'

EIGHTEEN

Crystal heard Rex snarl. Something was going down. And not something good.

'What's happening, Cor?' she spoke into her police microphone. Then in a louder voice she ordered, 'Report in, Cory.'

Alice stared up at her inquisitively. She'd caught Rex's warning growl as well.

'*Can I help you?*' Crystal heard her brother's startled voice, not directed at her.

Crystal closed her eyes, performing mental gymnastics over assigned routes. She spoke again into her microphone, 'You're on Harvard, right, Mike?'

'Roger that.'

'Cory has a situation at the bus stop on Fourteenth,' she said. 'An altercation of some kind. That's all I know.'

'OK – I'll be there in a flash.'

'Be careful,' she said, and then instructed Detective Alba they were all meeting at the bus shelter on Fourteenth ASAP.

'Oh shit, I'm on the opposite end,' Alba replied. 'Give me a minute.'

Crystal headed toward Fourteenth herself with Alice in the lead. She began directing the squad cars to converge on the bus shelter but paused when Cory spoke again.

'*It's him*,' Crystal heard Cory say. Her blood froze. '*It's him, Crys.*'

NINETEEN

I stepped back, pulling a stubborn Rex with me. He sensed danger, wanted to throw down, but it wasn't a fight we could win. I backed up another step, leash clenched in my right hand. Bus man advanced, matching our retreat step for step. And though the man's face was shrouded, I could sense him enjoying my predicament.

If I turned and tried to outrun bus man on the sidewalk or street – well, that's an awfully big knife for him to stab and slash at me from behind – a sure way to die.

'Run!' I screamed, dropped Rex's leash, and tore sideways on to the grass. Rex took my cue and dived into the woods. Gold medalist Usain Bolt couldn't catch my springer spaniel, but I wouldn't be following him, not into the woods – that would be a second way to die.

Crystal is six years older than I am; nevertheless, while growing up I'd find ways to piss her off. The key to my survival was by placing an obstacle between us. As a fleeing child I'd make her chase me around the Chevy pickup until she got bored and gave up or Dad stormed out to put an end to the ruckus.

I needed to get behind the bus stop shelter. Fifteen more feet and this prick and I could play ring around the bus shelter all night long. I'd watch him through the toughened safety glass and if he switched direction, I'd adjust accordingly. But I didn't need all night. I just needed the shelter between us long enough for Crystal and the cavalry to arrive.

But bus man read my mind and sidestepped to cut off my path to safety.

Shit!

Now I'd have to take to the woods when a voice from out of nowhere screamed, 'Stop!'

Bus man and I froze, eyes still on each other, but there was Detective Heppner sprinting down Fourteenth, from where I'd come, gun in hand, and closing in on bus man's six. The cavalry had arrived and Heppner shouted, 'Put the knife on the ground! Do it right now!'

Bus man's held my gaze as he crouched in compliance so to set his blade on the sidewalk. My blood curdled as I read his mind. Heppner had gotten close, too close, with thoughts of cuffing the guy as though he were a shoplifter. Instead, bus man whirled about as Rex had done seconds earlier and, with the fast grace of a ballet dancer, he dived skyward. I watched in horror as Heppner realized his mistake, as the killer batted Heppner's gun aside as though shooing a fly, as the knife shot upward, under the detective's chin, as the killer's lightning thrust lifted Heppner off his feet.

Then the knife came out, Heppner crumpled to the sidewalk . . . and the killer turned again my way.

I'm sure I screamed as we stared at each other, and then I fled behind the bus shelter, my original plan, so he couldn't get at me with that goddamned blade of his. He stepped toward the shelter, toward me, and I realized he'd not yet finished. Sirens broke the air and the man turned on a dime, switching course, now dashing into the woods, heading where Rex had gone.

I froze there a moment, and then realized I needed to check on Heppner.

A second later I was on my knees, my hands cupping the wound under Heppner's chin, applying pressure as the detective made gurgling sounds, as his body shuddered and seized. I heard Rex off in the distance, barking his lungs out, and I prayed he'd not give chase. Then brakes squealed as squad cars arrived. The bus shelter now lit up like a Broadway stage. Police officers poured into the street as I screamed, 'Get an ambulance!'

A cop ran over with a first-aid kit and knelt by my side, saying, 'It's on the way.'

'He went in there,' I said, nodding toward the woods. Then I heard Rex cry out in pain. My heart broke, and I added, 'My dog's in there, too.'

Words were spoken, and a second later three of the officers jogged into the patch of trees with flashlights in their hands. Then two of the squad cars were back in play, peeling off to Thirteenth Avenue, to try and head off our attacker.

I kept pressure on Heppner's wound as the cop near me looked into Detective Heppner's eyes and felt for a pulse. There were no more tremors and I suspected if I let go, Heppner's head would loll to the side.

I felt a nudge on the back and there was Rex; my beautiful brave springer spaniel had returned shaken but safe from his exodus into the woodland. My eyes filled with tears and I spotted Crystal and Alice sprinting up Fourteenth Avenue, heading our way. A figure I took to be Detective Alba lagged a half-block behind. An instant later Crystal hovered above us, her face as white as tissue paper.

The officer who'd come with the medical kit looked up from Detective Heppner, caught my eye, and then turned to Crystal and said, 'He's dead.'

TWENTY

That goddamned barking mongrel nearly got him as he scrambled over a six-foot privacy fence and dropped into someone's backyard. The dog caught hold of his pant leg and he had to kick at its head with his free foot until the fucker yelped and let go. He wanted to turn around and stab at the critter through the chain-link, but figured he'd done enough *stupid* for one day.

Plus, he had to get the hell out of Broadview before the cops closed in or moved to shut the suburb down.

Time was of the essence.

The man flew across Thirteenth Avenue, cut between houses,

jumped fences, and did the same across Twelfth Avenue and then Eleventh, with more than a few motion-detector lights flipping on in his wake. He slipped out from between a couple of town-homes on to Tenth, glanced both ways, and then jogged a final fifty yards through a string of adjacent front yards until he slowed it down and strolled into the parking lot of the cheap-ass corner apartment complex where he'd left the old Saturn with the muddied-up plates.

Once inside the vehicle, the man dropped his sheathed Ka-Bar into a plastic grocery bag, like the kind you'd get at a dollar store. He then rolled up the bag and shoved it beneath the driver's seat.

He'd be hanging on to the commando knife.

Then off came the sweatshirt. He turned it inside out to avoid smearing any blood on the car's dashboard, steering wheel or seats, and stuffed it into a black garbage bag. His knit cap, Covid mask, gym towel, and pair of gloves followed suit. He then stuffed this bag under the passenger's seat.

It would be disposed of on the way home.

The man slipped into an old sport jacket he'd draped over the seatback, ran fingers through his hair, caught the flashing red and blue lights in his periphery and slumped down, his eyes an inch above the steering wheel. A squad car flew down the cross street on the far side of the apartment complex, answering a call with a silent alarm. The squad had to be doing close to ninety miles an hour, most certainly headed to a certain bus stop on Fourteenth Avenue.

The man left the lot, turning right on to Tenth Avenue, and then made an immediate left at the cross street, in the opposite direction from where the squad car was heading. He dared not speed or run a stop sign. Even as he put more and more blocks behind him, he would not feel safe until he reached I-290.

Then he'd start thinking about where to dump the garbage bag.

PART THREE
The Dead Years

If a dog will not come to you after having looked you in the face, you should go home and examine your conscience.

Woodrow Wilson

TWENTY-ONE

'Because of the forty-eight hour rule,' I said. 'Seemed a lot smarter than hand-to-hand combat,' I pointed toward a scowling Detective Hempstead, 'at your garage door.'

Once again we'd been summoned to attend SAC Surratt's task force at the FBI field office. Same windowless conference room, same cast of characters – CPD detectives, Cook County prosecutors, a glut of special agents – only this time there seemed to be more hostility aimed at Crystal and myself than at Detective Heppner's killer. It had been a trying past few days; highlights to include multiple interviews with several of Crystal's higher-ups at CPD's headquarters building on South Michigan Avenue. The interviews felt like interrogations, more suspect than witness, and as I sat alone on my side of the table facing a barrage of questions from less-than-pleasant inquisitors, I wondered if I needed to ask for an attorney.

It was a moot point . . . I couldn't afford one.

And if I had it bad, I'd just gotten a small taste of how Crystal's past several days had gone. She'd immediately taken responsibility for what occurred that night in Broadview. It had been her idea and, for the most part, she ran the operation. The buck stopped with her and the buck had gone horribly south, culminating with the remains of her own partner – Detective Michael C. Heppner – lying on a refrigerated slab in the Cook County coroner's office.

And now we were being forced to rehash the debacle once again, this time in front of Todd Surratt's task force. With no new developments on the table, the FBI task force hadn't met since that second morning – the meeting I'd not been invited to – when Agent Renn completed her briefing after everyone had viewed the Netflix documentary. Though the night in Broadview had been a CPD operation, Crystal had notified Agent Surratt out of professional courtesy before she'd left for Hempstead's house. Surratt felt the idea had merit and wished her well.

Crystal had been solemn, her answers short and to the point, but it was obvious my sister wasn't herself. I could tell she was bleeding inside, and I wasn't going to spend the meeting listening to Crys get railroaded by an unforgiving detective out of Area 1.

At least we'd scored two chairs and a table this go-round, better seating for today's inquisition. I brought Alice along again, figuring I'd need a therapy dog just to get through today's gathering. Alice sat on the floor between our feet, periodically glancing up at me – even my bloodhound could tell there was something seriously off about the meeting's tenor.

'It's my understanding there'd been a lot of discussion and everyone agreed on the forty-eight hour rule,' I said. 'Right, Crystal?'

My sister nodded without looking my way and spoke by rote. 'If we spotted somebody in the bushes or lurking by the side of a house – or if the dogs clued us in on their presence – we'd take the person in and *legally* hold them for forty-eight hours without charges while we figured out who they were and what they were doing there. If we dug anything up, we could hold them longer under *extraordinary circumstances* or bring probable cause for an arrest to a judge.'

Crystal's automaton delivery was accurate in a *here are the facts as we know them* manner; however, it lacked passion and was far from complete. I added, 'If we spotted someone sitting or slumped down in a car, we'd walk on by but run the plates. If the car was stolen, we'd call the squad cars. If the car wasn't registered at a Broadview address, or even if it was, we'd keep eyes on it. We were *passive observers* – neighbors walking their dogs or,' I glanced at Detective Alba perched at one of the cop tables, 'a guy out sneaking a smoke. And if the person in the car did anything strange, we'd call in the squads. Again,' I said, 'we were passive observers.'

'But if that's the case, and the unsub was scoping out Detective Hempstead's neighborhood, Cory, why would he attack you?' Surratt said. Though the SAC had been made aware of the Broadview operation, the FBI had not been involved.

'I keep asking myself that question,' I replied. 'Maybe he was hidden somewhere; maybe he had his own infrared goggles and spotted us leaving through Hempstead's backyard.'

Detective Alba added, 'Crystal switched up our routes, but if he kept spotting us on alternate streets over a period of time, that could have raised suspicions.'

Hempstead exhaled loudly, alerting the room of his ongoing disapproval. Long gone were the smiles and guffaws and gags about turning sixty. Now the detective out of Area 1 was loaded for bear . . . and he had my sister in his crosshairs.

I bit my tongue, turned back to Detective Alba and said, 'The bus stop's about thirty yards from where we turned the corner. Maybe he saw me dip my head to speak into my microphone.'

'What? You spoke into your front pocket?' This time I scored an eye roll and a smirk from Hempstead.

'It wasn't *blatant* like that,' I defended myself. 'It would have looked like I was glancing down to check on my dog.'

'If you were a real cop instead of *doggie daycare*,' Hempstead replied, 'this would all be over, we wouldn't be fucking around here today . . . and Detective Heppner would still be alive.'

I stared back at Hempstead for several seconds, struggling to keep the lid on. 'Detective Heppner saved my life. And I can never repay that,' my voice trembled, my eyes were moist, 'but I wish he'd shot the guy, at least in the leg or something to take him out of commission.'

'Heppner got in too close with the jewelry, right?' the detective working the Casey Oselka case asked.

I turned toward him and nodded. Jewelry was cop speak for handcuffs. I added, 'That and Heppner came in fast – remember, he'd been running full bore to get to us – and before he knew it he was within the unsub's reach.'

'Should have all been cops,' Hempstead insisted, 'not *doggie daycare.*'

'Rex alerted me to the attack in the first place. Without him,' I said, 'I'd be dead.'

'Then why are you defending your sister?' Hempstead replied. 'She damned near got you killed.'

The lid came off. 'You're an asshole,' I snapped, pointing at Hempstead as if the room didn't know to whom I was referring. Alice stood as though I'd issued a command. Sets of eyes turned her way and I felt Crystal place a calming palm on my forearm. I figured any future work with CPD or the FBI had just dried up, but I didn't care. '*Detective Pratt*,' I said, 'acted as a dispatcher, cool and professional. Heppner was nearby, so she sent him my way and then called in the squad cars.'

Hempstead wouldn't let it lie. 'Big sis screwed up big time. The killer's on the loose and a good cop is dead.'

I'm lucky Hempstead wasn't near me. I'd have kicked him in his ever-expanding scrotum. Instead, I shot daggers his way. 'You should thank your lucky stars Crystal was a step ahead of the unsub, 'cause guess whose murder we interrupted, asshole?'

'This *infighting* is not productive,' SAC Surratt said in a voice that could freeze lava. He stared at me a long second and then looked at Hempstead.

His point was made.

I took a deep breath and leaned back in my chair. Something occurred to me and I turned to Loris Renn. She had the black pant-suit going again but with a green scarf for today's meeting. 'You're not staying at your house, are you?'

The FBI profiler shook her head.

'Good,' I said and nodded, 'because *clearly* the guy's still pissed off about the documentary.'

'Cory, is there anything you can tell us about the unsub?' Surratt asked, trying to salvage the meeting, in search of something *productive*. 'Any physical attributes that stood out?'

It was my turn to speak by rote as I'd shared all this in my previous meetings with CPD higher-ups. 'The man was a little taller than I am. I had on hiking boots while he wore running shoes, so I'd say he's about six-one. I only saw a strip of skin around his eyes that wasn't covered – a white guy, but I didn't catch his eye color.' I turned to face Surratt. 'He was in good shape, quick, athletic, and based on what he did to Detective Heppner,' I said, 'he knows how to use that blade of his.'

'He didn't say anything when you confronted him?'

'No, and it was creepy as hell,' I said, and glanced around the conference room. 'Another thing, though – he knew the neighborhood. As soon as he heard the sirens, he darted into the woods, no hesitation at all, because he knew where the woods led, and that he'd get lost in the weeds. And that bus stop's two blocks from Hempstead's house. So he knew the area pretty damned well.' I collected my final thought. 'The guy's a planner . . . no way it was his first time in Broadview.'

TWENTY-TWO

The killer's father sat again on the cedar bench of the sauna room. A towel was draped about his torso, but he'd been distracted, lost in thought, and had yet to turn on the heating unit. Even without the warmth and steam, his mind was focused. The answer had dawned on him during his most-recent drive to the lake house.

Actually, the answer had always been there, staring him in the face.

He just needed to come to terms with it.

It was the only way out of this soul-crushing dilemma . . . it was the only way out.

He had to kill his firstborn son.

But unlike Abraham, it wasn't God commanding him to offer up his son as a human sacrifice, and, unlike Isaac, there would be no reprieve for his boy.

The situation may well be some *twisted* test of faith, but it was anything but biblical.

The father stared at the rocks, finally detecting the lack of warmth. He checked the room temperature, realized his mistake, shook his head and flipped on the heating unit, and then sat back down on the cedar bench. It would take a while to heat the room, but not long.

His son was a coldhearted killer. He'd tripped over the *truth* years ago, and then it had *miraculously* stopped, but now his son was at it again, with four dead in the past few weeks alone, including a Chicago police detective. And along with this *inconvenient truth* came the *unmistakable message* in the form of a smashed storage room door, a shattered display case . . . and another missing knife.

The message was loud and clear: *You're part of this, Dad. You're part of this.*

He'd never win father of the year, certainly not in the home that spawned his firstborn son. He'd burn in hell for not turning his boy in years ago, as soon as he realized what the kid had been up to. And he'd burn an eternity not only for his silence, but for some of the things he'd done in order to keep his demented offspring's shitshow from splattering all over his own life, from destroying him. Had he done *the right thing* back then, back when he'd put two and two together, he could have at least saved the final victim – the retired man – his son had beaten to death under the guise of the Dead Night Killer. And he certainly could have saved the lives of the four men killed in his son's recent effort.

His firstborn had to die. He should have done it years ago . . . but he'd been a coward.

Ultimately, the father had no other option. What dawned on him during his ride up to the lake house was that once his firstborn stopped playing Dead Night Killer games . . . he'd come for his younger half-sisters and -brother. *He'd use my knives against them,* the father thought, as it'd be the ultimate *Fuck You* to the dad his firstborn loathed with a passion born of hell.

The father felt the calming warmth seep into his muscles as the sauna began to work its magic. His decision had been made and set in cement – his boy had to die. With the hard part out of the way, he needed a plan. Something foolproof, as he'd be playing with fire. He sat in the heat and the steam and let some of the more intelligent possibilities play out in his mind.

He'd inherited a .22 pistol when his own father passed away. The pistol was unregistered, from a past era when registering handguns would have been scoffed at, and his old man had used it back when his old man had been a boy for target practice and shooting at squirrels and other critters. Not long after his father's death he'd taken the pistol to the firing range and had been surprised at how the ancient handgun had been meticulously cleaned and oiled, and how it remained in perfect working condition. He shouldn't have been surprised, though, his old man had always taken great care of his tools.

He possessed a weapon that could not be traced back to him.

Next, his boy couldn't know for sure if the smashed storage room door had been detected yet, if his message had been received. The family didn't frequent the lake house after October came to an end, once it became chilly outside, once the caretaking company had pulled the dock in. His son wouldn't know for certain, but with what had blown up in headlines across the country, he'd strongly suspect his father had visited the lake property. And he'd strongly suspect his father's motives if his father suddenly showed up in town for a *friendly visit.*

Exhibiting such uncharacteristic conduct, he thought, could prove hazardous to his own health and well-being.

No, he would have to finesse this.

Let's see . . . he could call his son, tell him he was in Chicago on business, no great stretch there, and that his driver – one of the many perks of his position – could chauffeur the two of them to whatever restaurant his son favored. Then he could arrive at his son's door a few minutes later, giving the boy less time to plan anything *nefarious*, and lead his son to believe a chauffeur waited patiently for them in the driveway. And when his son let him into the entryway, while his son grabbed his coat and keys, the father would shut the door behind him with one hand and shoot his son in the back of the head with his other.

There could be no hesitation.

His late father's .22 would not be as loud as some other handguns. With the doors and windows closed – it was November, after all – he doubted the noise would merit a 911 call. Nonetheless, he'd immediately vacate the property, walk to his car, and drive away. But an hour later he'd return and, if no squad cars or ambulances were parked out front, no authorities had been notified, he'd slip back inside and ransack the hell out of the place – grab his son's wallet, cell phone, and any laptops or PCs or doorbell cameras he might come across. He'd rip apart every nook and cranny searching for his Ka-Bar knives, for any souvenirs his son may be hanging on to, for anything in the least bit incriminating.

He'd scrub the house clean.

After all, he'd have all night to ensure a thorough job, to do it right.

The father shrugged at the irony – at how he'd likely wind up owning the house to do with as he pleased after his son's estate worked its way through probate.

Then, after his search of his boy's house was complete, and in the wee hours of the morning, before the city awoke, the father would have one final task to accomplish. To make it appear as though a burglary had gone awry, he'd drop his son's wallet, with its various bank and credit cards, as well as his son's smartphone on a sidewalk in a less than pleasant part of town . . . and let nature take its course.

TWENTY-THREE

I have a theory that all funerals are the same – misty-eyed spouses, heartbroken sons or daughters, grief-stricken friends and colleagues and relatives, melancholy tributes – and CPD Detective Mike Heppner's proved to be no different, right on down to the ham sandwiches and weak coffee, macaroni salad and dessert bars served in the house of worship's basement cafeteria.

Of course, most funerals lack the dark pall of murder hanging over them.

Detective Heppner's service took place at Wicker Park Lutheran church. The pews were packed, soon to be standing-room only, and I recognized both the mayor and the superintendent of police in the second row, directly behind Heppner's immediate family, followed by a multitude of officers in blue and detectives in suit jackets in the rows behind them.

Though he'd been her partner, Crystal had not been invited to speak, so she and I squeezed into a couple of seats in a backmost pew.

Turns out Heppner had a twin brother. I did a double-take at how much he looked like the late detective. Heppner's sibling spoke of Mike's love of family, of Mike's love of work – how the detective felt he truly made a difference in people's lives – and, of course, how Mike was the world's biggest Chicago Bulls fan. Heppner's brother informed the packed church that – unless you'd been invited – you do not show up unexpectedly at Mike's house during a Bulls game as he'd not answer the door. And, even if you were invited, you'd best not engage in idle chatter nor dare stand between Mike and his flat-screen during the play of the game.

Detective Heppner's captain then spoke to the family about how sorry he was for their loss, and of his years working with Mike Heppner, and how the detective will be deeply missed, and – though the captain had never once won – he'd miss Mike passing out the bracket pick sheets each year for wagering on March Madness. The captain ended his eulogy with how sad a day it was indeed for the entire Chicago Police Department.

Crystal trembled at the captain's last line, and I cupped a hand over hers.

The pastor both welcomed and thanked everyone for coming to pay their final respects to Detective Heppner. He informed the funeral-goers there'd be a reception in the basement cafeteria following the service. The pastor then went on to read a portion of scripture regarding God's comfort during such difficult times as these, and he finished his sermon speaking about what Mike Heppner had meant to the people who loved him most.

Crystal and I got separated as nature called and I beelined for the Men's restroom at the end of the service. We'd agreed to stay at the reception a short while, just long enough to pass our condolences on to the family. When I wandered into the cafeteria I spotted Crystal off in a corner talking with Detective Heppner's wife. I figured I'd give the two women a few extra seconds of privacy by grabbing cups of coffee for my sister and myself. After peeling creamers and stirring in sugar packets, I looked for Crystal, but she was no longer in the corner of the room. Instead, I noticed Heppner's widow standing nearby, now chatting with a group I assumed to be relatives.

I sipped at my cup and waited her out, making my stand by the coffee urns.

'I am so sorry about your husband,' I said, stepping her way as she broke clear from her kinfolk. Mrs Heppner was a petite woman with broad features, more handsome than pretty. I wasn't sure how to proceed in such a *delicate* situation, and wished Crystal was there to help, but I managed to mumble, 'My name is Cory Pratt, and I was with him the other night.' I cleared my throat. 'Your husband saved my life.'

Mrs Heppner stared up at me a long moment in what I figured was a valium-enhanced gaze. At first I thought she was going to say something, but instead gave me a quick hug and then stepped toward the food table to greet other mourners.

Once again I glanced around the cafeteria for my sister, but she was nowhere to be found. I suspected she'd gone to use the bathroom before the ride home, so I dumped both cups of coffee in a bin – no great loss there – and went to find her at the set of restrooms stationed outside the gathering area. After five minutes of loitering, I snuck back to the cafeteria's entryway in case we'd somehow managed to overlook each other in the cluster of funeral-goers, but Crystal had not returned to the reception area.

I glanced at my watch – where the hell did she go? – and then returned to the restrooms for some additional pacing. I took out my iPhone – I'd turned it off for the church service – figuring I'd check for text messages or voicemail when a group of women exited the bathroom and another idea occurred to me.

I cracked open the door to the Women's room several inches. 'Crystal?' I said in a low voice so as not to disturb others. 'Are you in there?'

'She's not,' a voice behind me said. Startled, I turned about and there stood Mrs Heppner, no more than a foot away. She stared up at me with that same valium-enhanced gaze and added, 'I asked the bitch to leave.'

TWENTY-FOUR

'Have you eaten?' the killer's father said into his cell phone as soon as his son answered the phone.

'Dad?' his son replied. 'You're in town?'

'Yeah, you know – the usual song and dance for work,' the father said. 'Are you hungry?'

'I'm always hungry. When did you get in?'

'About an hour ago.'

'Why didn't you let me know you were coming?'

'I was going to call you from the airport, but here's a first – the flight was on time. In fact they boarded us early.'

'You want me to come pick you up?'

'No need, work's got a driver for me.'

'The life of Riley.'

'I wish,' the father said. He added, 'Just a second.' Then he held his cell phone at arm's length and whispered, *GPS this address*, as though he were passing along instructions. He brought the phone back to his ear. 'You got a favorite restaurant?'

'Is the meal on you?'

'Of course. Feel free to up your game from Wendy's.'

'In that case the Fuller House is nearby. You'll love their salmon stir-fry,' his boy said. 'When will you get here?'

'In this traffic, anywhere between an hour and ten years.'

'Excellent. See you then, Dad.' The father was about to end the call when his son added, 'Lots to talk about.'

But the father hadn't just arrived about an hour ago. Rather, he had made it to Chicago several hours earlier, in midafternoon. Obviously, there was no driver assigned to him, nor was there an on-time flight to O'Hare. He'd driven all the way to Chicago by himself. He did this for two reasons. First, there'd be no record of his trip. He'd paid cash whenever he'd filled the gas tank on the BMW X5 SUV – no credit card trail. Second, and most importantly, so he could bring along his father's .22 pistol without anyone being the wiser.

It had been a full day's drive – he was too old for this shit – but he'd tossed and turned all night before giving up on sleep, rolling out of bed, and hitting the freeway by four o'clock. He'd stayed again at the lake house – his wife had begun making asides about him having an affair – but it made it easy for him to pick up and go. Sheila and his daughter had no idea he was taking a road trip. Colleagues assumed he was working from home, and he did suffer through a lengthy conference call via his smartphone and then led a much briefer one as he sped along the interstate. He'd made great time; of course he'd only stopped to fill the tank or take the occasional leak at a rest area or truck stop.

Though the father had never been to his son's home in Western Springs, a suburb fifteen miles west of the Chicago Loop, he had the address and plugged it into the Maps app on his cell phone, which led him directly to his boy's door a little before three o'clock in the afternoon. He drove slowly past his son's residence, and then went to kill time at a nearby mall.

A half-hour ago he'd driven past the house again. The sun was in its final vestiges and the exterior lights flicked on as he drove past. It was too uneven an hour for the lights to be activated on a timer, so he assumed his son had just gotten home from the office.

The father had then pulled into an empty elementary school parking lot in order to make the call to his boy. After he hung up, he checked the .22 pistol for the hundredth time, and then dropped it back inside the pocket of his overcoat. He then reached inside the glove compartment and retrieved a mini-bottle of Absolut Vodka, like the kind they serve on airplanes. It was one of two mini-bottles of vodka he'd picked up at the liquor store across the street from the mall where he'd spent the late afternoon killing time.

He twisted off the small cap and tossed back the fifty milliliters of vodka in one fell swoop. He felt it burn all the way down his throat.

A shot of liquid courage to take the edge off what he was about to do.

He'd drink the second bottle after it was done . . . when he was miles away from his boy's house.

The father wiped the empty mini-bottle down with a Kleenex, glanced about the empty parking lot, opened the driver's door a few inches and dropped it on to the pavement below his SUV. He didn't want risk running afoul of any open bottle laws. It'd be just his luck to get snagged over some damned thing like that.

The father put the BMW into Drive and headed to his son's house for the third time that day. He pulled slowly on to the street – it'd been nearly eight minutes since he'd hung up on his son – and a second later he parked in the driveway. He stepped from the SUV, his right hand in his pocket, gripping the pistol, ready for action in case his boy tried something. The garage blocked the view of his SUV, so his son wouldn't be able to see there was no chauffeur.

Feeling as though he were walking the plank on an ancient pirate ship, the father strode the walkway to the front door. He noticed the curtains on the front window were tightly shut. As he stepped on to the covered stoop, his focus turned to the oval of frosted glass that centered his boy's front door, trying to spot any shadow lurking beyond, inside the entryway. He hit the doorbell once, and then again, listening as it rang before noticing a single Post-it note pasted eye-level on the wooden section of the door, to the left of the glazed-glass oval. He glanced behind him, and then slowly opened the screen door with his free hand and read the note from his son.

Have to take a raincheck. Emergency at work. You know how that goes. We'll talk soon.

The father read the note twice, and then a third time before he reached for the door handle. It was locked.

Goddammit!

No work emergency had cropped up in the last eight minutes. The father had tipped his cards; he'd blown his chance.

His son now knew he was coming.

TWENTY-FIVE

'I'm going to quit my job.'

We'd picked up some drive-thru comfort food – burgers, fries, shakes – on the drive home from the funeral. Crystal wasn't hungry so I wedged everything into the refrigerator and let the two mongrels out to do their business while she went upstairs and changed into sweats. I puttered about the house, following up on email and voice messages for work, while Crystal cozied up next to Alice on the couch to watch some mindless television. Rex curled up on her other side, muzzle on Crystal's lap.

Time passed and – after I fed the kids and let them outside again, this time to play as well as tinkle – I couldn't take it any longer and popped a cheeseburger and my fair share of the french fries into the microwave and ate quietly at the kitchen table. Alice and Rex had resettled on the sofa, sandwiching Crystal, and the trio now watched a home improvement show – some young couple was remodeling their backyard – but I suspect none of them held any genuine interest.

My sister hadn't said a thing since we'd returned home. That is, until now as she stared at the television set and uttered those six simple words that contained such life-altering consequences.

'But you're a great cop, Crys,' I said. 'Your instincts are gold.'

She came over and took the chair across from me at the kitchen table. 'I've been a detective half a year and I just got my partner killed.'

And there it was . . . the dark place she'd been living in since the night in Broadview.

I know all about dark places – how they rob you of sleep, of appetite, the endless weight placed upon your chest until it's nearly impossible to breathe, the all-consuming guilt . . . the marring of your soul.

'You didn't get him killed.'

'Heppner died in an operation I'd devised and ran. No one at CPD will want to work with me . . . and I can hardly blame them,' Crystal said. 'Jesus, Cory, Hempstead was right – I almost got you killed.'

I shook my head.

She added, 'I'd never forgive myself if something happened to you.'

No longer hungry, I put down what remained of my cheeseburger and said, 'I should have sicced Rex on that bastard as soon as I realized who he was. Rex was practically begging for a fight, but that blade of his – he'd have hurt him bad.' I glanced over at my springer spaniel, still on the sofa. 'I sent Rex away. He was in the woods by the time Heppner showed up.'

'I get that, Cor. Believe me, I understand.' Her eyes were moist. 'It's just that I can't do my job if I'm a *pariah*.'

'But it's not your fault.'

She shrugged. 'It doesn't matter . . . I've had enough.'

'Crystal – you haven't slept a wink since it happened. I know you feel like shit, but what happened at Broadview was not your fault. You're not to blame.' I looked at my sister. 'And I can prove it.'

'You can *prove it*?' She stared at me, figuring I was just trying to BS her in order to lift her spirits. Maybe it was the pepper jack cheese I'd ordered on my burger or maybe it was the limp french fries, but something had dawned on me while I sat at the kitchen table, snarfing them down.

'Will you give me five minutes?' I said. 'I feel like I should map it out, like they do with football plays.'

She looked at me cynically, as though I were stalling for time in order to pull something out of my ass.

'First off, Crystal's plan sucked and she's an idiot because the unsub got there first and watched as we paraded through Hempstead's neighbor's backyard. OK, that could be true if the guy's on a rooftop a mile away with an infrared scope, but let's not go all Tom Clancy here.' I returned my sister's stare. 'There was an air-conditioning unit in the house next door to Hempstead's backyard neighbor that our guy could have been hiding behind, but the dogs would have alerted us as we came in or left. And they'd have spotted him if he'd been on his belly in the adjacent backyard, just like they knew the CPD officer was hiding under the canoe. And once you get beyond the adjacent backyards, there isn't a clear line into Hempstead's backyard, especially in the dark. So if the unsub was hiding two or three houses away, it'd be impossible for him to watch Hempstead's backdoor. Right?'

Crystal shrugged.

'OK then – Crystal's also an idiot and should be fired because the unsub, invisible man that he is, spotted us each walking around the block a time or two and figured it out,' I said. 'But you and I both know about Alice, right? She's Batman.'

Crystal nodded, and, at the sound of her name, Alice came into the kitchen, and lay down at my sister's feet.

'And Rex is Robin the Boy Wonder. He alerted me to the cannabis kids before I saw them. Rex also spotted a fox or something else nocturnal at one point in our walk. I didn't see it, and he stopped pulling at the leash, which means whatever critter it was sensed him and ran away. And we both know Rex alerted me to the guy at the bus shelter as soon as we turned the corner.' I glanced down at my bloodhound. 'I imagine Alice did similar stuff with you, right?'

'Mostly trash bins. Alice would be staring up a driveway several seconds before I'd hear someone start rolling their bin to the street.'

'Here's the deal – I trust my dogs with my life. If some guy's lying in a ditch, Alice and Rex are going to growl or head toward him. They'll alert us in some manner. Same thing if the unsub's ducking down between cars or – hell, I don't know – lying under a car or hiding in the bushes or creeping by the side of a house or whatever, Alice and Rex are going to alert us, fair enough?'

'Yes.'

'Forget about Heppner and Alba for a second. You and I and Alice and Rex are going up and down Twelfth and Thirteenth and Fourteenth Avenue, walking the streets surrounding Hempstead's house for over an hour. Rex and I did each block at least twice. So did you and Alice. I'd stroll down Thirteenth Avenue, and then you and Alice would walk Thirteenth ten minutes later. Yet the kids never growled or jumped up and down or headed on to any lawn,' I said. 'Do you know what that means?'

Crystal's eyes lit up. She realized I might not be talking out of my ass, after all. 'The case of the dog that didn't bark.'

'Sherlock Holmes, right?'

'Yeah, Sherlock figures out the watchdog didn't bark because the watchdog knew the perpetrator.'

'So if Alice and Rex didn't spot the unsub,' I said, 'then the unsub sure as hell didn't spot us.'

'It's a negative fact,' Crystal said, stood, walked to the refrigerator, and took out her cheeseburger.

'What's a negative fact?'

Crystal put the burger in the microwave and tapped a button. 'It's when the absence of one thing proves the truth of another. Just like in the Sherlock Holmes story.'

After a second I asked, 'So what do you think?'

'I think you're sweet, Cor,' she said, took her burger out of the microwave, and returned to her spot at the table. 'It makes sense in a way, but it's also a lot of wishful thinking.'

I shook my head. 'He's not the Invisible Man, Crystal. I suppose he could have been up in a tree, but most of the leaves have fallen – we'd have spotted him. He could have also been on a roof, but that would have made him vulnerable, easy to catch if anyone noticed and called the police. It'd be stupid. And our guy is anything but stupid.'

'You're sweet Cor,' she said again.

'I'm not done.'

'There's more?' Crystal asked, and took a bite of her cheeseburger.

'The unsub is either omnipotent like Jason or Michael Myers from those slasher movies or . . . or he knows me from somewhere.'

'He *knows* you?' Crystal put her burger down.

'Look, I was wearing Dad's old windbreaker, the one he had for five hundred years. I even had a poop baggie sticking out of my pocket to complete the picture. I screamed dog-walker, I screamed suburbia, yet the guy attacks me.' I dipped another fry in ketchup. 'Why the hell would he do that, out of the clear blue sky? I wasn't in the stupid documentary. And it wasn't just some random happenstance. It was because he recognized me, because he knew me from somewhere.' I put the fry in my mouth, thought for a second, and continued, 'Unlike our pal Hempstead, I don't piss people off as a way of life. If some guy recognizes me because I trained his St Bernard, he'll come over and say, "Hello". He's not going to attack me. The same is true with old classmates from high school, or the woman that cuts my hair, or the clerk at the frigging liquor store – they'd say "Hi", not come at me with a commando knife.'

Crystal stared at me, motionless.

'So in what *context* would the unsub attack little ol' me?' I asked, and then answered, 'In the context of him knowing about the work I do with CPD or the FBI. In the context of him recognizing me, realizing he can't get to Hempstead, and then figuring killing me will suffice. No other context makes sense,' I said. 'Do you see what I mean?'

My sister nodded.

'You didn't screw up. I didn't screw up,' I said. 'The unsub recognized me. He's on the inside somewhere.'

Crystal slowly leaned back in her chair. 'You were at the Gorski crime scene and at Oselka's house as well.'

I nodded. I saw where she was headed. 'There were probably a dozen police officers and detectives at each scene. Most were men.'

'And at the first FBI task force meeting we went to?'

I shrugged. 'I didn't count. I'm thinking fifty maybe – agents and cops and lawyers. Again, mostly men.'

'It could be a higher number,' she said, 'if you tack on anyone on the periphery who saw you coming or going to something they knew about.'

It was then I realized I had her, and that my sister wouldn't be handing in her resignation, at least not anytime soon. I grabbed her shake from the freezer and set it in front of her, and then walked to the drawer where I kept the doggie treats under lock and key. I gave a Milk-Bone to Alice at Crystal's feet and tossed one to Rex on the couch. He scarfed it up and turned back to the television. The segment on the young couple renovating their backyard must have ended as Rex's attention now lay with a different pair ripping apart their master bathroom.

Crystal should have never brought up Sherlock Holmes. It went straight to my head. Maybe I'd bag studying for some lame-ass IT job at Harper Community College. Instead, follow in my sister's footsteps and get a degree in Criminal Justice. I could practically see myself skidding an unmarked police car to a stop at the scene of the latest crime, double parking out front, and badging my way past a crew of patrol officers securing the site.

I was far too jazzed for this hour of the evening. I bounced into the family room as though I were a boxer entering the ring. A second later both dogs joined me. They recognized my mood and knew what was coming.

'Guess who you guys are?' I said and got down on my hands and knees. 'You're the dogs that didn't bark.'

We commenced roughhousing. I rubbed behind ears, shook paws, shoved the pups around, and playfully yanked at tails. 'Yes you are,' I said, scratching under chins. 'You're the dogs that didn't bark.'

After a minute of frolic, Rex came to a standstill, caught my eye a long second, and then bolted for the steps leading down to the basement.

'Oh no,' I said.

Crystal called from the kitchen, 'What's up?'

As if in answer to my sister's query, my springer spaniel came flying back out of the stairwell, knotted sock hanging from his mouth.

TWENTY-SIX

'Your pizzas are here, ma'am.'

'I didn't order any pizza,' a tart voice replied through the hotel room's locked door.

'You still love anchovies, don't you, Loris?'

'Is that you, Mac?'

'You're the only person I've ever known who likes anchovies on pizza,' David Macaulay spoke through his N95 mask. He stood outside Special Agent Loris Renn's room at the Holiday Inn Express on North Wabash Avenue, holding two cardboard boxes. 'I picked one up for you at Giordano's; of course I had to order a normal sausage for myself.'

Agent Renn opened the door and took in her friend. 'You're all bundled up, aren't you?'

Macaulay wore a black overcoat with the collar up, a gray scarf, Covid mask covering his face, as well as a Cubbies baseball cap. 'I may watch too many spy movies, but I figured driving around town for pizza and dressing up like this would lose any tail I'd picked up.'

Renn smiled. 'So who's following you?'

'To be honest, I've been scared shitless since that detective got killed.' He shrugged. 'I wouldn't want to lead anyone to your door.'

'You must have got my text?'

'It's how I knew you were staying here.'

'You should have called first?'

'I worked late, hadn't eaten yet, and thought this anchovy monstrosity would make for a pleasant surprise,' Macaulay said. 'But if you've got company,' he slid one of the pizza boxes forward, 'I'll *awkwardly* hand you this and sneak away with my tail tucked firmly between my legs.'

'Shut up, Mac.' Renn stood to the side of the door and let him in.

'But I got the sausage for me,' Macaulay said. 'You're the weirdo that likes fish on their pizza.'

'But I'm just taking one piece – an even trade.'

'It sounds like we're swapping baseball cards.' Macaulay handed her a slice of sausage pizza but waved away Renn's anchovy. The two sat at the circular table in the corner of the hotel room, next to the window. 'Sorry I didn't bring beer.'

'Cokes are fine.' Renn had run down the hall and returned with a couple of overpriced cans of soda and a bucket of ice. She looked at Macaulay and added, 'Maybe beer next time?'

'It's a deal.' Macaulay stuck out his hand and the two shook on it. 'So have you fibbies got any new leads on the case?'

Agent Renn looked at him and said, 'Nothing that's letting me return home anytime soon.' She continued, 'I lost the battle with

Surratt after the task force meeting the other day. He's got me camped out here full-time under a fake name.'

'Did you come up with *Suzanne Nichols*?'

'Yes.'

'Suzanne Nichols sounds like she writes novels for Harlequin.'

'Don't be such a smartass,' Renn said. 'Besides, I enjoy a good bodice ripper.'

Macaulay chuckled. 'Anyway, I think your being here is a good idea. No risk of the bad guy following you from work.'

'Yeah, but this place has got me climbing the walls.'

Macaulay glanced around the room as though seeing it for the first time. Renn had moved her laptop and corresponding cords off the corner table in order for them to eat. He noticed the bed was made and said, 'You've got maid service.'

'Lucky me.'

'Do you get a free breakfast?'

Renn nodded.

'Is it a good one? Or is it one of those chintzy continentals?'

Renn stared at Macaulay. 'Would you like to stay and find out?'

'Yes, Loris, I would,' Macaulay answered almost immediately. 'It is *imperative* I find out about their breakfast buffet.'

Renn closed herself off in the bathroom – to take a quick shower and brush the anchovies off her breath – while Macaulay tried making sense of what TV channels the Holiday Inn Express offered. He settled on a station showing an old Humphrey Bogart movie in black and white when Renn opened the bathroom door. With only a towel draped around her body, she walked over and sat next to Macaulay on the bed. She put the tips of her fingers on Macaulay's cheek, and then they kissed a long second.

'Loris,' he said when they came up for air. 'There's something I need to tell you.'

She sat back. 'What?'

'I've not been *completely* honest with you.'

She sat further back on the bed and crossed her arms. 'Are you seeing someone else?'

'Oh God no,' he said, and exhaled. 'It's the cancer, Loris . . . it's come back.'

TWENTY-SEVEN

'What you're saying has a certain logic to it, Cory, but there are a dozen scenarios on how the unsub could have tripped over the trap set for him.' A skeptical Special Agent in Charge Todd Surratt sat behind his desk and stared back at us with the expressionless eyes of a leader not ready to commit. 'Maybe he never left his car. Maybe he parked four houses up the street and spots Hempstead's neighbor and his family jump in the car and leave for the evening, but later notices Detective Heppner and Detective Alba as they arrive at the house. Then, later still, he sees you show up with the dogs and the red flags go up.'

'That's a long time in his car,' I said. 'Remember, none of the neighbors noticed anything suspicious, like some guy sitting in a car for the length of an *Avengers* movie.'

'I'm playing devil's advocate here,' Surratt replied. 'We know he's cased the neighborhood and, let's face it, he did a pretty damned good job of that, so maybe he drives by and spots you walking the dogs around the side of the house, and that's when the red flags go up.'

Crystal shook her head. 'I should have placed an officer inside to let the team in the front door and then out the back, but it seemed less intrusive to have Hempstead's neighbors lock it down and stay with their relatives for the night.'

'I'm not so sure about that being the case,' I said. What had seemed like brilliant Aristotelian-like logic back at the house was being met with a giant 'Meh' by the special agent in charge of Chicago's FBI field office. 'We were instructed to walk up to the front door and then slip around the side of the house. I can't speak for the detectives, but I checked the street to make sure no cars were coming by when the dogs and I slipped around the house.'

I glanced down at Rex as though to confirm that's how it went down. He'd been sitting quietly on the floor between Crystal and me. He looked up as though to say *I don't remember any cars driving past either*, but that may have been wishful thinking on my part.

Surratt didn't mind my having Rex in his office. He knew he was part of the team.

Surratt then looked at his watch. Never a good sign. Another less-than-stellar sign was how Surratt hadn't taken a single note – nothing scribbled on his notepad, nothing tapped into his laptop – since we'd shown up at the field office on West Roosevelt Road earlier that morning and begged a few moments of his time.

I glanced around Surratt's office – nothing grandiose, just an average-sized room, a couple of guest chairs in front of a nothing-special desk, a table and a few more chairs in one corner. Considering Surratt's position, he could have set his workplace up like something you'd see in the White House Oval Office, but the SAC was anything but pretentious and the room screamed bare-bones. It looked like where you'd locate a mid-level manager whiling away the work week.

Surratt shrugged. 'Maybe he spots one of you walking up the driveway, but then notices there aren't enough lights on in the house for someone having company over. Maybe he drives by a little later and spots you or Crystal leading dogs out from between the houses and, again, the red flags go up. Like I said, a dozen scenarios of him spotting something and putting two and two together.' Surratt glanced again at his watch. 'I hate to give you the bum's rush, but I found out this morning Roland Jund is coming in for the task force meeting.'

'Who's Roland Jund?' I asked.

'He's the director of CID – the FBI's Criminal Investigative Division.'

Crystal added, 'Jund oversees investigations into serial killers.'

'Wow.'

'Wow is right,' Surratt said. 'Director Jund works out of DC. He called early, even before you two showed up. Told me he's in town visiting family, but wanted to stop by *as a show of support* and *to lend a helping hand* – which is bureau-ese for he's here to micromanage.'

'What can Jund do here that he can't do in DC?' Crystal asked.

'Just his presence puts an exclamation point on how important this case is, and how we can't let this son of a bitch slip through the cracks.' Surratt shrugged again. 'The FBI could use some good news for a change. Half the country thinks we're America's version of the Stasi and the other half thinks we're a bunch of boobs who screwed up warnings about 9/11, the Boston Marathon bombing, and a half-dozen mass shootings. Jesus, we're the clowns that blew off the US Females Gymnastic Team's claims of sexual assault, and Director Westbrook . . .' Surratt stopped mid-sentence to turn my way. 'You know Mitchell Westbrook?'

I nodded. I'd caught the man on cable news a few times, mostly getting grilled in congressional hearings on Capitol Hill. 'He's the director of the entire FBI, right?'

'Yes – Mitchell Westbrook is the director of the *entire* FBI,' Surratt affirmed. 'And Director Westbrook is trying to rebrand the Bureau – make us appear more competent, more trustworthy – but it can't just be a PR stunt. People are sophisticated enough to see through crap like that. So, yes, the Bureau could use a victory or two.' Surratt leaned forward. 'Roland Jund is Director Westbrook's eyes on the ground. And we can be damn sure the director will be watching every move we make.'

We processed that in silence a few seconds. I hoped Surratt didn't have to shell out copays on the blood pressure meds he no doubt popped like Chiclets.

Surratt's smartphone had been sitting atop his desk and it must have vibrated as he tapped at the screen and said, 'Speak of the devil. Jund is here.' Surratt stood. 'I'm going down and greet him.'

'Thanks for meeting with us,' Crystal said, standing.

I followed suit. 'Thank you, sir.'

Before Surratt opened the door to his office, he turned and faced us. 'Look, clearly you're not bringing up your theory in the task force meeting. If it happens to be true – and I don't believe it is – you'd let the cat out of the bag, but, also, that kind of news might be met with a laugh track.'

Crystal and I nodded slowly.

Surratt caught my eye. 'I need you to promise me something, Cory.'

'What do you need?'

'Don't get into it with Detective Hempstead, OK?' he said. 'Don't take the bait.'

TWENTY-EIGHT

'Don't mind me,' CID Director Roland Jund spoke to the packed conference room after a brief introduction by SAC Surratt. 'I needed a place to drink my Starbucks,' he held up the coffee company's super-sized cup for all to see, 'and Todd said he had just the place for me.'

With that, Jund took a seat and rolled his chair away from the table, his back now against the wall. Jund was on the tall end of short or the short end of medium height, graying hair, and a broad chest. Swap out his suit for jeans and flannel and the director of the FBI's Criminal Investigative Division could be an aging lumberjack.

'Let's begin,' Surratt said, taking back the reins of the meeting. He again stood inside the rectangle of tables and glanced down at his smartphone. 'Agent Loris Renn won't be joining us this morning. It appears she has a conflicting appointment.'

'Yeah, an *appointment* at the hotel's spa,' someone on the FBI side of the room chimed in, generating a handful of chuckles.

'Right, we all know how hotel spas and salons are in my budget,' Surratt replied and the meeting commenced.

As we'd arrived early, Crystal, Rex and I were the first ones in the conference room and commandeered a table facing the entryway. Crystal set up her laptop on her side of the table and I had Rex sit on the carpet under my side. Then, as task force attendees began to straggle in for the morning's meeting, Rex and I took a position near the conference room door. Several members stared as though they should be handing me a ticket for entry, while others may have mistaken me for a Walmart greeter, but I smiled benignly, shook more than a few hands, and mumbled, 'Good morning.' Detective Hempstead, nonetheless, puffed up his chest and glared at me as he strode past, as though we were opponents in an upcoming cage match.

I wore my hiking boots, the same pair I had on that night in Broadview, and did my best to keep my posture straight. Crystal and I figured a good pair of running shoes had, more or less, the same heel height as a pair of men's dress shoes. My job was to stand near the entryway before the meeting began so my sister could track any of the male task force members who were my height or taller as they filed in through the conference room door. Though we recognized a handful of the police officers in attendance, as well as a couple of agents, we knew next to none of the Cook County prosecutors. To make matters worse, no one wore name tags; however, Crystal had a system. She had a spreadsheet containing three columns – one for cops, one for FBI agents, and one for attorneys. Based on whichever area of the conference room any men my height or taller sat in, they would merit a checkmark under the corresponding job title column.

Rex's job, with any luck, was to alert me if he caught the scent off the man who'd accosted us at the bus stop shelter in Broadview. The thing of it is, though, my pups are trained in human remains detection, in finding cadavers, dead bodies. If the Grim Reaper marched into the conference room for today's meeting, Rex would be all up in his grill. However, in terms of Rex processing or tracking other scents . . . well, that's not his forte.

I just hoped the little guy would recognize the scent of the threat from the other night.

Jund and Surratt were the last to enter the conference room, with Surratt shooting question marks my way and saying, 'Please take a seat, Cory.'

A detective from one of the cop tables was talking about finger-prints lifted off the safety glass at the bus stop shelter. I knew the police were dotting their i's and crossing their t's, but I also knew this was a dead-end as the killer had been wearing a thin pair of gloves the night Heppner was killed. I took the moment to tilt Crystal's laptop in my direction and glance at her spreadsheet. Under the cops' column, there were eight checkmarks. Under the FBI column, there were eight marks as well. Under the attorneys' column, there were only four.

A total of twenty men on the FBI special task force that were either my height or taller, and who would have recognized me had we had a chance encounter near a bus stop on a dark November night.

Although there would be some overlap with the officers currently in the conference room, we'd have to do something similar regarding the police officers and detectives that had been working the Gorski and Oselka investigations while I'd been present. Crystal figured we could further filter potential suspects per their age; that is, if a police officer at the Gorski scene was in high school during the Dead Night Killer's heyday – seven years ago – they'd fall to the bottom of our list even if they were my height or taller.

Admittedly, what had again appeared as brilliant Aristotelian-like logic back in Buffalo Grove last night seemed a bit silly now that it was being put into practice.

Another CPD detective spoke of how the police had gone door-to-door in the blocks surrounding Detective Hempstead's house to see if any of his neighbors had security cameras set up that caught a view of the street. Several homes had doorbell cameras that captured their immediate stoop and a portion of their driveway. Cameras at a few other houses were able to video their curbside mailboxes as well as a portion of the street. Unfortunately, as the sun went down in the evening, the video quality from the cameras extending toward the street deteriorated to the point of being useless.

The detective was then able to share the video off his laptop with the screen mounted on the conference room wall. There were two instances of a blur near the neighbor's mailbox that could have been a nighttime jogger, but, then again, it could have been Sasquatch. Although the video was grainy and dark, and appeared as though it had been filmed inside someone's mouth, everyone in the room glanced my way as though I were a referee ruling on a tough call.

Was it the attacker who killed Heppner?

Hell if I could tell.

I shook my head.

The conversation then turned to the canvassing of Hempstead's neighborhood. We'd been down this road in the previous meeting as, outside of reports of minor vandalism, none of Hempstead's neighbors had anything of value to further the case.

'Do we know who the vandals are?' Detective Hempstead asked the detective leading the Broadview investigation.

'Basically kids,' the detective responded. 'Junior-high-school-age kids.'

'You should talk to them,' Hempstead said. 'Little shits always know what's going on in the neighborhood. If that fucker was

jogging around my house for days on end, them little shits would
have seen him.'

I didn't like Hempstead, but I had to agree with the point he
made. Even Surratt nodded.

The meeting continued and I glanced about the room. Every FBI
agent, CPD officer, or attorney was listening intently; many were
taking notes, while a couple others appeared primed to jump in
at the next lull in conversation. I glanced over at Director Jund only
to find him staring directly at me, as though I'd just been caught
with my hand in the cookie jar. I quickly turned away. The director
of CID had offered nothing over the past hour, he had just been
sitting there, his back against the wall, sipping his Starbucks . . .
and watching. I angled my head so I could catch him in my periph-
eral vision. Jund was listening, but his head moved slightly, every
few seconds, and I suspected he was making some kind of individual
assessment of every attendee seated or standing in the conference
room.

I leaned back in my chair, hoping I'd cut the mustard.

As the minute hand curved dangerously close to the top of the
hour, Surratt summarized the meeting, and ended by asking, 'Any
questions?'

Crystal raised a palm. 'Seven years ago, right before he disappeared, the Dead Night Killer beat his final victim to death. Until
that point he'd kill his victims with an upward thrust of his knife
from right below the chin.' Crystal made a stabbing motion underneath her jawline. 'Seven years later – although he used subterfuge
with Tim Gorski and Casey Oselka – he's returned to his original
MO with Derek Ambler and,' she paused a beat, 'Detective Heppner.'
Crystal shook her head. 'What happened seven years ago that caused
him to change his MO and disappear?'

Surratt said, 'I think the answer to that question would go a long
way toward solving the case.' He then pointed at the table where
Crystal and I sat and added, 'Could you two stick around a minute.
We need to talk.'

Jund had left to see a man about a horse, likely to do with his
Starbucks Venti, and Crystal, Rex and I stood by as Surratt called
Agent Loris Renn's cell phone for what he said was the third time
that morning. 'It just keeps flipping over to voicemail.'

'Maybe she's in the middle of her appointment,' Crystal said.

'I talked to her at six o'clock last night and she was doing just fine,' Surratt said. 'There was no mention of any doctor's appointment.' He looked at his phone again. 'And she's not returning my texts, which would be pretty easy to do if you're sitting in a waiting room.'

Surratt had shown us the text message he'd received from Agent Renn earlier that morning, informing SAC Surratt she'd not be able to phone in to today's meeting as she had to attend a doctor's appointment.

'So you're asking us to swing by the Holiday Inn Express and make sure she's OK?' I said, still a bit confused over what he wanted. I had an obedience class in a couple of hours in Evanston. I added, 'But if she's at a medical appointment, she won't be in her hotel room.'

'I'd go,' Surratt said, 'but I'm giving Director Jund the nickel tour, and I suspect he's going to be a fount of questions.' Surratt knelt down and ran a hand along the back of Rex's neck. 'Loris not returning my calls or texts is out of character. The likely explanation is her battery's dead, but after what you told me this morning – your *theory* about it being someone close to or inside the investigation – is, quite frankly, unsettling . . . and I want to make sure she's OK.'

'I've got it covered, Cor,' Crystal offered. Due to my upcoming training, we'd driven to the task force meeting separately. 'You can head on off to your class.'

I looked at my sister, figuring Rex and I could make Evanston if we left Alice at home. Hopefully, my bloodhound wouldn't leave me any presents in return. 'No worries,' I said. 'I can make it work.'

'I'll text you the name she's checked in under,' Surratt said and stood up.

Rex's head turned toward the conference room door. I followed his gaze and there stood CID Director Roland Jund in the entryway, an inquisitive look on his face. He'd been so quiet it'd taken my springer spaniel to hear him return.

Jund said, 'Am I interrupting anything?'

TWENTY-NINE

When Rex and I entered the hotel's lobby we spotted Crystal at the reception desk, standing off to the side and using the hotel's house phone, likely dialing Agent Renn's room. Crystal had beaten us to the Holiday Inn Express, parked her Honda out front and hung a CPD tag from her rearview mirror that would make even the most despotically minded of tow-truck operators freeze in their tracks.

I, on the other hand, had to circle the block twice to find a legal spot for the Silverado.

Rex and I crossed the atrium to peek into their dining area, and watched as housekeeping finished taking down the breakfast bar and wiping countertops. It reminded me I'd skipped breakfast this morning and wondered if I could bribe one of the maids to toss a couple hard-boiled eggs and a mini box of Froot Loops my way. As for Rex, he would have emptied my entire savings account for the briefest of shots at whatever remained inside that bin of bacon.

'Sir,' a desk clerk or concierge behind the reception desk called at me from across the foyer, 'dogs are not permitted in the hotel.'

I turned his way, but Crystal flashed her badge and was already chatting with the clerk. I heard her mutter something about 'police dog' and 'there'll be no mess.' The two continued their discussion so Rex and I took the opportunity to follow arrows on walls as they led us toward the hotel's Fitness Center. After a couple twists and turns, we tripped across a window allowing us to peer inside the hotel's gym. Exercise equipment included a couple of treadmills, a stationary bike, one of those elliptical machines that costs a million bucks, some free weights, yoga mats, and a solitary weight ball.

Unfortunately, Agent Loris Renn wasn't working out at any of the stations.

Neither was anyone else for that matter.

'Suzanne Nichols is in four-twelve,' Crystal said after Rex and

I had worked our way back to the reception area and informed her that the Fitness Center was a dead-end.

'Suzanne Nichols is Agent Renn's pseudonym, right?'

'Yeah,' Crystal said. 'If I ever had to hide out, I'd go with a man's name just to keep my stalker on his toes.'

'I'd go with Dr Seuss and sign in as *Bartholomew Cubbins*,' I said. 'Or maybe go with *Scott Lang*.'

'Who's Scott Lang?'

'That's *Ant-Man*,' I replied. 'Duh.'

Crystal smiled and said, 'Agent Renn's been driving a bureau car. If she's not in her room, I'll get the model and plate number and check out the hotel's garage. It's a couple blocks up the street.' Crystal must have seen the look on my face, so she added, 'I won't need you for that, Cor. If Renn's not in her room, you can head out to your training.'

We shared an elevator with a kid who looked all of five years old. He'd run ahead of his parents and leapt in with us right before the doors slid shut. With a surprised look on his face at discovering Rex, my sister and I were also in the elevator, he turned and pressed the button for the second floor, then paused, and a second later pressed the button for the third floor. He mumbled 'Sorry', and then stared at Rex while the elevator doors opened and eventually closed on the second floor. The boy said 'Bye' to Rex, and took off like a race car as soon as the doors to third slid open.

Crystal said, 'You drove Mom and Dad crazy doing stuff like that when you were his age.'

'I did?' I said, and then felt the familiar weight upon my chest – a strange brew of melancholia and self-loathing – that now and again comes along with the memories.

'Yeah, but they just figured it was all part of that *on the spectrum* thing.'

'Give me a break,' I said, glad that Crys had switched from reminiscences to ribbing me.

When I was in second grade, my teacher – Miss Berenson – had my mother come in to discuss my classroom behavior. I don't remember specifics, and I'm likely guilty as charged of having been a pain in Miss Berenson's ass, but she'd asked my mother if I'd been diagnosed somewhere *on the spectrum*, wondering if I had an autism spectrum disorder. My parents laughed it off, figuring

Miss Berenson wanted me medicated in order to make her job easier. They quickly transferred me into a different classroom and life went on, but my sister-tormentor overheard them discussing the situation and that type of ammunition was too good for Crystal to leave alone.

If I die first, she'll be sure to bring it up in my eulogy.

Crystal chuckled as the elevator doors on fourth slid open to yet more wall arrows. A quick glance informed us that room four-twelve was off to our right. I checked my watch for about the twentieth time as we headed down the hallway, performing mental gymnastics, figuring another ten minutes at the Holiday Inn Express wouldn't make me late to teach my obedience class in Evanston. In fact, Rex and I had plenty of time to spare.

But then I noticed the change in Rex's demeanor. His nose rose in the air, and then his pace picked up as though he knew where we were headed. Rex peeked back my way, caught my nod, and sprinted ahead toward what I strongly suspected was room four-twelve.

Crystal and I shared a glance, and began jogging to keep up with my human remains detection dog. You see, unless a room is hermetically sealed – damned near airtight – Rex can catch the scent through the walls or the crevice under a door.

As feared, Rex pulled to a stop and sat outside of Agent Loris Renn's hotel room. He looked back at me and then pawed the hallway carpeting outside the hotel room door.

Crystal and I shared another glance, and then she dropped her hand beneath her jacket, near her holster. I ignored the Do Not Disturb sign that hung from the door's handle and knocked on the door. I leaned in to listen. No movement, no sound. I knocked again, louder, and then louder again before checking the door handle. It was locked.

'I'll get the manager to come open the door,' Crystal said, turned around, and headed back toward the elevator.

'Crys,' I said. She stopped and looked back. 'You better call Surratt as well, so he can get a team over.' I stared down at Rex as he sat facing the hotel room door and realized I'd be doing no training in Evanston today. 'We both know what's in there.'

THIRTY

David Macaulay – 'Mac' to his friends – hadn't outright lied to Loris.

The cancer had indeed come back, but he hadn't *just found out* as he'd led Loris to believe. He'd lied about the timing. He had known about it for more than a few weeks, since the results of the CT scan of his abdomen indicated, in oncologist vernacular, *lung cancer metastatic to the liver*, or, in layman's terms, the lung cancer that he'd fought years earlier had now spread to his liver. Unlike a local recurrence – where the cancer would return to his lung, near the site of the original tumor – his diagnosis was that of a *distant recurrence*, where the cancer cells reappear far away from the original site, such as in the adrenal glands, lymph nodes, bones, brain or, in his case . . . the liver.

Evidently, it's not uncommon for cancer to spread to the liver.

Lucky me, he thought – *I'm a dead man walking*.

The damnedest thing of it all was he felt great. Never better. He had no symptoms whatsoever. There was no loss of appetite, no accompanying nausea, no pain under his ribcage. No jaundice, no manic itching.

No symptoms at all.

If not for that goddamned CT scan, life would be a bed of roses.

Sure, Macaulay felt great . . . however, his cancer doctor assured him in no uncertain terms – it wouldn't last.

With that in mind, his first question for the oncologist was, 'How long have I got?'

After a lot of medical mumble jumble regarding the extent of the metastases, the status of any cancer that may be in the rest of his body, his general health, the mutation status, the doctor finally coughed up something Mac could sink his teeth into. 'In patients such as yourself – those with metastatic lung cancer to the liver and EGFR-positive tumors – the median survival rate is eleven point seven months.'

So he had a year.

Maybe more, maybe less.

The oncologist went on to discuss how, historically, treatments for this disease had been largely palliative, to relieve symptoms rather than attempt a cure, but that had changed in recent years and there were now some options to pursue that could possibly reduce symptoms and extend life for patients with his diagnosis.

Fuck that, he thought when the doctor brought up the treatment options. He'd not be mounting that hamster wheel again. There'd be no more Docetaxel and Carboplatin and Pemetrexed through a chemo port to kill off the affected cells. There'd be no more radiation therapy to shrink any goddamned tumor. There'd be no more surgery – the lobectomy of his lung from seven years back had been all sorts of shits and giggles. And as for the endless diet of carrots and kale, cabbage and squash, leafy greens and broccoli and bell peppers . . . never again.

Perhaps notions of the infamous *cancer diet* was what sent Macaulay scampering home with the Kung Pao Chicken the day he'd been notified of the results of the CT scan. Perhaps the news of his cancer having returned had led Macaulay, subconsciously at least, to stream the Dead Night Killer documentary on Netflix.

No, he'd not be going through that living hell all over again on the off chance he'd beat the odds. Sure, perhaps the cancer would pass into remission again, for another year or two, only to bounce back, but next time to appear in his brain or adrenal glands. Nope, Macaulay thought, the odds were definitely not in his favor.

The house always wins.

And he needed to get his affairs in order.

Seven years ago his oncologist told him he'd been fortunate they'd caught the lung cancer before it had progressed beyond stage two. Macaulay originally had an appointment with his general practitioner to tell his tale of woe – chest pains when he laughed or coughed, a loss of appetite, some minor fatigue. Immediately, a string of tests were ordered and, within days, he was meeting with an oncologist.

A treatment plan had then been devised – and confirmed via a second opinion – and Macaulay had been cautioned that though he had a tough row to hoe, he should never give up hope as, like many of the patients that had come before him, he, too, could make it to the promised land.

The night before Macaulay reported for his first round of chemo, he'd paid a visit to Rick Schabacker – the recently retired man who'd butted ahead of him in line at a gas station – and they'd gotten to Schabacker's crux of the matter in record time. But, instead of putting the retiree out of his misery, something inside Macaulay snapped. All the pent-up fear and frustration and denial and acceptance surrounding his cancer diagnosis reached a crescendo . . . and then the volcano erupted.

He couldn't stop pounding on the man even if he wanted to.

And he didn't want to.

It was sheer physical exhaustion that brought the Rick Schabacker evening to a close.

He was lucky he'd worn gloves that night or he'd still be there scrubbing away DNA.

Commentators on the Netflix documentary posited the reason the Dead Night Killer had not been heard from in years was because he'd either died or been imprisoned for a different offense. Nothing could be further from the truth. The rounds of chemo and radiation, and the surgery to treat his bronchogenic carcinoma had drained everything out of Macaulay, like a puddle of rain evaporating in the summer heat. It had fried the barbarism or blood lust or whatever you wanted to call it out from him. After the treatment, and after he'd been deemed cancer-free, it had taken the bulk of a year for Macaulay to feel like himself again, and by then the urgings had dissipated into nothingness.

His demons had been excised.

That is, until the news of his reoccurrence . . . and then it were as though he'd been reborn, the old urgings reawakened, and, in retrospect, Macaulay came to view these past seven years – *the dead years*, as he'd come to call them – as though he'd been in a deep coma, sleepwalking through a meaningless life.

Macaulay had explained as best he could to Loris how he didn't plan on pursuing these *other treatment options* his oncologist had discussed with him. How his mind was made up, how he'd decided to go the palliative route in order to relieve symptoms and reduce any pain.

But Agent Loris Renn had gone mother hen as he somehow suspected she might. She wanted to sit with him and his oncologist and hear about these other options. She pushed for treatment as

Macaulay was a *relatively* young man and in *pretty good* shape. After this discussion ate into an hour of the evening, he'd asked if they could talk of other things, and Loris grudgingly acquiesced. They lay in bed all night, dozing now and again, lightly kissing, snuggling, and chatting about anything other than Macaulay's medical condition.

At the first light of dawn, he whispered 'OK' into Loris's ear, and told her he'd listen to the cancer doctor with an open mind, and do his best to switch out of *denial* mode. This put Loris in high spirits and, when he explained that she was the only person he'd told about his cancer reoccurrence and that he'd like to keep it confidential, Loris said, 'Of course', and immediately texted her boss to inform him that *she* needed a chunk of the morning off to go to a doctor's appointment.

Loris wanted to bounce out of bed, grab some coffee, and start the day, but he told her he'd forgotten a final surprise he had in store for her, and that she needed to stay in bed and keep her eyes closed while he went to his stack of clothes, in a heap at the foot of the bed, and fetched it.

Smiling widely she shut her eyes.

Loris didn't deserve any of this, and he'd be sure to make it quick.

Macaulay had been wary about reentering Loris's life after all these years, and wished to God she'd never partaken in that absurd little docudrama or had been ill the day they came for her interview. Quite frankly, he liked Loris a lot – perhaps it was love, he didn't know – and might have been sated had he indeed gotten to Detective Hempstead that night in Broadview.

But at least Loris wouldn't suffer. There'd be no strife. There was no need. Macaulay already knew Special Agent Loris Renn's crux of the matter – though Loris could love with all of her heart and mind and soul . . . Loris was married to her job. She was wedded to the Federal Bureau of Investigation.

That was it.

That was Loris Renn's kernel of truth.

He returned to the bed, sat next to her, and said, 'You're peeking.'

'No, I'm not,' she had replied, leaning back against the headboard.

'I can see your eyes,' he said as he slid the knife from its scabbard.

'No, you can't,' she had insisted.

He did it swiftly, hoping it was only the briefest of pinpricks. Loris's eyes fluttered open, but by then there was no one home.

He had laid her body back down on to the bed, as gently as possible, and then pulled the covers over her face.

Loris could rest now.

It was over.

He took Agent Renn's smartphone with him as he left the hotel room that morning. Within minutes it had been smashed and disposed of, its SIM card snipped into little pieces and flushed down a public toilet. The handful of text messages Loris sent him had gone to a burner phone, which he'd destroyed right after he found out she was staying at the Holiday Inn Express.

Macaulay thought how caring and kind it had been of Loris, wanting to come and discuss treatment options with his cancer specialist.

It touched his heart.

Yes, Macaulay felt the picture of health . . . but his oncologist assured him it wouldn't last.

Sometime soon, possibly tomorrow, the cancer would catch up with him and he'd be forced to take the pain meds, but as for now . . . he was the Dead Night Killer . . . and he had affairs to get in order.

PART FOUR
The Dead Night Killer

All knowledge, the totality of all questions and all answers, is contained in the dog.

Franz Kafka

THIRTY-ONE

'Where the hell are you?' Sheila said in lieu of hello. 'Jessica and I drove out to the lake house last night with sandwiches and homemade cookies, and you were nowhere to be found.' His wife added, 'And, *yes*, we asked around – none of the neighbors have seen you any time lately.'

'I'm in Chicago,' the killer's father spoke into his smartphone. 'I'm sorry I didn't—'

'Chicago?' his wife cut in. 'You've led us to believe you were at the lake house all this time.'

'Sheila – you need to stop talking.' His tone left no room for debate. 'You've got to listen to me, OK? It's very important.' The silence over the phone was deafening, and he knew he'd pay for it later. 'I need you to pack a bag, grab Jess, and leave the house immediately.'

After a lengthy pause, Sheila said, 'You're scaring me?'

'Look, I need you and Jess to spend the week at Kimmy's in Delaware. It'll be like a mini vacation, OK, but I need you two to leave the house right now.' Kimmy lived in a suburb of Wilmington. She was Sheila's favorite cousin; the two had practically grown up together.

'Are you in Chicago for work . . . or are you there to visit David?'

'I came to see David.'

'And?'

'And we'd set up a dinner meeting, but when I got to his house, he wasn't there?'

'Jesus Christ.'

Although Sheila had met his son from his first marriage on several occasions – only in passing and in very public places – she'd had decades of listening to him talk of how the kid was troubled, and she'd witnessed how her husband had done his best to keep his firstborn at arm's length, preferably with half of the country between them. If Sheila only knew the full story, all of the bits and pieces he kept hidden from the world, she and Jess would have been out the door in an instant.

'Call me when you get to Kimmy's,' he said. 'You and Jess should make it there in a couple of hours.'

'Can't you call the police if you're worried about what David's up to?'

'Look, Sheila,' he said, 'I can't reach him at his house or his office, and he's not returning my calls. I don't know where David is, but there's nothing I can say to the police. It doesn't rise to that level.'

'You're having your family *flee* from their home and *it doesn't rise to that level?*'

'I'm sure it's nothing.' He felt like he was walking a tightrope. 'It's just best to be on the safe side, that's all.'

'But a man *in your position* – for the love of God – there's got to be more you can do.'

'That's why I'm in Chicago,' he said more harshly than intended. 'David has always despised me, Sheila. You know that. And,' his voice trembled, 'I don't know what he's capable of.'

'Jesus Christ,' she said again. 'He's always been poison.'

'We'll have a long talk about this tonight.'

'What about Erin and Carson?'

'I'll reach out to them as soon as we hang up,' he replied. 'I can't imagine they'll be too disappointed about missing a few days of class.' Erin was completing her graduate degree at Columbia while Carson was in his senior year at the University of Pennsylvania. 'Besides, all that stuff can be done online these days.'

There was another lengthy pause before Sheila said, 'I'm frightened.'

He took a deep breath. 'I know you are, Sheila. Just get Jess to Wilmington,' he said. 'And one last thing – don't tell anyone where you've gone.'

THIRTY-TWO

CID Director Jund wound up being part of our planning session.

We sat in SAC Surratt's office the evening after Agent Renn's body had been discovered and discussed the possibility of her death being an *inside job*. How else does the killer ferret out that Agent Renn was hiding in room four-twelve at the Holiday Inn Express? How else does the killer recognize and attack me at a bus stop shelter in Broadview on the night he'd come hunting Detective Hempstead?

The meeting began with Surratt showing me footage taken from a security camera in the ceiling of the fourth floor hallway at the Holiday Inn Express that captured a man holding what appeared to be two pizza boxes outside Agent Renn's hotel room. A few seconds later Renn allowed the man to come inside. Unfortunately, the figure was shrouded in a black overcoat and scarf, a Covid mask covering his features, and a Cubbies baseball cap pulled low over his forehead. There was a second video Surratt played of the man placing the Do Not Disturb sign on the door's handle as he left the hotel room the following morning; sadly, he wore the same disguise.

I shook my head and said, 'He's all costumed up.'

'Unfortunately, he's in the same get-up when the camera catches him cutting across the hotel lobby.'

I tried to gauge the man's build as he stood outside the door to four-twelve. 'He seems like my height or taller.'

'We blew up some images and those pizza boxes were from Giordano's. We pulled on that string, but the feed from their restaurant is worse than the hotel's – costumed up, head down, and he pays in cash,' Surratt said. 'It wasn't a pizza delivery . . . and Loris let him in without any hint of a struggle. In fact – per the video – Loris leaves the room and comes back a minute later with cans of pop from the vending machine.' Surratt dropped his pen on to his notepad. 'She knew him.'

The four of us took a minute to absorb that piece of information.

'Her phone is missing,' Jund added to the despair. 'Fingerprints are also a bust. Looks like he wiped the place, probably used a couple of the hotel's washcloths.'

A pall had been cast over the meeting. There were no offers of coffee or other refreshments, no witticisms were bandied about, no camaraderie or lightheartedness. Instead, we were all business, deadly serious, as we'd discussed the killer's stature – my height or a little taller – as well as how Crystal and I had created a list of men on the FBI's special task force that met that criteria. We showed Jund and Surratt how there were eight individuals seated at the police officer tables that fit the bill, eight agents on the FBI side of the room, and four attorneys from the Cook County State's Attorney's Office. We did the math – a grand total of twenty males who were my height or taller who'd been assigned to work on the task force.

Crystal cross-referenced the task force attendee list with the DMV database to get the names of the CPD officers who were my height or taller. She then added three additional names to the police officer column taken from the list of male officers who had been at either the Tim Gorski or Casey Oselka crime scenes, where the officers would have seen and/or interacted with me and therefore could have recognized who I was if they spotted me on a street in Broadview. Crystal had pared these three policemen down from a lengthier list based on their heights recorded on their driver licenses, also lifted from the DMV. She further whittled down the list by tossing out any officers who were too young – those who'd been in high school or, in two cases, junior high – at the time the Dead Night Killer had initially been active nine years earlier. Granted, having the unsub turn out to be one of these three patrol officers was a long shot, a horse with little or no chance, but best to take no chances.

By the time Crystal, Rex and I left the FBI field office, it was nearly one o'clock in the morning. We'd just have time to swing home, let the dogs out, grab a quick nap, maybe a morning shower, and then be back at the building on West Roosevelt by seven a.m. It was imperative we be there by seven as three sets of gatherings would be scheduled, the first wave beginning at eight o'clock sharp.

The first wave would include the eight male FBI agents that fit our criteria. Surratt knew their names based on Crystal's descriptions. Most of these agents worked out of West Roosevelt and would most certainly respond to SAC Surratt's request for their attendance.

The second wave would include Crystal's list of the eleven CPD officers. Surratt would move heaven and earth, even if it meant contacting Chicago's Superintendent of Police directly, to ensure these officers arrived later in the morning.

The final wave would be the four male prosecutors from the Cook County State's Attorney's Office. As Kimberly Wray, who headed the State's Attorney's Office, was herself a member of the special task force, this would be somewhat easier than rounding up the CPD officers.

Crystal had carried the bulk of our late-night meeting, with Surratt helping to clarify a point or two, or to ask an additional question. Other than that the SAC had been uncustomarily quiet, clearly in emotional turmoil over the death of Agent Renn, but as Surratt was the special agent in charge and, as heartbreaking as the day had become . . . the show must go on.

After Crystal's phone call, both Surratt and Jund came running to the Holiday Inn Express, along with agents from the Evidence Response Team. And both leaders had witnessed the horror that was Agent Loris Renn's lifeless body lying alone in the hotel room's queen-sized bed. Rex and I stood outside the hotel room door, staying out of the forensic experts way, and watched as the room turned into a beehive of activity. An agent had already taken my statement – not much for me to add beyond Rex having alerted us to what lay inside the hotel room, and then having the hotel's manager swing open the door to room four-twelve and confirm our darkest fears.

Surratt eventually stepped out into the hallway, took a deep breath, and said, 'You don't need to hang around here, Cory. I've got a thousand things to do,' he glanced back into the hotel room, 'but it's very important that you and Crystal and I connect later today.' Surratt turned back to face me and said, 'I think you know why.' Loris Renn had reported to him since he'd been assigned to lead the FBI's Chicago Division nearly two years earlier. Surratt added, 'I've never lost an agent.'

It was clear Roland Jund, as director of the FBI's Criminal Investigative Division, had been around murder scenes before. The

CID director carried himself in a more detached manner as he chatted with members of the forensic team – nodding his head in agreement on this point or that, and directing agents toward additional surfaces to dust for prints.

This was not Jund's first rodeo.

Far from it.

Before we'd discussed how to approach the next day's gatherings, I took a minute to tell them about my other dog, Alice, and how special my bloodhound was, and how she *might* be able to connect the killer's scent from Agent Renn's hotel room back to the killer.

'Will the scent from the pillowcases be strong enough for her or this guy?' Jund asked, looking down at Rex as he lay curled up at my feet, napping on the office floor.

I shrugged. 'We know the killer stayed there overnight, so he had to sleep or lie somewhere,' I said. Surratt would have the evidence bags containing the pillowcases from room four-twelve waiting for both Alice and Rex to sniff before each meeting. 'I can't imagine the bathtub or floor being much fun.'

Jund looked at me. 'Kind of like how the wardens track escaped prisoners in the old movies.'

'Rex is a good boy, but Alice – she's an incredible sniffer dog, sir,' I said. 'We'll walk both Alice and Rex past these men and see if any kind of scent or chemical signature trips their trigger.' I stared at the director of the CID. 'I think it's worth a shot.'

'It's not the *thinnest of straws* I've ever grasped at,' Jund said after a second, and I knew our idea had gotten the green light. He added, 'I've seen dogs do the damnedest things. Unfortunately, the only thing my wife's pug ever did was eat my recliner.'

THIRTY-THREE

'Respectfully, sir, this is bullshit.'

Surratt stared at the agent with the intensity of a thousand dying stars and replied, 'We're doing this as a precaution, Jim, to err on the side of safety. It'll take five minutes out of your day.'

'But we never knew where Loris was staying,' the agent seated at a center table in the conference room persisted. 'That information wasn't made available, obviously, and none of us are stupid enough to have gone looking for it.'

'Like I said, Jim, five minutes of your day.'

There was no getting around, however subtly Agent Surratt parsed his words, that the eight FBI agents in the room – each seated two tables apart so as not to throw off Alice's or Rex's sense of smell as both of my dogs would be stopping by each one of them – were under suspicion of killing Detective Heppner in Broadview as well as executing their colleague, Agent Loris Renn, in her hotel room at the Holiday Inn Express. No matter how delicately SAC Surratt finessed it, the required attendees read between the lines. It didn't help matters that four members of the FBI Special Weapons and Tactics Teams stood by, positioned evenly about the conference room, one in each corner. It further didn't help that these men from SWAT were all giant-sized Goliaths, each large enough to make David reach for his slingshot.

The SWAT team may have been overkill, as Surratt himself appeared ready to handle any and all resistance.

After sniffing at a pair of pillowcases inside an evidence bag, I walked my dogs around the rectangle of tables, slowly, feeling much like the sleuth at the end of those movies based on Agatha Christie novels. As we passed their tables, Alice and Rex sniffed at each of the agents, often licking a proffered hand. I focused on my bloodhound's reaction as we paused by each of the agents. I finished orbiting the conference room, ending with the openly frustrated agent – Agent Jim – who had initially objected to our little experiment.

Once Jim was cleared, he stared at SAC Surratt and held up his palms as though to say, 'See, I told you so.'

I couldn't argue with the displeased FBI agent. My pups' reactions were a complete lack of a reaction to any of the men seated in the room. Neither dog had connected the killer's scent from Agent Renn's hotel room or the pillowcases to any of the agents spread out at the conference room tables.

'Thank you all for coming,' Surratt said to those seated. 'This was as I expected.'

Agent Jim stormed out of the conference room followed closely by six of his colleagues; however, the last agent stopped to have hushed words with Surratt as Crystal, Alice, Rex and I shuffled off to the side to allow them privacy. I rubbed behind Alice's ears, whispering how she was a good girl, and watched as Surratt stood motionless in the entryway as the agent's tones became less and less hushed, as the agent emphasized his points by making gestures with his hands. I didn't need subtitles to know what the conversation was about and actually heard the FBI agent say, 'Perhaps a séance next time', as he stomped out of the room.

Roland Jund had sat in the same chair he had during the previous task force meeting, rolled back against the wall, sucking on a Starbucks, observing everything, saying nothing, and not lifting a finger in Surratt's defense with either of the two pissed-off subordinates.

The next wave of eleven CPD officers – three patrol officers from the Gorski and Oselka crime scenes as well as the eight assigned to the task force – came two hours later. That sniff-and-tell session went marginally better. Surratt gave his same introductory speech, placing extra emphasis on this being *precautionary in nature* and that he *didn't expect results*; however, the presence of the SWAT members continued to belie that message. Perhaps because police dogs were woven into CPD's culture, or perhaps because the officers were getting a paid break from performing real work, the friction was limited to a couple of chuckles and a handful of rolled eyes.

Alice, Rex and I swept the room for the second time that morning, and, for the second time that morning, we came up empty. There was no alerting on either canine's part – no warning growls, no pulling of a leash – nothing. I began feeling more court jester than protagonist in an Agatha Christie movie.

Roland Jund sat through this second wave as well, same chair rolled against the wall – again observing everything and offering nothing.

Rex, on the other hand, was in hog heaven. He'd gotten so many pets and ear scratches from the various police officers, he looked at me as if to ask why we'd forgotten to bring his knotted sock.

The friction in the third wave – the male prosecutors from the Cook County State's Attorney's Office – was on par with that of the CPD officers. This was likely due to their boss, Kimberly Wray, being in attendance, and standing in the entryway with Surratt as

Alice, Rex and I again orbited the tables and, for the third time that day, struck out. Surratt dismissed the Cook County attorneys as well as the SWAT team members, but hung outside the conference room's entrance chatting with Wray.

'It was worth a shot, kid,' Jund said and patted my shoulder. I suspected he'd forgotten my name. 'Like I said,' Jund continued, 'I've grasped at thinner straws.' And then he was gone, likely to relieve himself of his mega Starbucks or, quite possibly, the entire investigation.

Alice, Rex and I stepped out of the conference room and watched as Crystal paced around the rectangle of tables as though searching for anything left behind before joining us. She held a couple sheets of paper in her right hand. We stood a few feet from Surratt and Wray until there was a lull in the conversation and Crystal said, 'Seven male prosecutors were in attendance yesterday – four of which we brought back today – but the task force member list indicates eight men from your office.'

'Huh?' Wray said.

Crystal shared a sheet she'd been clutching. 'Here's the seven men who attended yesterday's meeting,' she said, and then held up a second page, 'and here's your team from the member list showing eight men. Our count was off by one.' Crystal looked at Wray. 'Who didn't show for yesterday's meeting?'

'Oh, that would be Mac,' Wray said. 'David Macaulay – he's ill.'

'Ill?' said Surratt.

Wray turned to him. 'This is strictly confidential, OK, as I'm likely breaking HIPAA laws – David's fighting cancer.'

'But he's been attending most of the meetings,' Crystal said, and I suddenly remembered David Macaulay as the good-natured gentleman from our first gathering who'd let me know I'd been speaking loud enough for everyone in the conference room to hear.

'Short-term disability only pays sixty percent, so Mac wanted to keep working until he no longer could . . . which is now.' Wray glanced from me to Crystal. 'I know you will respect David's privacy. The poor guy can't catch a break. He almost died of lung cancer a few years back, and it's metastasized – now it's in his liver.'

The three of us nodded and mumbled the usual trite adages – *so sorry to hear that* and *aw, man, that's rough* – that you say when you're at a loss for words. *Metastasized* is the last thing anyone would want to hear come out of their doctor's mouth.

Wray added, 'Mac's a dear friend of mine and a brilliant colleague. In fact, he's one of the few I've been grooming to replace me should I prove dumb enough to run for mayor. It breaks my heart to say this, but I doubt if he'll be around in six months, much less this time next year.'

THIRTY-FOUR

Special Agent Loris Renn's funeral was held at Holy Name Cathedral, one of the largest Roman Catholic dioceses in the United States as well as the seat of the Archdiocese of Chicago. The cathedral dominates the corner of State and Superior streets, a half-block south of Chicago Avenue, and though Crystal and I made it with plenty of time to spare, outside of a couple of task force meetings, we didn't know Agent Renn and so took seats in the back.

With Detective Heppner's funeral not far back in the rearview mirror, the single suit I owned, a navy-blue wool I snatched at a blowout sale at a JCPenney factory outlet, was getting quite the workout. It'd not been dry-cleaned in, well, ever, but I'd only worn the suit about ten times and never once to shuck corn or dig a ditch.

Crystal and I sat quietly, reading about Agent Renn's life in the funeral program as the church filled. Turns out Renn had been a lifelong overachiever. She'd received a Gold Award in Girl Scouts in her junior year of high school. She'd graduated summa cum laude with a Bachelor of Science in Psychology from Loyola University, and earned further honors a few years later with a Doctor of Psychology degree in Clinical Psychology, also from Loyola. Agent Renn had begun working for the Federal Bureau of Investigation the year before achieving her Psy.D, and had been with the bureau ever since. Per the program, Renn was thirty-nine years old. There was no mention of her being married or having children.

I recognized various task force members as they arrived and took their seats. Needless to say, none of our fellow members were fighting to squeeze into the back row next to us. I watched as Surratt and Jund and a slightly familiar-looking gentleman entered the cathedral, walked down the aisle, and took their seats behind Agent Renn's parents and siblings.

I nudged Crystal and whispered, 'Who's that third guy?'

'Mitchell Westbrook,' she replied. 'The director of the FBI.'

Right, I knew I'd seen him before, getting grilled in Senate hearings – the director of the *entire* FBI. 'Good of him to show up.'

It had been a mind-numbing past week. There'd been no news regarding the case, no phone calls requesting my presence at additional task force meetings, no updates from Surratt . . . nothing. Me and Alice and Rex tossed ourselves back into our regularly scheduled obedience classes as well as volunteered to fill in for a couple of my dog handler colleagues in an effort to recoup some of the income I'd lost due to my recent string of missed training sessions. Work had been a great distraction – I loved keeping busy – but I did so with a heavy heart.

It was impossible to erase the image of Loris Renn's lifeless body lying on the hotel room's queen-size bed.

I sat in the pew and half-listened to the funeral readings and psalms, and dabbed at my eyes as one of Agent Renn's nieces sang a moving rendition of 'In the Arms of an Angel'. I glanced about the cathedral as the priest stepped up to the pulpit. Latecomers stood in back, and I spotted a man I somehow knew. He was dressed in a black suit and tie, leaning against the rear wall, hands at his sides, looking weary. I tried placing him when he caught me staring and nodded my way. The lightbulb went off over my head and I nodded back.

It was David Macaulay – the prosecutor from the Cook County State's Attorney's Office who was battling cancer. If he were ten yards closer, I'd wave him over to take my seat.

I nudged Crystal again. 'That guy is here.'

'What guy?'

'David Macaulay – the liver cancer guy.'

Crystal glanced over her shoulder, nodded a second later, and then turned back to the sermon.

When SAC Todd Surratt walked up to the podium to give his eulogy for Agent Renn, he got my full attention. Surratt had always appeared polished, comfortable in front of crowds, born for public speaking . . . but not today. Today, Surratt looked gutted. He'd occasionally cease speaking, there'd be an awkward pause for several seconds, and then he'd draw a slow breath and start in again as he spoke of how it had been a great joy and honor to work with Loris, how hard Loris worked, how she excelled in her career as a criminal profiler, how Loris's insights were brilliant, second to none, and how Loris would be terribly missed.

I thought Surratt had finished his eulogy as he stood at the podium and looked out over the congregation. Then he coughed into his hand and continued. He began speaking of good and evil, and though how '*hic sunt dracones* or here be dragons', good will ultimately triumph due to the Loris Renns of the world – because the Loris Renns of the world far outnumber the dragons.

Surratt gripped the podium with both hands, stood another second, and said, 'We're going to catch him.'

Crystal and I waited for our row to empty. We would not be going to the graveside service, nor would we be returning to the cathedral for the luncheon-slash-reception. Too many task force members might still be sore at us for what had gone down in the task force conference room and, after what had occurred between Crystal and Heppner's widow at the detective's funeral, neither of us cared for another scene.

I glanced around for David Macaulay as we exited our pew so I could stop by and say hi, but the Cook County prosecutor was nowhere to be found.

THIRTY-FIVE

*M*y dream has morphed.
No longer am I a child in the backseat of the automobile.

I'm now staring into the rearview mirror. It takes an instant or an eternity to realize that those are my eyes – my adult eyes – returning my gaze . . . and that it's me behind the car's steering wheel.

The dream is present-day, and I turn my attention to the road ahead of me.

Sleet slaps down on the windshield, ceaselessly. The wipers run full bore, sweeping faster, and faster still, but the visibility is nil – it's darkness – and I begin to wonder if there's even a road below me at all.

Suddenly, blinding lights are heading my way as the car skims along the ice. Though it makes no sense, I find myself turning back to the rearview mirror.

Mom and Dad are in the backseat . . . and they're staring my way.

Though it's three o'clock in the morning, I let the dogs out the lower level's sliding glass door. I wipe a forearm across my eyes and watch as Alice and Rex seize the opportunity for a middle of the night sniff and pee. Then I smell the cigarette smoke as it drifts down from the deck above me, and I realize I'm not the only one awake.

'Busted,' I say as I step on to the main floor. Crystal is standing inside the frame of the sliding glass door that leads to the deck. My sister has been quitting cigarettes for years or, if you listen to her whenever she's caught, she's very slowly taking up smoking. Either way, Crystal doesn't smoke often, and she never smokes inside the house.

Crystal drops the cigarette into the makeshift tinfoil ashtray she holds in her other hand, crushes the foil together, and asks, 'What are you doing up?'

'Rex was stirring,' I lied, 'so I let him out.'

'You sure? You've been through a lot lately.'

'I'm fine,' I said. 'What are you doing up?'

'Couldn't sleep. Something tugged at the back of my mind, and I found myself thinking about a sergeant I knew when I first started at CPD. I didn't know it at the time, but he was a cancer survivor.' Crystal slid the deck door shut. 'I knew him when he found out the cancer had returned and had moved into his lymph nodes.'

I shook my head. 'The poor guy.'

'He died about eight months later, but here's the thing, Cor – when I talked to him, he was in shock because he felt great. Once you've beat cancer, though, you need to get tested a couple times a year, maybe even more.'

'Yeah – in case it returns.'

Crystal walked into the kitchen and dropped the crushed tinfoil into the kitchen bin. 'He told me he felt *as healthy as a horse*, even though the tests indicated it was already in his lymph nodes. He'd never have known if not for the tests.'

'I'm sure as time went by he'd start feeling ill.'

'Yeah, the cancer was certainly there and would have gotten to him sooner or later had he done nothing.'

I nodded, not sure where this was headed.

Then Crystal spelled it out. 'I'm thinking about David Macaulay. And I'm thinking about how my old sergeant could have still kicked anyone's ass the week or two before he went in for treatment.'

I turned that over in my mind. 'But Macaulay's in treatment and, well, we all know how chemo beats the shit out of you.'

'How do we know Macaulay's *in treatment*?'

'His boss – that Wray lady – told us so.'

'When you tell your boss the cancer's back and you're taking medical leave, it's not like you hand in chemo receipts or submit your radiation schedule to prove you're getting treatment.'

'He looked pretty wiped out at Renn's funeral.'

'So? Here's me looking wiped out, Cor.' Crystal leaned back against the wall, held the back of a hand against her forehead, and drooped her eyes as though she were falling asleep. Clearly, my sister could moonlight as a mime.

I stared at Crystal. 'You think the guy doesn't have cancer?'

She shrugged. 'I'm sure he does . . . or did. In fact, I'd be very interested in knowing when Macaulay was *originally* diagnosed.'

'Why?'

'Remember the whole mystery surrounding the Dead Night Killer, how he seemed to have fallen off the edge of the world seven years ago?'

I nodded, knowing where Crystal was headed.

'A cancer diagnosis might do that to you.'

THIRTY-SIX

'Why are you asking?' the head of the Cook County State's Attorney's Office inquired.

Crystal, Alice, Rex and I sat quietly in Special Agent in Charge Surratt's office as he spoke with Kimberly Wray through the speakerphone. The SAC had broached the topic of David Macaulay's cancer.

'Just tying up loose ends,' Surratt said.

There was a long silence before Wray replied. I could almost hear her thinking. 'I don't know – Mac fought lung cancer five or six years ago,' Wray finally answered. 'Give it a rest, though, Todd, will you? Mac's not your man – that's absurd on its face,' she'd added before hanging up.

Once again Crystal and I had shown up in the lobby of the FBI field office on West Roosevelt Road, hats in hand, and begging for a minute of the SAC's valuable time. Unlike our previous visits, Agent Surratt looked as though he'd bitten into a lemon. At first he didn't even bother bringing us up to his office; rather he led us around a corner to a spot near a drinking fountain and restrooms.

Crystal knew we might only get a few seconds and dived right in. 'Before he disappeared, the Dead Night Killer beat his last victim to death with his hands. It was brutal. And a total switch-up from his normal MO. Then he takes a powder for seven years.'

'We know all this,' Surratt said and glanced down at his watch.

'And we've all wondered why he went away, right?' Crystal said. 'Well, what if our psycho got diagnosed with some form of cancer, say, seven years ago? That's a pretty damned life-altering event.'

Surratt stared up from his watch.

Crystal continued, 'But what if he's already got someone in the queue – someone he's been following, stalking – and he says, "Screw it," and figures he'll get one more before he's sucked into the medical hell that awaits him.'

Surratt's hands were now on his hips. 'And then his anger gets the better of him . . . and he beats the poor guy to a pulp.'

Crystal had already checked the DMV database; she dropped the hammer. 'Macaulay is taller than Cory – he's six one.'

A half-hour later we were seated in Surratt's office, eavesdropping on his conversation with Kimberly Wray.

Surratt looked at us after Wray hung up. 'I was hoping she'd end this line of inquiry by saying Macaulay fought cancer last year. But saying *five or six years ago* is a bit lackadaisical. *Five or six years ago* sounds an awful lot like it could stretch to seven.'

'Which would fit with the Dead Night Killer's hiatus.' Crystal added, 'Where do we go from here?'

'Well,' the SAC responded, 'if Mr Macaulay won't come to the mountain . . .'

We drove out of the FBI underground parking garage in a black SUV. Crystal sat in the passenger seat, riding shotgun and acting as navigator, while Agent Surratt himself piloted the vehicle. Rex sat in Crystal's footrest. We were heading to David Macaulay's home in Western Springs, GPS-ing an address I assumed Crystal got off the DMV database.

I rode in the backseat of the SUV. Alice sat in the middle, and one of the Goliath-sized SWAT members who'd stood conference room guard for our pillowcase meetings sat on the other side. He nodded when I said 'Hi'; otherwise the agent sat motionless looking out the window. I got the definite vibe he didn't want to waste time on small talk, so I pulled back from asking how much he could bench press. I figured the SWAT giant wanted idle chit-chat kept to a bare minimum in case someday he had to break my neck. Of course the guy wasn't all bad – about fifteen minutes into the ride, I glanced over and he was rubbing Alice behind her ears.

She'd love him forever.

SAC Surratt figured if Macaulay wouldn't come to the mountain – for whatever reason – then we'd bring the canines to him. The pillowcases in the evidence bag sat on my lap. Our hope was that Macaulay would open the front door and the dogs would either get a hit off his scent or they wouldn't.

If they didn't, we'd apologize for pestering him, wish him the best of luck, and maybe even offer to take him out to lunch.

But if Alice or Rex linked the pillowcases from Agent Renn's hotel room to Macaulay, then Surratt and SWAT giant would bring him in for further questioning . . . and deal with whatever fallout the head of the Cook County State's Attorney's Office might toss their way when the time came.

The ride took forty minutes. We circled the block and doubled back after spotting Macaulay's split-level. His two-car garage protruded out from the house, and if we came in from the opposite direction, we could turn the SUV into his driveway and be blocked from his front windows.

Agent Surratt parked in the center of Macaulay's driveway, the bumper of the SUV nearly kissing the garage door. Without a word,

SWAT giant popped out of the vehicle and on to the strip of grass between Macaulay's driveway and his neighbor's yard. I leaned out my window and watched as the big guy strode over and peeked in the side garage door window. The giant must be a magician because a second later he had a flashlight in one hand and shone it inside. A second later SWAT giant returned, shaking his head.

Macaulay wasn't married, so an empty garage hinted strongly of his absence.

SWAT giant spoke briefly with Surratt, and then he was off again, back on the strip of grass, only this time he was heading into Macaulay's backyard to keep an eye on any backdoors or windows in case Macaulay was in fact home and decided to make a run for it.

Surratt and Crystal powwowed, while I took the dogs out and waited by the rear of the SUV. The two were planning on how best to address Macaulay in the event he was home and, in the further event, he went batshit crazy. Crystal had her sidearm, a Glock 22, her police Taser and handcuffs, whereas I, on the other hand, came armed with an industrial-sized can of pepper spray and about a hundred and twenty-five pounds of canines.

I imagined Agent Surratt was armed as well and, of course, this was his play.

We were at Macaulay's front door a few seconds later, ringing the bell, Surratt in front, game face on, with Crystal a step back and off to the side, hand on her holster. I stood at the bottom of the stoop; Alice and Rex sat at my heels, awaiting commands. Once again I wore dad's old windbreaker, my hand in a pocket, gripping the canister of pepper spray. I could hear the doorbell from where I stood, but sensed no movement inside Macaulay's split-level.

My dogs had yet to alert – no pawing at the ground, nudging, sniffing or staring in my direction. Not surprising; unlike a hotel room at the Holiday Inn Express, Macaulay's house had brickwork and siding, weather-resistive barriers to protect building materials from water penetration, insulation and vapor retarders and drywall.

Surratt then opened the screen door and checked the handle.

Locked.

Something caught my eye; a yellow slip of paper floated out on to a Welcome mat when Agent Surratt opened the screen door.

'Hey,' I said, but Surratt had already noticed it.

He picked the yellow slip up, read the message and showed it to Crystal. I leaned forward to also take a peek.

Have to take a raincheck. Emergency at work. You know how that goes. We'll talk soon.

'The stickum must have worn off,' Crystal said. 'Macaulay's supposedly on medical leave – not dealing with any work emergency – so that Post-it could have been there awhile.'

'Or he comes and goes through the garage door,' I said, 'like we do, and the note could have been there a month.'

I walked Alice and Rex around the house to see if we could detect any signs of life. There were none. Drapes and curtains and blinds were all tightly shut. I didn't see SWAT giant until he stepped from behind a corner bush. I nearly jumped out of my skin but Alice jogged to him, in search of more ear rubs, no doubt. I told SWAT giant the house appeared empty and we trekked back to Surratt's SUV.

The only thing the trip had accomplished so far was Rex taking a leak on one of Macaulay's deck posts.

'His mailbox is jam-packed,' Crystal informed us when we were all back in the vehicle. Then she turned to Agent Surratt and said, 'What now?'

In response, Surratt took a folder out of his briefcase, flipped through it, found a page and held it up. 'Task force member contact list,' he said. 'I'm going to give Macaulay a call.'

'Won't that clue him in?' I asked.

'If Macaulay's our unsub, I suspect he's already clued in. If he's not, he'll call me back.'

I scratched the back of Alice's neck and listened as Surratt first called David Macaulay's cell phone. It must have kicked straight over to voicemail as Surratt began speaking nearly immediately. 'Hi David. Todd Surratt calling. Sorry we missed you at the meeting the other day. Kim said you're on medical leave – sorry to hear that as well – but if you could contact me as soon as you get this message, I'd sure appreciate it.'

Surratt then dialed Macaulay's work number and left an all but identical message there in case he was checking his voicemail.

Crystal then handed Agent Surratt a piece of scratch paper.

'What's this?'

'Macaulay's home phone.'

'Been working the DMV, I see.'

Crystal nodded and we listened as Surratt called Macaulay's home number. It rang for a while before Surratt left a third message.

The agent returned his iPhone to his breast pocket and said, 'We're going to get a surveillance team out here to keep eyes on his house. Work something out with some lucky homeowner about five doors down so we can sit in their driveway and watch the street. Who knows?' Surratt said and looked back at me. 'If I spooked him with all the phone messages, maybe he'll come running home to grab a go bag.'

THIRTY-SEVEN

'What an unexpected surprise,' Kimberly Wray said after being paged to the lobby of the Cook County State's Attorney's Office. She looked down at Alice and Rex and added, 'They won't be making a mess, will they?'

'No,' I said. 'They'd outlast me in that regard.'

Wray turned her attention to Special Agent Surratt. 'To what do I owe this *ongoing* pleasure, Todd?'

'Can we talk somewhere in private?'

Wray stared at Agent Surratt as though trying to untangle a knot. 'We can go to my office.'

Based on the letters stuffed inside his mailbox, which was a delivery or two away from spilling out on to the street, David Macaulay hadn't been home in god knows how long. And though it'd been less than a day, Macaulay had yet to return any of Agent Surratt's phone calls. Definitely not something your average Joe would put off if contacted by the agent in charge of the FBI field office in Chicago.

Unfortunately, there was nothing solid Agent Surratt or my sister could use to *get a warrant* for Macaulay's home so we'd fallen back to square one. Crystal had made a half-hearted case for rigging up some kind of *wellness check* with the Western Springs Police Department in order to crack Macaulay's front door and slip Alice and Rex inside, at least into Macaulay's entryway, to see if his scent tripped any triggers.

'Total gray area,' Agent Surratt had said. 'Macaulay was recently spotted at Agent Renn's funeral, actually by both of you, and he didn't appear under emotional duress or in deep despair.'

Crystal nodded, and then added, 'Funny how Macaulay was the last one there and the first to leave, as though he didn't want to speak with anyone.'

And that's when it dawned on me.

If you remove sleep from the equation, folks tend to spend the bulk of their days at work – in their office or cubicle – as opposed to farting around at home. In Macaulay's case – as lawyers spend their days going over legal briefs or case law or whatever it is they do – his scent would be plastered all over his office.

So we play the canine card one last time.

In his role as the head of Chicago's field office, Special Agent in Charge Surratt had been to the Cook County State's Attorney's Office on numerous occasions, mostly for meetings with Kimberly Wray. And Surratt recalled a string of offices inhabited by Wray's topmost prosecutors that lined the hallway leading to Wray's corner office.

I had the evidence bag of pillowcases stuck inside a satchel normally used for all the paperwork associated with running an obedience class. I knelt down before my two pups in the first-floor lobby of the State's Attorney's Office as we waited on Kimberly Wray and let Alice and Rex take a final sniff. I can't say if our four-legged friends suffer déjà vu, but I suspected if I forced the two to smell these pillowcases for the hundredth time, they'd go feral, answer the call of the wild, and head for Alaska.

As soon as Ms Wray led us out from the elevator, my bloodhound's nose popped up – air scenting – and I whispered, 'Go, girl.'

Alice raced down the hallway with Rex hot on her tail. They spun around a reception desk, and disappeared down a back corridor.

'What the hell are those two doing?' Wray said to me.

'They caught a scent.'

Wray gave Surratt a frosty glare, then turned and strode down the hallway, muttering words and phrases that would earn the most wholesome of family entertainment an R rating. Wray rounded the reception area and took the hallway my dogs had sprinted down.

'That leads to her office,' Surratt said as the three of us followed the head of the State's Attorney's Office.

As soon as we turned the corner, I spotted Alice and Rex, about halfway down the hall, both sitting upright, looking back at me, with Alice patting on the carpeting in front of a closed office door with her front paw. More ominously, there stood Kimberly Wray, a defiant stance in front of the same door, her arms folded across her chest.

Crystal and I were irrelevant as her eyes shot daggers at SAC Surratt. 'You have got to be kidding me.'

'Whose office is this?' Surratt answered with a question.

'You know goddamn well whose office this is.'

A few more steps and we all knew. There was a nameplate at eye level – David Macaulay.

Wray continued, 'What game are you playing at here, *Agent Surratt*, with this little farce of yours?'

Surratt held her gaze, but said nothing.

'Aren't we the sly ones,' Wray said and looked down at Alice and Rex. 'These mutts are supposed to be telling me something, huh? Cancer-ridden David Macaulay is hiding inside his office because, yeah, that makes a lot of fucking sense?'

Wray turned the handle on Macaulay's office door and shoved it open. Alice wriggled inside with Rex a foot behind her. They ran once around Macaulay's desk and came to a halt in front of his side closet. Both looked my way as Wray hit the light switch, illuminating a desk and several chairs, and beyond that a window overlooking South California Avenue. The room was minimalistic, radiating a frugal government budget, not unlike SAC Surratt's FBI office.

'Are they telling me David's taking chemo in his coat closet?' Wray said and flung open the door.

Macaulay's closet wasn't big enough to hide in, much less receive chemotherapy. Two sport jackets hung from a rack, a Bears cap from a hook, and, more importantly, two pair of well-worn dress shoes sat on the floor, one pair black, the other brown.

Agent Surratt held up both palms and said, 'Kimberly—'

'Do not fucking *Kimberly* me,' Wray cut him off. 'You think this little ruse of yours means a damned thing?' Her eyes then flashed toward me. 'What's in the bag?'

'It's for—'

'Open it,' she demanded, 'right now.'

Agent Surratt gave a nod, and I opened the satchel for Wray to inspect.

Her gaze returned to Surratt, her face reddening. 'I can't even begin to process what just occurred.'

There was a second of silence in Macaulay's office. My sister and Agent Surratt and I *were* processing *what just occurred*. And we all knew what we'd witnessed. The scent in David Macaulay's office matched the killer's scent from Agent Renn's hotel room.

'Hey!' Wray barked at Crystal. 'What the hell are you doing? Get away from Mac's desk.' Wray stepped forward as my sister backed up. 'Jesus Christ – have any of you dipshits heard of the Fourth Amendment? This is as *unreasonable* a search as a search can be.'

'This is government property, Kimberly,' Surratt said softly, perhaps hoping a calming demeanor might rub off.

It didn't.

'A warrantless search of a government employee's office with no probable cause?' Wray snapped back at Surratt. 'You really want to go down that rabbit hole?' Wray then glared at Crystal until my sister backed further away from Macaulay's desk. 'How many times do I have to say this to you? Mac has cancer, for Christ's sake. I hope to God he's visiting the Grand Canyon before they hook him up to chemo. I hope he's maxing out his credit cards in Vegas. Mac's a good guy. He's not the Dead Night Killer, for fuck's sake . . . he's my friend.' Wray's eyes were moist. 'Let the poor guy die in peace.'

Agent Surratt looked down at the floor and said, 'We'll get out of your hair.'

I hustled Alice and Rex out into the hallway, followed by Crystal and Surratt. The five of us headed toward the reception desk on our way to the elevator atrium, when we heard Macaulay's office door slam shut.

'If I wake up tomorrow and find out Mac's been identified as a suspect or a person of interest, I'll have your ass on my wall, Agent Surratt,' Wray shouted from behind us. I watched as both receptionists spun their chairs our way as though they were on a Tilt-A-Whirl. 'This dog thing's a goddamned joke, Surratt, and you're a laughingstock. I'll be shocked if you've got a job this time next month.'

Not a word was said until we were all seated in Surratt's black SUV.

'Well,' Surratt said, buckling his belt, 'that certainly could have gone better, but I have to agree with Kimberly on one point. If we've not caught Macaulay by this time next month, I'll be heading the field office in North Platte, Nebraska.'

We drove a few miles before Crystal said, 'Where the hell is he hiding?'

THIRTY-EIGHT

D avid Macaulay was forced to figure out how the automatic pool cover functioned as what remained of the good doctor had begun to ripen.

He'd gotten to the crux of the matter – to Dr Greg Fienhage's kernel of truth – during his first night's stay at the oncologist's mini mansion on a modestly secluded hillside in the village of Wilmette, fifteen miles north of downtown Chicago. Unfortunately, the good doctor's home was not on Lake Michigan itself, but Macaulay recognized he was hardly in a position to be particular.

He'd originally dragged Dr Fienhage's remains, still bound to a dining-room chair, to the doctor's three-season porch in the hope that the November chill would conceal any stench. Overnights were chilly, but daytime temperatures still reached into the fifties. Further, since he needed to stay at Dr Fienhage's home a few more days, he didn't need the oncologist's progressing residue sitting out in plain view in case anyone came looking for the good doctor.

They might get the wrong idea.

But the problem provided Macaulay a project, something to keep him busy, and he soon figured out how the controls worked to electronically open and shut the doctor's pool cover. He himself would never purchase a house with a backyard pool, certainly not in Chicago where you open it around Memorial Day and shut it down soon after Labor Day. Too much cost and maintenance for three months of enjoyment. But to each his own, and Dr Fienhage could clearly afford it. Macaulay noticed the pool water was set an inch below the skimmers. Macaulay wasn't sure if Fienhage's pool service dumped antifreeze into the water when they closed it for the season, but he lay on the pool deck and dipped down some fingers. Not that he'd ever want to drink the water, considering the range of chemicals dumped in it for the winter months, but it certainly felt icy.

Perfect for what he needed.

Dr Fienhage's backyard was shrouded by a variety of trees and shrubs and landscaped inclines. The nearest neighbor was a hundred yards away, but he hiked the six foot privacy fence to verify he was free of prying eyes. Then he used the dining-room chair as a make-shift dolly, dragging his favorite oncologist across the pool deck, and dropping him into the pool's deep end.

Then Macaulay hit the switch and marveled again at the auto-mated pool cover as it extended itself slowly across the pool's surface.

What'll they think of next?

Dr Fienhage had first made Macaulay's *list of recipients* seven years earlier when the oncologist had sat him down in an examin-ation room and explained the treatment options for his lung cancer diagnosis. The next day Macaulay found out where the oncologist lived, how the doctor had been divorced and remarried, how he had a daughter in junior high, and how the man enjoyed the finer things in life, including European travel and sporty cars.

In fact, Macaulay hid his vehicle on the far side of Fienhage's eight-car garage – four stalls, two deep, with endless storage shelves along the rear wall – and soon found he enjoyed tooling around Wilmette in the doctor's 911 Carrera.

Of course during Macaulay's *dead years*, his old list of recipients had been tabled. But the oncologist had once again won a spot on Macaulay's list – his *new* list – the day Fienhage sat Macaulay down and explained how the scans revealed that Macaulay's cancer not only had returned but had metastasized to his liver. To Macaulay's delight, he learned that the intervening years had found Fienhage divorced once again and, with his daughter attending her junior year at the University of California in Berkeley, the good doctor lived all alone in his Wilmette mansion.

Macaulay had shown up at Fienhage's residence the fourth night after his sleepover with Loris Renn at the Holiday Inn Express. Before that he'd been staying at a Super 8 in Northlake, which, though they kept his credit card on file, he'd paid every day in cash to keep them from running it. He slept with one eye open at the Super 8. He knew it was just a matter of time before he required new lodgings . . . untraceable lodgings.

So he'd shown up on Dr Fienhage's doorstep one evening with a box of steaks and a bottle of Silver Oak Alexander Valley Cabernet Sauvignon.

'It's highly unusual for a patient to come to my house,' Dr Fienhage had said, though his eyes lit up at the bottle of wine.

'You can trust me, doc,' he had assured Fienhage. 'You know I work for the State's Attorney's Office.'

'Well, since you've come bearing gifts, would you like to step inside for a glass of the Sauvignon?' Dr Fienhage had asked him.

'I just wanted to stop by and thank you for all you've done, and to let you know I'll be making an appointment to see you about those *treatment options* you brought up.'

'That's a good decision,' the doctor had agreed, and held up the bottle of wine. 'You sure you won't stay for a glass?'

'Well,' Macaulay had smiled. 'I don't think one glass will hurt anything.'

Later that evening, Macaulay worked with an immobilized Dr Fienhage far more gently than he'd done with *the others*, providing the good doctor with a false sense of hope, just as the doctor had once provided him. Plus, he needed a few favors from Fienhage before they got down to brass tacks. Macaulay had Fienhage read a script to the voicemail of one of the women who ran scheduling at his oncology office. He also had Fienhage read a damned near identical script to two of his clinic partners. The script concerned Dr Fienhage's mother, and how the poor dear had just passed away in Vancouver, Canada – where Fienhage was from – after suffering a series of debilitating strokes, and how he was now heading to the airport to be on the next flight out, and how he was sorry for leaving them short-staffed, but, as his father had passed years earlier, and his being an only child, his mother's death would tie his hands for the foreseeable future. He hoped to be back in two weeks, if possible, and it'd be best if they texted him as he suspected he'd be constantly in and out, making funeral arrangements, writing an obituary, as well as figuring out what in hell he was going to do with his mother's condominium.

A little later into their midnight palaver, after these administrative tasks were complete, Dr Fienhage shared the password to his iPhone with Macaulay so Mac could keep the doctor's oncologist partners apprised of the progress being made in Vancouver.

Later still, they unearthed Dr Fienhage's kernel of truth. It was predictable. What the good doctor valued most in life was how others perceived him. Macaulay figured Fienhage must have had an insecure childhood, as the man dedicated his life to building this façade of himself as the learned clinician and brilliant oncologist, the dedicated father, the connoisseur of fancy cars and fine wines and even better cuisine.

But underneath the façade, Dr Fienhage felt much the charlatan – he suffered from a severe case of imposter syndrome – and deep down he feared that, someday, he'd be found out as being nothing special, as being a fraud . . . a nobody.

'I believe we are all our own worst critics,' Macaulay had told the doctor in his final minute of life. 'You've heard the old adage *fake it till you make it*, and by all accounts you've made it. I am one of your success stories, Dr Fienhage. We're past the point where we can be brutally honest with one another, so let me ask you a question – did you ever think I'd be around today, all these years later?'

The good doctor slowly shook his head.

'I think that might be something you should consider. Close your eyes and think about all the good work you've done in the world. The work you could never have accomplished if you weren't who you said you were . . . if you were *truly* a fraud.'

He'd let Dr Fienhage linger with that notion a second, even watched as the oncologist's face relaxed and his color lightened before he drew their session to a finale.

When studying Dr Fienhage's driver's license, it occurred to Macaulay that he and the doctor were generally the same height. Although he was slimmer than Fienhage, there were several outfits from the man's walk-in closet, likely purchased years earlier, that fitted him to a T. So when he cruised around the city in the 911 Carrera, he took two sets of wallets with him. One was his own – for his daily withdrawals from his checking and savings accounts, as much as the ATMs would permit, at least until CPD or the FBI shut that down – and Dr Fienhage's wallet in case he ever got pulled over as the 911 was undeniably built for speed.

For now Macaulay sported a baseball cap, but, in a few days, right before he headed out for the University of Pennsylvania, where some family business required his utmost attention, he'd dye his hair black so as to match Fienhage's. He'd also bring along the doctor's eyeglasses for whenever he utilized the man's credit cards and needed to look more the part.

He'd monitored the headlines closely – both on cable news and the Internet – and was pleasantly surprised every day his name didn't lead the broadcast. But that wouldn't last much longer. He'd recently called a colleague from a phone at a Wilmette library, and learned how the FBI had used that dog handler's pooches to try to ferret out if Detective Heppner and Agent Renn's deaths were the result of an *inside* job. Macaulay's colleague chuckled as he relayed the story, as though it was the punchline of a joke, but Macaulay realized his days in Chicago were growing very short, indeed.

He also remembered spotting the kid with the dogs at Loris's funeral.

Smart boy.

Too bad he hadn't killed him at the bus stop in Broadview.

Macaulay's thoughts turned toward his father . . . and he knew there was one last thing he had to do before he left Chicago.

Macaulay had never once spoken of his father, not even back in the days of boarding schools or throughout his years at the University of Chicago. Instead, he'd tell anyone who'd asked that he had been raised by a single mother after his old man had deserted the two of them – run for the hills – back when he was way too young to even remember the SOB. Which was marginally true, as dear old Dad had all but abandoned the two of them well before Macaulay was six.

Macaulay had left his iPhone at his home in Western Springs. The call log would list the phone call he'd recently received from his father. Next to his iPhone was his old cell phone, one he'd used years earlier, which contained some interesting text messages from his father that would not present the old man in the best of possible lights, rather serve to implicate him in those nasty events from seven years past.

And, underneath the two smartphones, lay a copy of David Macaulay's birth certificate, containing both his father's surname and signature.

Given those *revelations*, dear old Dad's future – his retirement years – may not turn out as golden as his father likely envisioned.

Yes, eventually the FBI would be coming for David Macaulay.

But sooner rather than later, Macaulay would be departing Illinois.

Before he left, though, he had to say goodbye to his father.

What kind of son would he be if he didn't?

And to do that, he'd have to find a way to invite the old man to this impressive new mansion of his.

It was imperative that Macaulay let his father know he had no need to worry, that Macaulay would never hurt him – at least not physically – and that there'd be no closure between the two of them of the sort Dr Fienhage had found in the deep end of his swimming pool.

Father had no need to fear.

As for Mac's half-brother Carson . . . well, Carson was a different matter entirely.

THIRTY-NINE

*T*his time the dream skips all preliminaries. It cuts to the chase as though sentient and realizes it needn't waste valuable time setting the table.

It knows I know what it's about . . . and it doesn't care.

Immediately, I'm behind the wheel, struggling, nerve endings taut as piano wire, my eyes locked in the rearview mirror – Mom and Dad are watching me, a mixture of sadness and horror in their gaze. Then I feel that never-ending sense of sliding, more flight than skidding, as the oncoming headlights grow brighter, harsher . . . a hundred suns . . .

I'm tangled in bed sheets, writhing, screaming myself into consciousness.

'Cory,' I hear as a hand touches my shoulder. 'Wake up, Cory.'

I shoot up in bed as my sister steps back, her eyes wide, jaw dropped. Alice is at her side. Rex has fled in the commotion, likely slithered under the double bed.

'Are you OK?' my sister asks. 'You were screaming.'

I wipe my brow with a forearm. It comes back moist.

'You were having a nightmare. I could hear you from upstairs.'

I nodded and took a deep breath, not quite sure if I could speak.

'You've been through a lot, Cor.' Crystal searched my eyes. 'Heppner died right in front of you, and then Agent Renn in that hotel bed.' She shook her head. 'I should never have sucked you into this madness.'

'It's not that, Crys.' I dropped my feet over the edge of the bed and took another breath. 'It has nothing to do with the case.'

She backed up a few more feet, looked at the chair by my desk, but then opted to plump down on a bean bag Mom had picked up a million years ago and stared at me. 'Then what's going on?'

'Do you ever dream of Mom and Dad?'

'All the time,' she replied. 'I love those dreams. I try to make them lucid. Even if I'm half awake, I try to let them know how we're doing, and that we're OK.' She continued, 'Did you just have a Mom and Dad dream?'

I shook my head. 'I have these nightmares.'

Crystal thought for a second. 'I'm sorry to hear that, Cor. That was a *horrible* day – worst day ever. It was hell and you suffered trauma – we both did – and that can take a long time for a person to work through.' She tried getting comfortable in the bean bag chair, an impossible task. 'But you need to know that Mom and Dad would be so proud of you, Cor.' She then added, 'They were proud of you when they were alive.'

'I was an asshole that day,' I said. 'I'm the one who caused the *trauma*.' My face was wet with tears. 'The last thing I ever said to them was that they should *just fucking leave already*.'

Crystal stared at me a long while. 'All teenagers are *assholes* at some time or another, but Mom and Dad – they knew who you were. They loved you, Cor. If anything, they'd be happy you didn't go with them that night.'

'These nightmares I have – I'm in the car with them as it happens.' I look down at the floor. 'It's like I'm driving them to their deaths.'

'Oh my God, Cory – you've been keeping this bottled up?' She struggled in the bean bag to sit upright. 'We have people at work we can see, you know, after a shooting incident, or if something distressing occurs.' She hesitated a second. 'I can get a referral or set something up if you'd like.'

'You want me to see a *shrink*?'

'Don't knock them – they can help people sort out their feelings.'

'I pushed them from the house, Crys,' I said, louder than I'd intended. 'And when the weather went shit-ass crazy, I didn't warn them. I wrote them a text to skip dinner and take the back roads home, but I deleted it without sending because at that moment . . .' I choked back a sob, '. . . I hated their guts.'

Crystal looked at me with more curiosity than disgust. 'You've been living with this misplaced sense of guilt all this time?'

'I don't find anything *misplaced* about it.'

'The car accident was *not* your fault, Cor. Life doesn't work that way,' she said. 'I've wished a ton of ill will on you over the years – every time you stick me with your dirty dishes – but, hey, you're still walking around.'

We sat in silence and watched as Rex squirmed his way out from hiding under the bed.

'They called me from Applebee's that night to tell me not to go out.' She continued, 'Dad figured the highways would be plowed and sanded by the time the two of them left the restaurant, but the city got caught with its pants down. There were a ton of accidents that night.'

'If they'd taken the back roads, they'd still be alive.'

'That's not your cross to bear, Cory. It's not.' Crystal then shrugged and said, 'Besides, you know what Mom and Dad would say if they were here right now?'

'What?'

'Don't let Cor forget his meds for the spectrum thingy.'

I wiped my eyes a final time. 'I swear to god, Crystal, I'm going to record you one of these days, post it on TikTok, and get your ass cancelled.'

Crystal worked her way out from the bean bag. 'We're going to talk more about this, Cory – because you can't live your life from nightmare to nightmare, OK?'

I looked at my sister and nodded.

'Mom and Dad wouldn't want that.'

I didn't want to talk about it anymore, so I said, 'Alice ran all the way upstairs to get you?'

'No, I was on the main floor, toying with having a cigarette.'

'I bet you were more than *toying with* having one.' I glanced at the digital clock. 'What are you doing up at two in the morning?'

'Come upstairs and I'll show you what I found in Macaulay's office.'

I wondered what she meant by that, and then remembered Wray shooing her away from Macaulay's desk. 'Did you find his copy of the Fourth Amendment?'

'Right – 'cause James Madison wrote that with serial killers in mind.'

When we got upstairs, Crystal pointed at what appeared to be a handful of business cards laid out on the kitchen island.

'What the hell are these?'

'When you were all focused on Macaulay's coat closet, I was checking out his desk. He had a cup on the corner that read *Business Cards and Shit*,' Crystal said. 'So I palmed his business cards and shit when no one was looking.'

'I don't recall you sharing this with Agent Surratt?'

'After that ugly scene in the hallway – Wray ripping Surratt a new one – I figured I'd keep mum on this in case it didn't pan out. I figured the cards would be just the usual BS people hand you at business conferences or from insurance agents or whatever.' Crystal picked up one of the cards and handed it to me. 'But then I noticed this one.'

Instead of a business card, what Crystal handed me seemed to be more of an appointment reminder. It included a date and a time from mid-September. As I flipped it over I asked, 'What's this for?'

'An old appointment slip from Macaulay's oncology clinic,' Crystal said. 'We've got his doctor's name.'

FORTY

Shortly after his daughter Erin had been born, the killer's father heard through the grapevine that his first wife, Janine, had changed her last name back to her maiden name – Macaulay – and that she had done the same with their son David. The father imagined if he dug through the court documents he'd find where Janine had forged his signature in order to obtain his consent. He further imagined he could contest the change in his son's surname, but, quite frankly, he felt a tremendous sense of relief . . . and more so as the years passed by.

But considering David's *proclivities*, how many days would that change in surname buy him after his son got caught?

Sure, both Janine and her parents were deceased, and his wedding to her had been a simple affair – immediate family only, officiated by a county judge the week before he reported to boot camp. But there'd be some forgotten aunt or cousin lurking about the woodpile, or an old family friend on Janine's side, who'd start making phone calls as soon as the news of David's arrest exploded across the headlines of every newspaper in the country.

Either that or some enterprising reporter would get around to checking David's birth certificate, immediately noting his son's *original* last name . . . and eventually linking it back to him.

The truth would come out – the beans would be spilled – and life as he knew it would come to an immediate end.

The sins of the son shall, in no uncertain terms, be visited upon the father.

Christ, he thought – he'd be treated as though he were the father of Jeffrey Dahmer.

He'd have to resign in disgrace, of course. And no one would look at him in the same manner ever again, of course. There would be civil lawsuits from the families of the victims, of course . . . and, as long as we're being open and honest, about a thousand percent chance of him doing a lengthy stint in prison.

He'd be lucky if Sheila and the kids stood by his side.

The Ka-Bars utilized in the multiple homicides had been taken from his knife collection. He'd never notified the police that they'd been stolen. More damning, there existed a string of *infuriated-beyond-belief* texts he'd been foolish enough to send to David seven and a half years ago, immediately after he realized what his psycho kid had been up to. And if his son had hung on to those messages, or if a forensic specialist could pull those texts out of the ether – which they can – an air-tight case could be made that he knew exactly what his son had been doing all those years ago . . . and that he'd done absolutely nothing to stop him.

And how he'd continued to do nothing when David started up again.

His goose would be cooked. The father imagined even the most middling of prosecutors could stir together a half-dozen charges with which to send him away for, at his age, the rest of his natural life. Even counting his years of service in the military or the amount of work he'd done for charity, the father doubted he'd garner much sympathy from any state or federal judge, and even less from a jury.

The father had been staying at the Embassy Suites in downtown Chicago – not the best place he'd ever stayed, certainly not the worst. He barely ate, he barely slept. Days were spent with his laptop or on conference calls, going through the motions, providing the appearance of normalcy. Nights he spent lying in bed, counting the ceiling tiles, and repeatedly assuring himself he'd done nothing to deserve this living hell.

Tonight, as he tossed and turned, he made a decision. *Fuck it* – no more of this soul-crushing inertia, no more playing defense and hoping for the best. Instead, he'd go proactive. The father would get out ahead of this fucker. He'd devise a narrative – a half-page of bullet points – that would paint him in the best of possible light. He was a victim as well here, the father of an estranged son – a boy who'd hated him for decades – from a failed marriage dating back a lifetime ago, and he'd only recently tripped over evidence of what his deeply disturbed offspring had been up to. In the morning he'd hire the cagiest of defense attorneys to sell this narrative – to punch it home – as they brought their case to the authorities.

As for any grenades tossed his way by David, well; he and his legal team would roll with the punches.

He'd immediately resign from work – hell, he was spitting distance from retirement – so as not to cause the organization any prolonged embarrassment. But the takeaway in the press would be: Devastated father turns in estranged and troubled son.

It felt good, a sense of relief that the nightmare was finally coming to an end. Perhaps he'd actually get some sleep tonight. He turned over and was adjusting his pillows when his smartphone vibrated on the bedside table.

Who the hell would be contacting him at this time of night?

Sheila? One of the kids?

He grabbed the cell phone, saw he had a text from a number he didn't recognize, and tapped to bring it up:

Dad – As you are likely aware by now, my cancer has returned, metastasizing to my liver. Dr Fienhage's prognosis is most grim. Felt you should know. – David

The father stared at the text message for several minutes, realizing his son was using a burner phone. And, yes, word had in fact worked its way to him about his son's recurrence. Truth be told, it warmed the cockles of his heart. It gave him hope that the cancer would knock David out of commission, just as it had done seven years earlier, only this time it'd take his son out on a more permanent basis.

Dammit! – he began second-guessing his decision, and found himself slipping back into inertia and playing defense.

He recognized the name of his son's oncologist from the last go-round, from seven years earlier, back when his hunt for his son had ultimately led him to Northwestern Memorial Hospital the night after David had his lobectomy surgery. The father had shown up late that evening, bluffed his way past a nurse station, and found his son's room.

David was clearly medicated, groggy, hooked to an IV, but he recognized him and slowly nodded.

'Hello, Father,' his son had said. 'I wondered if you'd be stopping by.'

'So kind of you to tell me where you were,' he'd replied facetiously.

'I didn't think you cared,' his son had said.

He stood there a moment before saying, 'You've not made it easy . . . especially with what you've become.'

His son mumbled something incoherent.

'What?'

'Have you come to kill me?'

'I hadn't thought of that,' he said, looking from the monitor to the IV drip.

His son mumbled something again.

'What was that?'

'It's over.'

'It's over?'

'Yes,' his son had said and closed his eyes.

The father stood next to the hospital bed a few more minutes, watching his son as he breathed in and out, as his son drifted off into a deep and restful sleep.

Then he had slipped out of the hospital as though he'd never been there.

The father sat up in his bed at the Embassy Suites and switched on the nearby lamp. He read through the text message a final time and scratched at his cheek.

He wondered why David had provided his oncologist's name.

FORTY-ONE

'Would it be possible to meet with Dr Fienhage today?' 'I'm sorry,' the receptionist said. 'Dr Fienhage is currently out of the office.'

Crystal changed tack. 'The mother of a friend of mine referred him to me.' My sister stood in front of the reception desk at Lakeview Oncology Center – located off a harried Ashland Avenue – appearing sufficiently awkward and tongue-tied, while I hung back and, hopefully, looked the part of a concerned family member come along to offer support. 'They've found,' Crystal's voice trembled, 'a spot on my lung.'

'I am so sorry to hear that,' the receptionist said in a hushed voice with a look of concern. This was likely a situation she dealt with every day. 'Our clinic has a remarkable team of oncologists.' She began studying her computer monitor. 'I could fit you in with one of them later today or, possibly, tomorrow morning,' she looked up, 'if that would be OK?'

'Um, my friend Taryn – well, her mother battled lung cancer with the help of Dr Fienhage . . . and Taryn's mom is cancer free and thinks the world of him.'

Crystal's performance might not merit an Oscar, but possibly an Emmy. Nevertheless, it made me want to cringe, like when a character in a movie or on a TV show gets caught trespassing on someone's private property, so I glanced around the clinic's waiting room – soft lights, a fish tank the length of one wall, a few indoor plants, padded chairs and loveseats and side tables, a small station offering coffee, tea, hot chocolate and healthy snacks. There were a handful of patients waiting on appointments, some reading magazines, others staring at their feet.

No matter how lighthearted, hospitable or welcoming the oncology center made their waiting room . . . no one wanted to be here.

I turned back when the receptionist responded to Crystal, 'Unfortunately, Dr Fienhage is out of the country right now. We expect him back sometime next week, so I can schedule you an appointment then, but I'd hate to have to call you back and reschedule in case Greg is still away.'

My sister had conned me into coming along with her to the oncology center. In fact, we swung by the house in order to pick her up in the Silverado as Alex and Rex and I had just completed an early afternoon training session in Glenview. Crystal thought she'd be able to glean more information stopping by the clinic in person than over the telephone. If she could connect with Macaulay's cancer specialist, this Fienhage guy, she'd flash her badge, tell the oncologist we worked with David Macaulay – considering the FBI task force, this tale was not necessarily an outright lie – and that we knew about Macaulay's medical condition, but can't find the guy and were deeply concerned for his welfare.

Then she'd press the doctor to see if he had any idea where Macaulay might be.

The reason for the subterfuge came with a first and last name – Kimberly Wray. Sure, we wanted to find David Macaulay as soon as possible, but we didn't want to give the head of the Cook County State's Attorney's Office any additional ammunition with which to rip us and/or Special Agent Todd Surratt another new one.

'He's out of the country?' Crystal served that over the net as though it were a question, not a statement.

'Dr Fienhage is from Canada. He had to fly home to deal with a death in the . . .' the receptionist paused a second but then continued, 'to deal with a family emergency. As a result, Greg's status is a bit *up in the air* at this point in time.'

'Oh no – the poor man,' Crystal said, ladling it on. 'And I bet that's caused a lot of work for the clinic.'

'Tell me about it. I've been rescheduling Greg's appointments all week.' The receptionist shrugged. 'Just one of those things in life you have to deal with.' She then cleared her throat and added, 'If your *diagnosis* is *time sensitive*, it may be best to get your records transferred here and have you seen as soon as possible by one of our other practitioners, with the thought that Dr Fienhage can review your chart once he's back in the office.'

No way, I almost said out loud as I watched a single tear slip down my sister's face and lodge in the corner of her lip. *No way*. It was all I could do to keep from rolling my eyes. Now I realized how Crystal always had Mom and Dad wrapped around her little finger.

'OK,' Crystal whispered, wiped at her lip, and took a card from a holder on the countertop. 'My brother and I are going to grab a drink and discuss, you know, the best route for me to take, but,' she nodded at the woman behind the desk, 'I suspect I'll be calling you shortly to schedule an appointment with one of the other providers.'

'Absolutely,' the receptionist replied. 'Absolutely.'

After we left Lakeview Oncology Center, drinks wound up being a couple of Big Macs, Cokes and fries at McDonald's as an early dinner. Since Crystal was springing as payback for my chauffeur duties, I even soaked her for one of those baked apple pies. Though we'd gone through the drive-thru window, I pulled the Silverado into an empty spot at the far corner of Mickey D's parking lot for us to eat and chat about what we'd learned at the cancer clinic.

I even tossed a few pretzels at Alice and Rex to keep them from starting some kind of canine mutiny.

'You know what I mean, right?' Crystal asked and took a bite out of her Big Mac.

'Yeah, it seems a bit odd that Macaulay's oncologist runs off to Canada right when all this other shit is raining down.'

'It's not only *odd*, it's fishy as hell, Cor,' she said. 'And Lakeview Oncology seems all baffled in terms of when the guy's coming back. She may as well have told us Dr Fienhage was on Mars.'

'Should we call Surratt?'

'There's not much to tell him.'

I crumpled my hamburger wrapper and tossed it in the bag. 'So what do we do now?'

'Let me DMV Fienhage's address,' Crystal said, 'and then we'll swing by his house.'

FORTY-TWO

The killer's father glanced quickly behind him before breaking away from the timber steps leading down the steep hillside. The stairway would eventually connect with a cross street which, once traversed, would connect with a wooden walkway that eventually wound itself to Lake Avenue and, from there, to Gillson Beach on Lake Michigan itself.

But the father's destination was not Gillson Beach or Lake Michigan.

Using Google Earth he'd been able to bring up the area surrounding Dr Fienhage's Wilmette mansion on his smartphone. He needed to cut south across a couple hundred yards of woodland – trees, brush, undergrowth – before ultimately bumping into the eight-foot privacy fence surrounding the cancer specialist's backyard.

He hoped it was the only fence he'd have to scale as he sported plain-toed Oxfords along with his black suit pants and jacket, T-shirt and white button-down. For all practical purposes, he'd dressed as if it were another day at the office, though he had blown off wearing a tie. The father initially toyed with stopping to buy some hiking boots, jeans and a fall coat – possibly something camouflaged – but it was a sunny afternoon and he figured if today didn't go as planned, screw it, the last thing he'd give a shit about was ruining his dress clothes.

Fortunately, he'd been walking the trail alone – no one else had been out and about to witness him begin his descent down the sloped staircase, and no one had been out and about to spot him exiting said staircase.

The father had called Dr Fienhage's clinic that morning using the Embassy Suites' courtesy phone at the reception desk. He asked to speak with the oncologist, but had been informed that Dr Fienhage was currently out of the office on a family emergency and might be returning sometime next week. The news of the doctor's absence – and how he *might be returning sometime next week* –

fitted in with his deciphering of the text message his son had sent and, when the cancer center's receptionist asked if she could take a message for Dr Fienhage, he'd hung up the lobby phone.

Quite frankly, with what he knew about his son's *inclinations*, he suspected the good doctor would never be returning to his oncology practice.

Yes, the father knew he was walking into a trap.

This is what everything had boiled down to.

His son knew he would be coming – his firstborn having virtually beckoned him to the oncologist's estate – thus he carried his own father's unregistered .22 pistol fully loaded in his right-side pocket. In his left-side pocket, a ski mask. And around his neck hung a pair of binoculars.

But his firstborn would not know when and – praise be to Google Earth – his firstborn would not know where.

In a perfect world, the father would catch his son unaware. After all, he did have the high ground as the knoll continued its downward grade. Even after it met with Dr Fienhage's privacy fence, the slope continued at that trajectory for an additional twenty-odd yards before flattening out in order to encompass the doctor's underground swimming pool as well as a backyard deck the size of an aircraft carrier. Beyond that lay stone steps leading down to a lower patio, fire pit, and barbecue station the length of a midsize U-Haul.

As far as he could tell from Google Earth, the doctor's backyard was made for entertaining, so wouldn't it be nice to catch his boy dozing on a reclining chaise lounge chair, taking in the late afternoon sun on this perfect Indian summer of a November day, enjoying what could possibly be the last pleasant weather of the season. A scenario like that would be most serendipitous; of course he would need a rifle if such an opportunity indeed presented itself. Without a rifle, he'd have to find a portion of the wooden fence impossible to spot from the cedar deck, where he could slip quietly over, and work his way toward his slumbering son.

Two shots to the head would suffice, and then he'd get down to the more taxing work of getting rid of both David's body and David's vehicle. Of course carjackings in Chicago were becoming more prevalent – an epidemic, in fact – and, unfortunately, had taken on a more lethal tenor.

Perhaps David's vehicle could be found abandoned in some crime-ridden section of Rockford, Illinois, with David stuffed inside the trunk.

But the father was getting ahead of himself – wishful thinking – and he doubted such an effortless opportunity would present itself.

As soon as he was thirty yards out from Dr Fienhage's privacy fence, the father hit the ground and brought the binoculars up to his eyes. He adjusted them and scanned each section of the doctor's backyard, looking for movement or any sign of life.

He held the binoculars to his eyes for five entire minutes.

Nope – his clinically insane progeny was not to be found loafing about on the deck. In fact, the house appeared quiet, wrapped up tight . . . abandoned. Curtains to both sliding glass doors on the upper deck were stretched taut. Both glass doors were shut and, he assumed, locked. The father brought the binocs back into play, glanced around the landscape, scoping out the best location for him to slip into Dr Fienhage's backyard without being spotted by any prying eyes watching from any window. He found a place on the side of the yard, near where the fence connected with the backyard gate. *Damn*, he thought. The binoculars revealed a padlock on the gate, otherwise he could dance his way inside.

The father put down his binoculars and began second-guessing himself. What if the cancer specialist was truly out of town? What if his son's message, his slippage of his oncologist's name had been nothing more than that?

Well, it's too late, I'm already here and I need to find out, he thought to himself.

Using the burner phone he'd paid cash for at a nearby Walmart, he called Dr Fienhage's home number for the third and final time that afternoon. He listened to it ring and ring and ring until it flipped over to voicemail, just as it had done the two previous occasions. The father cursed inwardly as he took the ski mask from his pocket, stretched it over his head – yup, this is what his life had come to – and jogged along the side of the doctor's garage in order to peek around the corner and verify no cars were parked in the driveway.

It'd be just his luck to interrupt a family get-together.

The father then returned to the woods beyond the privacy fence and circled back until he reached his desired spot, the perfect point of entry. He stood before the eight-foot fence, wishing he'd brought along one of those mini-bottles of vodka to steady his nerves. Instead, he took a deep breath and soldiered up.

He was several exits beyond the point of no return . . . and, one way or another, he was going to see this thing to the end.

Once inside the fence, he'd quietly check the two sliding glass doors on the upper deck as well as the one on the lower patio and, if all three were locked down, he'd put one of the metal lawn chairs through a sliding glass window and hit the house like gangbusters. Pistol in hand, he'd pause inside, as that kind of uproar would trigger an equal and opposite reaction for anyone inside the house who might be shitting themselves or running for cover.

If there wasn't a peep, he'd still tear through each room, making certain the house was empty. Then, if the oncologist's home held no secrets, he'd quickly exit over the privacy fence and be jogging toward the hillside steps a minute later.

But, if his son were inside Fienhage's house, he'd kill him – even if it meant emptying the entire magazine into the goddamned psychopath – and then he'd retreat back up the hill with his binoculars and keep watch over the residence. If no squad cars or fire trucks or ambulances arrived within an hour, he'd return to the mansion . . . and clean up the mess.

The father shook his head and then jumped as high as he could, grasping ahold the top of two pickets. He pulled himself upward, a chin-up, knowing he was too old for this shit, his dress shoes a whirl of activity, seeking traction. He swung a leg over the top rail, somehow worked his body across to the other side when the figure appeared as though out of nowhere. Hands were on his jacket collar and suddenly he was airborne, and just as suddenly crashing down hard on to the cement of the pool deck. Immediately he knew something was wrong with his shoulder. He grimaced and lifted his head toward the man who had been lying in wait for him.

'What took you so long, Father?' his firstborn said.

FORTY-THREE

'Just get it over with.'

'What is it you want me to do?'

The killer's father was secured to a dining-room armchair, his wrists duct-taped to walnut armrests, his ankles secured to the chair's wooden legs, with more duct tape wrapped about his abdomen. He would be going nowhere. 'You know goddamn well – that bullshit thing you've got going with the knives you stole from me.'

'Really – that's what you thought I was going to do?' His son looked as though he'd been slapped across the face. 'You know I could never hurt you, Father.'

His son annunciated *Father* with great reverence, as though he were speaking to royalty or some kind of deity, but the father knew it rang hollow; his pathological firstborn meant anything but. And the father didn't need an X-ray to know the fall had shattered his right shoulder – it hurt like a son of a bitch – but he was a little out-of-focus on how he'd gotten fastened to an armchair in what appeared to be the great hall off Dr Fienhage's kitchen.

Of course the father could forgive his short-term memory being a bit hazy as, after David had flung him off the top of the privacy fence, he'd followed up by blasting him with a Taser gun.

'What do you think of my new digs?' David threw a hand in the air, signifying the oncologist's household.

'What have you done with him?'

'Who?'

The father glared at his son and said nothing.

'Dr Fienhage?' David said. 'Oh, he's enjoying his swimming pool.' His son sat on a leather ottoman a few feet in front of him. 'The good doctor's been so overworked lately; it's nice he now has time to take a well-deserved breather.'

'So what's that bring it up to now?' the father asked his son. 'How many innocent lives have you taken?'

David looked insulted, a second slap to his face. 'I'd quibble with the word *innocent*, but I'd rather talk about something else.'

'What could you possibly want to talk about?'

'Mother, of course.'

And there it was, the father figured as much – the time had come for a family reckoning. 'What about your mother?'

'You know she always loved you . . . even at the very end.'

The father felt his face begin to flush. 'Somewhere deep inside, Janine meant well,' he replied. 'But your mother had issues – mental health issues – that made living with her impossible.'

'Then why would you leave a six-year-old alone in her care?'

'You two were attached at the hip, a couple of peas in a pod. If I tried dragging you out of that house, you and she would have fought like banshees.'

David looked his father in the eye. 'Why didn't you get her the help she needed?'

'Jesus Christ,' he said, 'I tried – I tried for years. Your mother was bipolar – extreme swings, manic and depressive. Some of the medications helped, if she stayed on them . . . and her staying on them was always a big *if*.'

'So abandoning us would somehow *cure* that?'

The father's face reddened. 'You hated my guts by then. Janine had poisoned you against me, beyond repair.'

'You do know Mom rarely left her bedroom?'

He nodded.

David shuffled the ottoman a foot closer to his father. 'I was left alone with a mother who lived her life inside of a room.'

'Janine needed more help than I could *ever* provide.'

'I loved her.'

'Of course you did – she was your mother.'

David added, 'I doubt I'll ever *love* anyone as much as I loved her.'

The father sat quietly and stared at his son.

'She was all you said she was – bipolar disorder, depressive.' David moved the ottoman closer yet, their knees nearly touching. 'And she talked of death all the time, Father. Did you know that?'

He shook his head.

'She wanted it to end – she wanted that most of all – and would have taken action, had she not a child on her hands. By the time I turned fifteen, *death* was all Mom spoke of.'

The father blinked back moist eyes. 'Believe what you want but, in those early years . . . I loved Janine. If you saw any of the old pictures, you'd have seen it in my face.'

David continued as though he'd not heard his father's admission, 'She did all the research – you know – on what it would take. She begged me to do it, Father,' he said. 'She made me promise her I would.'

It slowly dawned on him what his son was saying. 'Dear God.'

'And I lived up to that promise.' David looked his father in the eye again. 'Mother wrapped herself in a blanket – like a straitjacket – so she couldn't put up a fight, however involuntary, like a drowning victim pulling down their rescuer. Then I knelt on her chest as she lay on the bed, just as she'd instructed, to make it impossible for her to breathe. I plugged her nose with my thumb and forefinger, as she'd also instructed, and cupped my other hand over her mouth. She wanted it to end . . . and it didn't take long. Not long at all as I sat there and cried my eyes out while she slipped away. But when it was over, Father, she looked happy. It was the first time in my life I'd ever seen her look that way. Mother was finally at rest.' David stared off in the distance a long moment. 'I guess that's my crux of the matter,' he finally said. 'My kernel of truth.'

Hair had risen on the back of the father's neck as his son spoke of his ex-wife's final seconds, but he failed to grasp the last part. 'What's that mean – your *kernel of truth?*'

'It doesn't matter,' David said, still staring off in the distance.

The father's mouth hung open as he looked from his son to his bound wrists. He hadn't imagined the horror and revulsion of the past few weeks could get any worse, but he'd been wrong. The only thing he'd taken solace in all these years since Janine's death was that his ex-wife had died *peacefully* in her sleep.

A gentle end to a tragic life.

And now even that wasn't true.

David continued, 'I called Grandma the day after it happened and told her that Mother wouldn't leave her bedroom. Nana came right over to check, and when she came out of the room she was as white as a ghost. Then she sat me down in the front parlor, Father.' David added, 'Do you remember the front parlor?'

The father nodded.

'Then Grandma made some phone calls and an ambulance and

police cars arrived . . . and they took Mother away in a body bag while I sat in the front parlor and watched. There was no autopsy as Mom had feared. We'd not used a pillow so there'd be no bits of fiber on her face or in her eyes or nose or mouth. To everyone involved, Mom simply passed in her sleep.' David concluded, 'People die in their sleep every single day.'

'Dear God,' the father said again.

'And you already know the rest of the story. I was sent to be with you, but you banished me – like a red-headed stepchild sent off to a faraway boarding school,' David said. 'You wanted nothing to do with me.'

'Even back then I was *terrified* of you,' the father said slowly. 'Are you telling me I shouldn't have been? For Christ's sake, David, did you hear what you just told me about Janine?' He took a breath and added, 'Look around; look at where we're at.'

His son glanced about the room, as if the key to life lay somewhere in Dr Fienhage's kitchen.

The father grimaced at the intense pain in his shoulder and said, 'So what happens now?'

'Well, first I'm going to get you a snack and then make sure you're well-hydrated as you're going to be here a couple more days,' he said. 'I have some *family business* to attend to without your interference.'

The father's eyes grew wide.

'Oh don't worry about Sheila. Nothing's going to happen to Mom's *replacement*. For all I know, you're on the prowl for wife number three and I'd be doing you a favor,' he said. 'And my sisters are safe as well. I'd never touch a single strand of hair on either of their heads.'

The father stared at his firstborn son; his circuits overloaded digesting what David was implying. 'I have them all in hiding – you'll never find *him*.'

'Carson may not be in his apartment, Father, but what's the name of the tavern he so loves on Chestnut Street? *Devil's Alley*? Your boy's killed quite a few brain cells there, that's for sure.' David paused a moment. 'Is he still seeing Elle? If so, he may not be staying at his apartment, but I'll hazard a guess on where he's spending his evenings. And you know how big a workout freak he is – how Carson goes to Life Time Fitness every day, sometimes

even twice a day. Seems a little excessive, don't you think, Father?
A bit on the vain side. He should be spending that time studying.'
David continued, 'Amazing what two thousand dollars and a private
investigator can get you in Pennsylvania – my half-brother's pattern
of life.'

The father struggled against his secured wrists.

'That's pointless, Father – you're only going to chafe yourself.'

'You fucking bastard.'

David shrugged. 'I imagine I am.'

The father tried to rock the wooden armchair, but gained no traction. He looked at his firstborn son and seethed. 'I'll fucking kill
you.'

'I hate to rain on your parade, Father,' David said and shrugged
again, 'but you kind of muffed your chance.'

'For God's sake, don't do it,' the father said, the tears beginning
to stream down his face. 'He's your little brother.'

'It does have a certain Cain and Abel ring to it, don't you think?'

'Please, David,' the father pleaded. 'Kill me – I'm the one who
screwed you over all those years ago. Kill me – but leave your
brother alone.'

David thought a second. 'Perhaps it's not so much Cain and
Abel, Father. Perhaps it's more the prodigal son returning with a
vengeance.'

'Please, David. I beg you . . . please.'

'I'm sorry, Father – but Mother would have wanted it this way.'

FORTY-FOUR

'Can you imagine shoveling this in wintertime?' I said as
we pulled up the bunny hill that was Dr Fienhage's
driveway.

'I'm sure he's got a service that does it for him,' Crystal said.
The driveway leveled out as we reached the top, revealing four
separate garage doors. Crystal added, 'Bet he's got a four-wheeler
in there for when it snows.'

I parked in front of the first stall, adjacent to the stone walkway that curved around some shrubbery as it worked its way toward the doctor's front entrance. I let Alice and Rex out of the backseat, and hustled them over to grass on the far side of the garage so no observant homeowner could spot them tinkling on the yard and get all bent out of shape.

Hey, it's happened a few times.

As the pups did their business, I glanced around the side of the doctor's garage. He had a patch of blacktop long enough to park a good-sized RV. Beyond that a wooden privacy fence, tall enough to challenge the most nimble of neighbor kids, cut from the corner of the garage, across the blacktop, and then worked its way up the hill and into the woodlands surrounding Dr Fienhage's property.

The doctor had a hell of a house, a hell of a driveway, and, from what I could tell, a hell of a backyard.

Evidently, there's money to be made in oncology.

Crystal opened her passenger door but remained in the shotgun seat as she tapped at her smartphone, giving Dr Fienhage's home phone a final ring. A minute later she shook her head, stepped out of the pickup, and joined us as I brought the dogs over to the stone footpath.

'Curtains are closed,' I said, pointing at the front of Fienhage's house. 'No one's answering the phone, he's not at work – so I'm thinking he's actually in Canada.'

'Well, if he is here,' Crystal said, stepping on to Fienhage's front porch, 'let me do the talking.'

'By all means,' I said. 'I wouldn't know what to say.'

Crystal stood to the right of Dr Fienhage's double-entry doors, dipped a hand beneath her blazer jacket – near her holster – and said in a whisper, 'It's a wellness check – we work with Macaulay, we know he has cancer, but can't find him and are concerned about his welfare. Then we see if Dr Fienhage knows where in hell Macaulay's holed up.'

I nodded, my right hand inside the pocket of Dad's old wind-breaker, gripping my canister of pepper spray as Alice and Rex circled about our ankles.

Crystal pressed the doorbell.

FORTY-FIVE

Macaulay set the backpack containing seven thousand dollars in cash from his ATM withdrawals as well as Dr Fienhage's wallet and credit cards on the kitchen island when the doorbell rang.

His eyes shot toward his father. 'You order a pizza?'

His father lifted his head. He'd been staring into his lap for what seemed an eternity, his spirit crushed. When the doorbell rang again, his father glowered his way and began to scream, 'Help—'

But Macaulay was on him in a flash, jamming a driving glove he'd found in the Porsche into his father's mouth. A second later he was dragging the armchair on its back two legs past the refrigerator and into the walk-in pantry. He shoved his father inside, chair and all, and quietly shut the pantry door.

Then Macaulay jogged up the carpeted steps and ducked into the first of the four upstairs guest rooms, the one with a bay window over the entryway. He pulled the shade back a half-inch and peeked outside as the doorbell continued to ring. The person at Dr Fienhage's front door was blocked by the roof of the porch, but Macaulay spotted some beat-to-shit Chevy pickup sitting in the driveway.

What the hell?

Is the yard service guy here to be paid? Wouldn't that be disbursed online or by check? Or does Dr Fienhage pay the mower guy in cash?

Then he spotted the dog – a bloodhound, like the one he'd seen with that dog handler at the FBI task force meetings – jog across Fienhage's front yard, followed in hot pursuit by a . . . springer spaniel. Red flags exploded in Macaulay's mind. The springer spaniel was not only the same type of dog from the night he'd killed that detective in Broadview . . . it was the same dog.

He knew this because he'd been ready to kill the goddamned thing at that bus stop shelter, and he'd then been forced to kick at its head when the mutt had him by the pant leg as he scrambled over a backyard fence, trying to make good his escape from the CPD snare.

What would the dog handler be doing here at his oncologist's house?

His question was quickly answered as two figures left the front porch, heading back toward their pickup truck. Sure enough, one was the dog handler from the task force meetings as well as the night in Broadview. Worse yet, the other figure was the dog handler's sister – the CPD detective, also from the task force.

What the hell?

There was no way they'd gotten a warrant to search Dr Fienhage's house. If they did they'd be here with a half-dozen squad cars, not just the two of them coming here in a piece-of-shit pickup.

So the two of them are chasing down a lead – they'd somehow gotten his oncologist's name and address – in an effort to see if the oncologist could point them in the right direction?

He'd been regularly checking Dr Fienhage's home voicemails. The good doctor had shared with him the required passcode, amongst other things he'd shared in their first and last night together. Lately, there had been several hang-ups with no messages. Macaulay assumed most of those were from his father but some, including the call from a few minutes ago, were likely from the detective and her kid brother.

Events were progressing faster than he'd anticipated. Macaulay was lucky he was on his way out the door, literally half a minute away from slipping behind the wheel of the 911 Carrera and leaving Fienhage manor forever. But now he'd wait another ten minutes, maybe he'd even slip down to the road and peek about, verify the two weren't watching the house like you see cops do on the TV shows, before he hightailed it the hell out of here.

Shit!

This meant he may not get to enjoy the doctor's credit cards – and the doctor's identity – for as long as he'd anticipated.

He continued watching as the two stood next to the rusting and dented Silverado, deep in conversation. He glanced at his watch. *Come on*, he rushed them along mentally; *get in the damn truck and leave.*

The dog handler whistled for his pups, and then he and his detective-sister headed toward the side of Dr Fienhage's garage.

Double shit!

FORTY-SIX

A lice and Rex scampered up the incline to explore the woodlands beyond Dr Fienhage's privacy fence while Crystal and I played *Three Stooges*. There was no side garage door for us to peer into; however, there existed two rectangular windows about eight feet off the ground, likely intentionally high to avoid burglaries or vandalism. Each of these windows was about four feet in length by two feet in height, and centered widthwise along the garage wall. Worse than being so high up, the windows offered no ledges or sills or fingerholds in which to limit our vaudeville act to a bare minimum.

So there I stood, my hands cupped at chest level, holding up Crystal's left foot, while her other foot steadied itself atop my right shoulder. 'Hurry up,' I pleaded. 'Very uncomfortable.'

'Can you stop jiggling?' she replied.

I almost teased Crystal about her weight – or queried her diet – but, valuing my life, I thought better of it. Plus, acting as human scaffolding required my full attention.

'This place is huge,' Crystal said. 'It's two cars deep. Empty shelving lines the back wall – I doubt Fienhage works on any of his vehicles.'

My arms quivered. 'Can you come down and tell me this?'

'Just one more second, Cor,' she said. 'He's got a monster SUV in the second stall, and it blocks whatever he's got going in the first stall. Third stall is something sporty.' She paused a second and added, 'I think it's an Alfa Romeo.'

'Jesus – what are you gonna recite the Gettysburg Address from up there?' I gritted my teeth. 'Get the eff down, already.'

Crystal brought her right foot back into my cupped hands and somehow I managed to slide down the garage siding until my sister was able to leap to the blacktop.

'He's got another car under a cover in the fourth stall, seemed like a midsized vehicle,' she completed her lengthy dissertation.

'You thinking it's Macaulay's Lexus?' I circled the blacktop, shaking the jitters out of my arms. Per my sister's consultation with the DMV database, Macaulay tooled around in a Lexus NX.

Crystal shrugged. 'I'm not sure I'd make that leap – it could be anything. Maybe Dr Fienhage really is in Canada.'

I peeked around the corner of the doctor's backyard fence and spotted Alice and Rex about thirty yards up the hillside, both sitting there facing a row of pickets, with Alice patting at the dirt beneath her with a front paw.

'No way,' I said.

Crystal looked at me. 'What?'

I whistled and the pair came galloping down the slope, spun leftward at a fencepost, leapt over landscaping block on to the blacktop, and sat in front of the padlocked gate to Fienhage's backyard. Alice resumed patting the ground with her paw.

Crystal stared at the two dogs. 'You've got to be shitting me.'

'Well,' I said, 'we have been wondering why the doctor's been incommunicado.'

'Are you sure they're not amped up over a dead rabbit?'

I smiled at Crystal. She knew enough about HRD dogs to know what had occurred. 'Sure, Alice and Rex like dead rabbits as much as the next dog, but that's not what they've alerted to.'

'Well, hell,' Crystal said. 'Let me get my kit.'

I watched my sister work on the padlock a minute before asking, 'Can't we just call this in?'

Crystal had returned from the truck with a small black bag she had buried in the bottom of her purse that she called her *lock-picking kit*. She held up something called a tension wrench, and she inserted its bent end into the padlock opening while mumbling something about applying pressure to the lock cylinder. Then Crystal showed me something called a rake tool due to one side containing ridges, which she then shoved into the padlock's key slot and commenced jiggling around with both picks.

'If we call it in,' Crystal said, 'we'll have to deal with Kimberly Wray and the State's Attorney's Office.'

'Won't breaking in get you in trouble?'

'If I get fired, I guess I could take up burglary,' she said. 'But it doesn't appear we'll have to worry about that because I suck at this.' As Crystal twisted and turned the tension wrench and slid the rake tool in and out of the padlock, she told me of a burglary ring of thirteen-year-olds they'd busted up a few years back, and how all of the kids were proficient with these lock-picking tools. 'If one of those little shits was here right now, we'd already be inside.'

'So you ran out and bought a kit?'

'You'd be amazed what you can get online these days.'

I hiked back to the Silverado and peered down the driveway, half expecting a string of squad cars swarming in to place Crystal and myself in handcuffs. I cut across Dr Fienhage's front yard to the landscaping boulders that held up an embankment on the home's far side. Like the windows in front, the side windows were shut tight with the blinds drawn.

If my dogs had indeed discovered human remains – which I knew they had – I figured Macaulay would be long gone. Who'd want to hang out with a corpse?

When I returned to the side of the garage, Crystal stood there holding the open padlock in one hand and her picks in the other. '*Voilà*.'

'Are you sure about this, Crys?' I said. 'I'd hate for you to get in trouble.'

'If we find a dead rabbit, the padlock goes back on and we get the hell out of here, and pray there're no hidden cameras that caught me doing this,' Crystal said. 'But if we find someone in there,' she nodded toward the back property, 'like, say, Dr Fienhage – I don't think he'll be in any condition to demand a prosecutor press charges.'

I nodded at Crystal's logic . . . and swung open the gate.

FORTY-SEVEN

Macaulay shot down the staircase, snatched the Ka-Bar Mark 2 off the kitchen island, sprinted to the doorway at the end of the great hall, threw it open, and slipped into the murky darkness of Dr Fienhage's garage. He didn't flip a switch;

the only light entering the parking stalls came from the late afternoon sun filtering in through a line of windows set high on the far wall.

Macaulay crossed the garage in an instant, hoisting himself on to a cabinet countertop that ran the length of the side wall. Like the shelves lining the back wall, most of the cabinet's drawers and cupboards were empty. A blue cast-iron vise sat alone on one countertop edge while a dusty Coleman cooler sat on the opposite end. He doubted either had been used much, if ever. White pegboard lined the wall above the countertop yet only held a half-dozen tools – a hammer, a series of different-sized wrenches, a screwdriver – as though Dr Fienhage had stopped by the nearest hardware store upon moving in, tossed a handful of tools into his cart, hung them for show on the pegboard, and then lost interest in ever touching them again.

But Macaulay was interested in none of that. He wanted to see what the lady detective and the dog handler were up to along the side of the house. He stood on the countertop; shuffled sideways to one of the high-set windows, and glanced through the pane of glass.

Shit!

He twisted sideways, his back pressed tight against the pegboard, holding his breath. Right as he'd peeked out the window, he spotted the top of the sister-cop's head – her dark brown hair – as she emerged along the side of the exterior garage wall. A second later and they'd have been staring eye to eye.

There was no way the sister-cop could spot him from her angle, so Macaulay stood motionless and listened as the two spoke.

'Hurry up. Very uncomfortable.'

'Can you stop jiggling?'

Macaulay chuckled inwardly, and realized how hard he was squeezing the handle of his commando knife. A knife he considered, after many years of intimacy, to be more an appendage of his right hand than a mere accessory.

Then the familiar urge kicked in.

These two had taken away his prime objective in Broadview that ill-fated night, making it impossible for him to get at that prick detective – John Hempstead – who'd been part of the Dead Night Killer documentary. Later, the dog handler and the sister-cop discovered Agent Loris Renn a full day sooner than he'd planned for. And, as he'd heard from a colleague in the State's Attorney's Office, dog man and sister-cop had attempted some kind of Perry Mason denouement using the dog guy's mutts and some linen from Loris's hotel bed.

Goddamn this brother-sister combo, poking about Dr Fienhage's just as he needed to vamoose.

He squeezed the Ka-Bar's handle tighter still.

'This place is huge. It's two cars deep. Empty shelving lines the back wall – I doubt Fienhage works on any of his vehicles.'

The impulse began to pound in his head – was damn near uncontrollable. Every fiber of his being wanted to swing the Ka-Bar Mark 2 in a wide arc, smashing through the double panes of window glass, and sinking five inches of blade into the center of sister-cop's overly curious forehead.

How would that make for a Perry Mason denouement?

Fuck it, the killer side of him was going to do it. Macaulay readied himself.

'Can you come down and tell me this?'

'Just one more second, Cor. He's got a monster SUV in the second stall, and it blocks whatever he's got going in the first stall. Third stall is something sporty. I think it's an Alfa Romeo.'

Don't do it, the rational side – the lawyer-prosecutor side – of Macaulay fought for control. Think it through. You kill the sister, then what? You'd have to run back to the door to punch an opener so one of the stalls would open. By the time you got around to the side of the house, the brother would be up the hill and dialing 911 . . . and then you're screwed. Goodbye to assuming the doctor's identity, goodbye to driving to the University of Pennsylvania to powwow with your half-brother. And, after all is said and done, it'll wind up like an episode of *Cops* where they'll drag you out of some dumpster you're hiding in.

Think it through for Christ's sake.

'Jesus – what are you gonna recite the Gettysburg Address from up there? Get the eff down, already.'

The lawyer-prosecutor side of Macaulay seized control. He leaned back against the pegboard and slowly exhaled. There's nothing the dog handler and the sister-cop can do. In another minute or two, they'll jump into their rickety piece-of-shit Chevy and head out on the highway. Ten minutes later, he'd follow suit. Macaulay had a lengthy drive to UPenn ahead of him, but he'd tackle half of it this evening.

He thought about the road trip. The long drive would be a blast because everything they've ever said about driving a Porsche 911 is a hundred percent true.

Macaulay scrunched down and sidestepped back to the window. He tilted his head so only his left eye would be exposed as he peered down to watch as the two called it quits. Instead, he stared in disbelief as the dog handler's two mutts sat in front of Dr Fienhage's padlocked gate, gazing into the doctor's backyard, toward the swimming pool. The bloodhound patted insistently at the blacktop with a front paw while the brother and sister looked on in surprise.

Oh shit, Macaulay thought . . . *cadaver dogs.*

The sister-cop then disappeared from view. He listened as the door to their pickup opened and, a few seconds later, shut. A moment later she returned to view with a small black case in hand. Half a minute later the sister-cop worked the padlock like a dental hygienist scraping plaque.

Goddammit, Macaulay thought.

He should have killed her.

FORTY-EIGHT

A quick glance around Dr Fienhage's backyard got me thinking I'd made the correct decision in heading back to school. The cancer doctor had an upper deck the size of Brazil and an in-ground swimming pool you could dock a yacht in. I doubted I'd ever be able to afford anything this elegant, no matter how many classes I aced at Harper Community College, but perhaps someday I'd be able to spring for a bite-size version of the hot tub the wealthy oncologist had positioned on his deck between the two sets of sliding glass doors.

Fienhage had a Jacuzzi big enough to contain a Subway franchise.

Alice and Rex immediately sprinted toward the deep end of the swimming pool, took their seats on the edge of the pool deck. Crystal and I watched as Rex joined in with Alice this time as they both pawed at the concrete beneath them.

We followed in our pups' footsteps. Crystal's focus lay on the back of Dr Fienhage's house, her right hand on her holster. The sliding glass doors were shut, inside drapes pulled tight. Similar to the front of Dr Fienhage's mansion, drapes or curtains or shades were all drawn on upper-floor windows. As we approached the pool's deep end, I glanced at the red stepping stones leading down to Fienhage's lower yard – a patio stretched out from yet another sliding glass door, culminating in a circular fire pit, upscale lawn chairs, and a barbecue station large enough to feed Rhode Island.

I reached Alice and Rex first. Though dusk was swiftly approaching, it'd been a warm November day and I caught a small whiff of what had tripped their trigger. If the scent were any stronger, I'd have sat down with them on the pool deck and patted the concrete.

Instead, I nodded at Crystal and said, 'Yup.'

She glanced backward a final time as she knelt next to the dogs. Then we both tried lifting up the tarp covering the swimming pool, but it seemed to be fastened with some kind of mechanical unit keeping it securely in place – evidently built sturdily enough to withstand the heavy snow and ice of the often fierce Prairie State winters.

'He's got one of those automatic pool covers,' Crystal said, and glanced beyond the shallow end where a wooden fence hid the pool heater, filter, pumps and whatever the hell else. 'I'm sure there's a switch for it somewhere.'

'Somebody's in the pool, Crys,' I said, bent down and slipped both palms under the tarp, gripping it firmly. 'I think it's OK for us to break some shit.'

She nodded and I raised my legs, pulling upward. There was tightness, then a series of popping sounds, then a gap big enough for Crystal to lean forward between the tarp and pool's edge, and peer down into the water.

A second later she said, 'Now I know why Dr Fienhage hasn't been answering his phone.'

Then my dogs began to growl.

FORTY-NINE

oddamn cadaver dogs!
GMacaulay cut to the rear of the garage, ducked around the shelving, and stood beside the door accessing Dr Fienhage's backyard property. He watched in anger as the two mutts darted to the side of the swimming pool's deep end and performed that fucking thing they did – patting the ground with a front paw – to indicate a discovery had been made. The dog handler and his sister-cop trailed the dogs, but the sister-cop kept glancing back at the house. At one point, though he doubted she could spot him, Macaulay stepped backward as her eyes scanned past the garage door window.

Shit!

Macaulay was burned if he made a run for it. In five minutes CPD and the FBI would be notified of Dr Fienhage's fate, and then all things Fienhage would be monitored and tracked – the doctor's bank accounts, his credit cards . . . his vehicles.

Goodbye Porsche 911.

Then Macaulay's face would be plastered all over the news. He wouldn't be able to walk into a Starbuck's without the baristas speed-dialing 911.

Worse yet – his father would be released from his imprisonment in Dr Fienhage's kitchen pantry and able to warn his *other* son to get the hell out of Pennsylvania.

Macaulay's plan to destroy whatever remained of dear old Dad's life would turn to shit . . . and all because of this meddling brother-sister combo.

Fuck!

All of his plans down the toilet.

. . . But wait, the killer side of him seized control . . . *it doesn't have to be that way.*

Macaulay felt his grip tighten around the handle of the commando knife as the dog handler and sister-cop tried peeling back the pool cover. Their backs were to him as they fumble-fucked with the winter tarp. Macaulay only had to make it twenty-something yards. He could cover that ground like a halfback – take one out immediately, and then kill the other.

And if either of the yapping mutts got in his way – Macaulay clenched his Ka-Bar Mark 2 blade and readied himself for battle – well, they weren't exactly pit bulls or German shepherds or Dobermans.

He'd pig-stick them, like a wild boar hunt.

Macaulay quietly opened the backyard garage door.

FIFTY

C rystal and I twisted left, but Macaulay was upon us. Crystal took a foot to her chest, hard, launching her backward, down through the gap I'd made with the pool cover, plunging her into frigid water. Then Macaulay was before me, a flash of a blade in the setting sun, suddenly a blur of black and tan between us – Alice – as eighty pounds of bloodhound latched her jaws to Macaulay's elbow. Alice's leap bought me an instant to jerk my head sideways as his knife flashed upward, just missing my chin.

The momentum threw me off balance. I stumbled backward, the deck no longer beneath me, and dropped to the pool cover. I sank down, a tarp over quicksand, but watched as Macaulay smashed at Alice's nose with his free hand. She fell to the concrete with a yelp as Rex lunged forward, dodging in and out, barking, spinning and snapping at the man who'd attacked his pack.

'Run,' I screamed as I flailed at the tarp beneath me, a fish on a dock, grasping at wrinkles of green plastic for support.

Thank God Alice and Rex heeded my command, bolting down the steps to Fienhage's lower yard, leaving Macaulay slashing at the air where they'd just been.

But then Macaulay's attention turned back on me. And he was no longer the jovial task force member or cordial colleague attending Loris Renn's funeral. Macaulay's face now a mask of fury and determination. He bent down, reached forward with his free hand,

and grasped the hem of my jeans. My eyes widened as Macaulay began dragging me back toward the pool deck where we both knew what loomed.

'Cor!' Crystal shouted, muffled and distorted beneath the tarp, her view blocked from current events.

'He's on the deck!' I screamed, praying she'd bob to the surface, gun in hand, praying she'd read my mind. 'He's on the deck!'

Crystal read my mind, but so did Macaulay as he released my jeans and threw himself to the concrete as three shots blasted through the pool cover.

Boom! Boom! Boom!

And then Crystal came up through the opening in the tarp. She was close by, so I grabbed the back of her blazer as well as a fistful of hair, and shoved her toward the pool deck as Macaulay scrambled to his feet and flew toward the door to the garage from where he'd sprung. Shoving Crystal forward drove me downward. Ice-cold water flooded the back of my windbreaker and shirt. I shuddered as I rolled and twisted in the sagging tarp and frosty water, flailing and floundering as best I could to get out of the swimming pool . . . knowing full well what lay beneath me.

Crystal made better progress; the top half of her stretched atop the pool deck as she sighted her Glock 22 and pulled the trigger.

Boom!

The window of the back garage door exploded a split-second after Macaulay had slammed it shut behind him. Then Crystal was up and running. Alice and Rex were back in play, joining Crys in hot pursuit of the man who'd tried to kill us. Somehow I got three fingers on the pool deck and that was all I needed. A second later, I was up and sprinting after the trio.

Crystal didn't wait to see if Macaulay had locked the backdoor. Two shots – one for the deadbolt, one for the handle.

Boom! Boom!

Then she kicked the busted door in and entered the garage with me at her heels. Suddenly the roar of an engine filled the room, and we both tripped backward, stumbling into a pile as Macaulay gunned a sports car straight for us, clipping the side of a back shelf.

'Back,' I screamed at the dogs to get them out of the way, and shoved Crystal up and forward as Macaulay shifted what I saw was a Porsche 911 into reverse. The garage door for the first stall had nearly completed its upward trajectory and I realized what Macaulay was about to do.

Dammit!

If I'd only parked the Silverado with its nose to the garage door instead of near the pathway to the front door, there'd be no opening and we'd have had the bastard boxed in.

Like a bat out of hell, Macaulay slammed the Porsche into the gap between the side of Fienhage's garage door and my Chevy's bumper, obliterating the trim and railing off the door, scraping the shit out of both sides of the sports car, and destroying the left panel of my pickup truck. There was a second when I thought Macaulay'd stalled out – he stared back at us with pure hatred – then ducked down in his seat and goosed the gas pedal as Crystal planted a bullet in the center of the driver's side windshield.

Boom!

But then Macaulay was through, and gunning it down the driveway's steep incline as Crystal tore ass after him. I hustled after her, working the pepper spray out from the windbreaker's pocket, not sure exactly why, when I heard two more shots.

Boom! Boom!

But a second later Crystal was jogging back toward me, shaking her head, and cursing.

FIFTY-ONE

'Alice,' I said, embracing my bloodhound with both arms. 'You saved my life.' I hugged her and scratched at her back. Rex wandered over, his tail swinging back and forth, wanting to be part of the group hug. 'Yeah,' I said and rubbed under his chin, 'you threw down, too, Rex. I saw that. You knocked him off his A game.'

Crystal had taken my iPhone, which was damp but somehow operable as opposed to her smartphone, which was soaked through with water as well as whatever chemicals they dump in pools to winterize them. I doubted her cell phone would ever work again, whether Crystal dropped it in a container of rice or not. She was now circling the Silverado and talking with her captain, calling in the troops.

Crystal's first phone call had been with SAC Todd Surratt, to alert him to what had just gone down at Dr Fienhage's residence – Surratt promised his team would be here ASAP – before she contacted her tribe at CPD.

My sister had been shivering, her lips blue, during her call with Surratt, so I rummaged about in a duffel bag I keep on the back floor of my pickup and fished out an old jean jacket, a pair of sport sandals I wear in summer, and a beach towel I led Crystal to believe was much cleaner than it truly was. Between phone calls she tossed her soaked blazer and shirt in the back of the truck while I looked away, tossed on the jean jacket, buttoned it to the top, and lifted the collar for that additional two inches of warmth. Her wet shoes and socks also went into the pickup's cargo bed after she strapped the sandals over her bare feet. Crystal then used the beach towel to pat down her pants as best as possible, and then wrapped the damp towel around her waist.

I headed back into the garage – into the tattered remnants of Dr Fienhage's first stall – and took the cement steps to the door leading into the doctor's house.

'Cor!' Crystal called from the driveway. 'Wait for me.' She then said a few more words into my iPhone and tapped off. She headed my way, her pistol back in her hand. 'Let's make damn certain there are no more surprises.'

I snuck along behind Crystal, guarding her back with my can of mace, as she took a minute to clear the master bedroom, guest rooms and upstairs office. We took another minute to clear the lower level, and a few more seconds to circle the main level before returning to the kitchen. I'm glad there were no added threats lurking as I wasn't sure how they'd play out.

Perhaps Crystal would shoot them and I could salt their wounds with pepper spray.

I peeked into a backpack sitting atop the kitchen island. 'Well,' I said, 'at least he won't get away with his pot of gold.'

Crystal headed toward me to see what I'd found when we heard a muffled moan. I almost hit the ceiling while Crys drew her Glock like an Old West gunfighter. Then we heard a series of grunts and sounds of movement, wood scraping on the tile floor, followed by a long moan . . . all sounds emanating from a closed pantry door, a place I assumed opened to shelves of canned goods and cereal boxes. Crystal motioned to the handle and I edged along the side as we listened to yet another muted moan.

Then I grabbed the door handle and threw open the pantry.

A man sat with his back to us, strapped in an armchair. Jesus – had we interrupted Macaulay performing one of his *sessions*? I looked at Crystal as she reholstered her weapon. I grabbed the wooden sides of the armchair and dragged it out from the walk-in pantry.

I'm not sure if siblings can die of shock at the exact same moment but that's damn near what happened as I twisted the armchair around to face us. We heard the squad cars pull into Dr Fienhage's driveway, but Crystal didn't run out to greet them. My sister and I remained glued to the tile of the kitchen floor.

We both knew the man who was duct-taped to the armchair with what appeared to be a leather glove stuffed inside his mouth.

It was Mitchell Westbrook . . . the director of the Federal Bureau of Investigation.

FIFTY-TWO

M y butt hurt.

I'd spent much of the past two and a half hours either perching on Dr Fienhage's front stoop or the lip of my pickup's tailgate, keeping an eye on Alice and Rex, and answering the sporadic question posed to me by a CPD detective or FBI agent. Crystal, on the other hand, was allowed free rein to journey back into Fienhage's house and partake in the ongoing homicide investigation. Fortunately for Crystal, somewhere along the line someone tossed her a dry pair of sweatpants to slip into.

Initially, I'd yanked the glove out from Director Westbrook's mouth and began peeling off the strands of duct tape securing him to the chair as Crystal ran out to greet the arriving CPD officers.

'How'd he get you?' I asked the FBI director.

Westbrook shook his head and said, 'I think my shoulder's broken.'

At that point Crystal returned with a half-dozen CPD officers – some detectives, other higher-ups, I couldn't keep track.

Westbrook mumbled, 'Restroom' and repeated how he thought his shoulder was busted. Crystal and another detective helped him up from the armchair and then into the front corridor which contained the main floor's bathroom.

Trying to be helpful, I went to Dr Fienhage's freezer, fumbled about the racks, and pulled out a jumbo bag of frozen peas.

'What the hell are you doing?' said a guy in a suit, black hair and a mustache.

Startled, I held the bag of peas in front of me as though it were a newborn. 'This might be good for the FBI director's shoulder, at least until the ambulance gets here.'

He followed up with, 'Who the hell are you?'

Fortunately, Crystal heard the commotion and came to my rescue. 'That's my brother, sir. His HRD dogs clued us in on the body in the swimming pool,' she said, pointing toward a sliding glass door leading out to Dr Fienhage's backyard. 'He was also involved in the struggle with David Macaulay.'

The suit and mustache still looked like he wanted to squeeze my throat. 'Let's get you out of here,' he said. 'And keep your dogs under control so they don't shit up the crime scene.'

I handed Crystal the bag of frozen peas and headed outside in time to spot a dark sedan and two black panel vans driving up a patch of grass in order to get around the various CPD squad cars – the FBI had arrived. The black vans pulled around to the side of the garage, near the back gate, whereas the sedan parked in front of Dr Fienhage's fourth garage stall. I watched as agents poured out from the two vans and expected to spot Special Agent in Charge Surratt step from the sedan; instead, CID Director Roland Jund stepped out from the vehicle's backseat, caught me staring and said, 'Hi Dogger' as he strode past me on his way into Dr Fienhage's house.

See – I knew Jund didn't know my name.

A short while later, squad cars were switched about so an ambulance could back its way up the driveway and park with its rear

facing the second garage stall, right next to my Silverado. A couple
of paramedics stepped out from the cab and headed into the house,
one carrying a trauma bag.

Then Crystal came out and whispered, 'David Macaulay is
Westbrook's son.'

'What?!'

'Shh,' she said.

'How come he's got a different name?'

Crystal shrugged. 'Previous marriage or something. Westbrook
said they'd been estranged for decades.'

'So Macaulay kidnapped him and hauled him here?'

'Director Westbrook said his son informed him his cancer had
returned and requested he meet him at the home of his oncologist
in order to assist him in weighing treatment options,' Crystal said.
'Estranged or not, Westbrook showed up a couple hours before
we got here, Macaulay let him in the front door, and then attacked
him when his back was turned.'

'Where's the director's car?' I glanced at all the vehicles now
packing Dr Fienhage's driveway. 'There weren't any cars when we
showed up.'

'Westbrook told us he took an Uber,' Crystal said. 'Jund's been
in there asking him a dozen questions – kind of weird since
Westbrook is Jund's boss.'

'Where the hell is Agent Surratt?'

'He got a warrant for Macaulay's house. He's there right now.'
She turned to head back into the house and said, 'I got to go.'

I glanced again at all the vehicles lining Dr Fienhage's driveway.
Just my luck – I'd been blocked in and forgotten. I'd already done
some triage on my pickup, pulling it forward and backward a few
feet to verify it still ran. It did but I'd definitely need some bodywork
done on the bumper and left front panel, where Macaulay had
smashed the Porsche against it as he fled the scene.

Realizing I'd be spending the rest of my life in the doctor's
driveway, I rooted about in the back of the pickup, grabbing a
handful of paper bowls and a plastic bin of dog food I keep on hand
in case of, I guess, situations like this. I dumped a big scoop into
two bowls, set them on the blacktop below my tailgate, and let Alice
and Rex chow down. Then I splashed a bottle of water into two
more bowls for the pair to lap up after dinner.

I leaned back against the side of my pickup, contemplating my place in the universe, and received about the tenth surprise of the day. Kimberly Wray walked up the driveway – there was no more space up here to park – and into the brightness kicked off by the garage floodlights. She was alone, still in her dress clothes, and heading my way.

Wray stopped about ten feet from me, looked from the squad cars to the FBI vans to the ambulance, and then turned back to me and said, 'Is it true?'

I slowly nodded.

Without another word, the head of Cook County State's Attorney's Office turned about and headed back down Dr Fienhage's driveway.

I watched as Wray disappeared into the darkness, then heard footsteps and spun toward the garage. The paramedics were assisting a pale-faced FBI Director Westbrook through the garage, and from there up into the back of the ambulance as CID Director Jund and Crystal followed in their wake.

I stepped over to join them.

'I need to have this looked at.' Westbrook sat on the bed in the ambulance and grimaced.

'One more second, sir,' Jund said, evidently receiving a call on vibrate as he held a smartphone up to his ear and walked back into the garage for added privacy.

I glanced at Director Westbrook, noted he had some kind of ice pack strapped to his shoulder. I wanted to go back inside Fienhage's house, grab the lieutenant or captain with the mustache, drag him out here, point at the ice pack, and ask the big dope why he gave me such a hard time about the frozen peas.

But that would be small of me.

Jund spoke on his cell phone a few more seconds, hung up, and joined us at the back of the ambulance. 'That was SAC Surratt, sir.'

Westbrook said nothing.

'He was calling from David Macaulay's house.'

'He got a warrant that fast?'

'Yes,' Jund said. 'They've been ripping the place apart.'

'Fine.' Westbrook grimaced again. 'You can update me at the hospital.'

Jund looked at the director of the Federal Bureau of Investigation a long moment, and then said, 'With all due respect, sir – you have the right to remain silent . . .'

FIFTY-THREE

Well, that certainly didn't go as planned.

Anything but . . .

Macaulay sat in a Chipotle on East Lake Cook Road in Wheeling. After ordering a Barbacoa burrito and a large Coke, he had exactly twenty-seven dollars left in his wallet and forty-two cents in a front pocket. Tragically, his backpack of cash had been left sitting on top of the island in Dr Fienhage's kitchen.

Before ordering his meal, Macaulay had snuck into Chipotle's restroom, locked the door, and converted the small lavatory into a first-aid station. He removed his jacket and rinsed the dried blood off his right elbow as best he possibly could with the lukewarm water that came out of the tap. Then he smothered the bite marks left by dog boy's bloodhound with a palm full of liquid soap from the wall dispenser, soap he strongly doubted was antibacterial. Then he pressed a fistful of paper towels against his wound a full minute before putting his jacket back on and heading out into the restaurant.

Later he would need to do a better job of cleaning and dressing the wound.

The allure of tooling about in a Porsche 911 had faded in Macaulay's crazed flight from his oncologist's home in Wilmette to the Chicago suburb of Wheeling. The sports car was hot as hell – the police were certainly searching for it by now – and it might even contain some type of tracking system that CPD or the FBI could tap into. So, he'd abandoned the bashed-up 911 in a corner spot at a Walmart and hiked the half-mile to the taco shop.

Macaulay figured he'd best eat while he could, before his face became a mainstay on the cable airways or above the fold in many of the nation's newspapers. Fortunately, Dr Fienhage had left a Porsche driver's cap – a promotional knickknack from the car dealership – sitting on the passenger's seat, so Macaulay wore it pulled down around his eyebrows. He'd also been lucky enough to have left the fleece hiking jacket he'd appropriated from Fienhage's entryway closet in the sports car.

His Ka-Bar Mark 2 sat in its sheath in the jacket's breast pocket.

After smashing free of Fienhage's garage, he'd initially steered the Porsche toward the township of Proviso in order to make it to his storage shed so he could swap out the Porsche with the aged Saturn he had parked there. Then Macaulay realized just how screwed he was. Though the key to opening his individual storage unit was a five-digit combo, he didn't have his magnetized key card to gain entrance to the rental facility or, lacking that, the fake ID he would need to bluff his way inside.

Goddammit, he cursed internally as he exited the freeway – he had a thousand bucks and a change of clothes in the Saturn's trunk. When the investigators got around to searching his house, as Macaulay knew would happen sooner rather than later, they'd find his key card as well as a handful of fake IDs, amongst other items of value, stuffed behind an air-vent cover in his office wall.

With the Proviso rental facility out of play, Macaulay had pulled the sports car into the parking lot at a strip mall lot, closed his eyes, and rubbed at his temples.

That's when it occurred to him – a way out of this vice-grip.

And a most-ironic manner of escape at that.

Macaulay took Dr Fienhage's smartphone out of his pocket, tapped a few words into Google, and there it was – topping the list of results. Entering *Cory Pratt* and *Dogs* into the search engine came back with something called the *COR Canine Training Academy*. Macaulay tapped open the website and, sure enough, there was a picture of Cory Pratt in front of what appeared to be a room in a warehouse leading a dog obedience class. And there she was, sitting at Pratt's feet – the goddamned mutt that had sunk her teeth deep into his elbow at the side of Dr Fienhage's swimming pool.

A second later Macaulay scored a minor victory filled with all kinds of potential.

Pratt's Canine Training Academy website included a Contact page, and the Contact page included an address in Buffalo Grove. Macaulay jotted down Pratt's address on his forearm, and then left the Porsche long enough to drop Dr Fienhage's powered-up cell phone into the truck bed of a nearby F-150, just as he'd seen done in countless movies.

No one would see this coming.

Brother and Sister Pratt had destroyed his plans for a reunification with his half-brother, Carson, in Pennsylvania, just as they'd fucked up his night in Broadview. It almost brought a smile to his face as he drove to the Walmart in Wheeling and abandoned the good doctor's sports car.

Cory Pratt was a young man in a business where a portion of his clientele likely paid in cash. Hmm, perhaps young Pratt might have a little something lying about with which to replenish Macaulay's missing backpack of cash. Either way, he would get the young man's ATM PIN and, with any luck, Pratt only used the old Chevy heap of shit to cart his dogs around to training sessions. With any luck, young Pratt would have a young man's car tucked away in the garage at his home in Buffalo Grove.

Macaulay dropped his burrito wrapper into the garbage bin, took his half-drunk carton of pop and went to the counter to ask the cashier if he could use their phone to call a cab as his car had broken down. That shouldn't be a problem – Macaulay found people liked to help. Pratt's house was less than three miles away. His twenty-seven dollars should be more than enough to get him there with some left over for a reasonable tip.

He'd have the cab driver drop him off at the nearest cross street, of course. He couldn't imagine Pratt beating him there from Wilmette, not after the debacle at Dr Fienhage's house and all that would entail for the young dog handler, but better safe than sorry. Plus, he'd not want any prying eyes to spot him being dropped off in front of Pratt's home.

He suspected he'd get there with plenty of time to get set up in the dog handler's backyard; after all, Pratt would want to let the dogs out a final time before going to bed . . . and Macaulay would be there waiting for him.

Even if he took his own sweet time as the two of them worked their way toward young Master Pratt's kernel of truth, Macaulay would have at least a day's head start, maybe even two, before that meddling sister-cop of Pratt's stopped by to find out why Cory wasn't answering his phone or returning her calls.

If only he could be there to witness her reaction when she beheld what had become of her younger brother.

FIFTY-FOUR

I didn't get home until midnight.

And thank God at that – I thought I'd have to notify Social Security to have my retirement checks forwarded to Dr Fienhage's residence.

Crystal chose to hitch a ride to the station with another detective, not caring that she still wore too-large sport sandals, some stranger's sweat bottoms, and my dusty old jean jacket. She told me not to wait up – spoiler alert: I wasn't planning to – and that she'd be home at quarter past whenever.

Alice and Rex were both antsy, and they danced around my legs as I stood in front of the open refrigerator, weighing my options. They wanted to go outside for their final sniff and pee of the evening, but I was hungry as hell so I grabbed a pack of hot dogs, mustard, as well a bottle of Rolling Rock. Considering the day's events, I figured I'd earned a beer. I flicked the light on the range above the stove and tore open the hot dogs packet, shook four of them on to a microwavable plate, and then surrendered to the canine terrorists' demands.

'All right, already,' I said and led Alice and Rex out of the kitchen, across the hardwood floor and to the door that led down the stairs, down into my domain. 'But you two'd better take long-ass pisses because I plan on sleeping in.'

We took the carpeted steps as I performed mental gymnastics. We had an orientation session in Oak Park at ten o'clock in the morning. I factored in an hour drive, probably less as it wouldn't be rush hour. So, conceivably, I could sleep until about eight fifty. Considering the *sensitivities* of my morning clientele, it would behoove me to take a morning shower, but that would cut into my slumber; however – a quick sponge bath, a dousing in cologne, and a fresh pair of jeans and shirt should do the trick.

The three of us hit the lower level – my man cave – and the dogs scampered across the family room to the sliding glass door that opened to the backyard, their domain. I crossed the room with visions of hot dogs and beer dancing about in my head, flipped the lock on the sliding door, switched on the exterior light, and slid open the door as Alice and Rex darted outside, spun about, and began to growl.

Macaulay's first blow caught me square in the mouth, hard. I tripped backward, hit the coffee table, and wound up on my ass. Macaulay was now inside, kicking at the gap between the sliding glass and the doorframe, forcing my dogs to stay outside as he shoved the door shut. Rex yelped in pain as I shoved myself up from the floor, but then Macaulay was on me, a fist hammering at my stomach. I tried sucking air, couldn't, and figured this was all she wrote as he slipped around me, the blade of his knife up against my throat, drawing a trickle of blood, as my dogs howled outside the basement door.

'You'd better shut them up,' Macaulay said. 'Or I'll open the door enough for them to jam their heads in . . . then I'll stab their eyes out.'

FIFTY-FIVE

W e'd reached an uneasy truce.

Macaulay pretended he wasn't going to kill me . . . and I pretended to believe him. But he knew that I knew that he knew that I knew – or however the saying went. After all, we'd both been part of Special Agent Surratt's task force, and we were both *intimately* aware of his modus operandi. I wondered what had occurred during the Dead Night Killer's midnight visits . . . and now I was gaining firsthand knowledge.

My deepest concern was what my sister would find when she came home from work – when she eventually came downstairs to check on me.

And how it would haunt Crystal for the rest of her life.

After I commanded my dogs to settle, they both sat in front of the sliding glass door, staring in at us with the occasional whine by Alice or whimper by Rex. Off-balance, and with his blade to my throat, Macaulay marched me into the furnace room, spotted all the items sitting atop my workbench, and said, 'I knew a guy like you would have a ton of duct tape.'

Upon returning to the family room, his fist slammed into my stomach, once again knocking the air out of me. As though he were a rodeo champ roping a prize steer, he bound my ankles with a couple yards of duct tape. I lay on the carpeting, panting for breath, as he disappeared into my bedroom. A second later he dragged out my desk chair and asked, 'You sleep down here?'

I sucked enough air into my lungs to say, 'Fuck you.'

'Wrong answer,' he replied, kicking me in the side of my head. Alice and Rex howled and spun and clanked against the sliding glass door as though trying to smash their way inside.

An instant later I was in the chair, duct tape circling my torso, fastening me in place.

'They're doing it again?' Macaulay said and held his knife in front of my eyes – the implication clear.

I stared at my pups, mouthed 'Stop,' and made a ceasing motion with my right hand.

Alice and Rex sat back down.

'You really don't want me to worry about neighbors calling the cops,' he said. 'Now, do you want it in the stomach again? Or the face?'

I shook my head. Both my face and abdomen throbbed in pain, and the coppery taste of blood lingered in my mouth.

'Well then – hands out front.'

Macaulay bound my wrists just as he'd done my ankles, and then he tossed the roll of duct tape over his shoulder as though it were an afterthought.

That was the moment I became completely defenseless.

'Sorry about the fisticuffs, Cory. May I call you Cory?' he asked rhetorically. 'You see, I'm never able to let my hair down until we achieve this point.' Macaulay swung Dad's old recliner around to face me and plopped down. 'Shall we try the Q and A again? Do you sleep down here?'

I shook my head.

'The bed's not made.'

'I'll sleep down here when the dogs are sick, so I can get them outside before they barf on the carpet,' I said, praying he'd think I lived alone.

'But the bed's not made.'

I shrugged. 'I'm a guy.'

'You should still make it,' Macaulay said. 'Neatness is next to godliness.'

'I use it more as an office than a guest room.'

Macaulay crossed his legs and continued, 'This is a bit awkward for me, Cory. I hate discussing financial matters with anyone – a bit tacky, don't you think? – but you and your sister took a certain something from me and, financially speaking, it's left me in a *vulnerable* position.'

'I looked in the backpack at the doctor's house.'

'Well, then you know.' He tapped the flat of the blade against a kneecap. 'I imagine your training academy deals in cash transactions, right?'

I nodded. 'Some of my customers pay in cash.'

'I imagine a young guy like you not wanting to report all of those cash transactions to Uncle Sam,' he said. 'A guy like you might want some *walking-around* money.'

It occurred to me where he was going with this. 'I don't do that, but I have some petty cash in a desk drawer in there,' I said, nodding toward my office-slash-bedroom. 'I use it to make change for the customers who pay in cash.'

Macaulay was back in the office-slash-bedroom an instant later, rifling through the desk drawers. He came out with my laptop under an arm and thumbing through the envelope of petty cash with his hands. 'Cory, Cory, Cory,' he said as he sat himself back down in the reclining chair. 'There's only enough in here to get me to the end of your driveway.'

'That's almost three hundred dollars.'

'A lot of inflation lately – three hundred doesn't go as far as it used to,' he replied. 'What are we going to do about this, Cory?'

As long as I kept him talking, I figured, it'd keep him from killing. 'I've got fourteen grand in a savings account.'

'That's the spirit, Cory,' Macaulay replied. 'Now we're talking.'

Fifteen minutes later he looked up from my commandeered laptop. I'd provided him my bank codes so he could see I hadn't been lying about the fourteen thousand dollars. If I didn't survive the night, the least of my concerns would be Harper Community College not receiving the second half of their tuition. I'd given

Macaulay my PIN number as well and he'd appropriated the debit card from my wallet. 'How much does your bank allow in a single ATM withdrawal?'

'I have no idea. I only grab about forty bucks at a time.'

'I shall find out.' He tossed my laptop on to the couch, and then glanced around the basement family room as though for the first time.

Macaulay had already taken a quick lap around the main level in order to peek in the garage. He'd spotted Crystal's Honda HR-V next to my Silverado pickup, returned with a grin on his face, and asked where I kept the keys. I sent him to the drawer in the kitchen where my sister and I kept our spare keys in case either of us needed to take or move the other's vehicle. I listened as he rummaged about in the drawer, as he walked down the hallway, as he again opened the door into the garage. Macaulay must have clicked the key fob as I heard a corresponding beep emit from Crystal's HR-V.

After that he'd come back downstairs to work my laptop and worm his way into my bank account. But now I watched as the wheels spun behind his eyes, and suspicion spread across his features. He scratched at a cheek and said, 'I suppose the truck's a tax write-off.'

I half-nodded.

'Don't look so glum, Cory,' he said. 'I'll abandon the Honda in a couple of days – you'll have it back in tiptop shape, but riddle me this,' he looked me in the eyes, 'how's a guy like you afford an HR-V and a house like this?'

I said nothing.

'Forgive my forwardness – and don't get me wrong, a dog handler is an *honorable* profession – but a home like this in Buffalo Grove has got to be what? Four hundred grand, maybe more?'

'I inherited it.'

'What?'

'My parents died . . . and I inherited the house.'

Macaulay stared at me a moment and said, 'I'm sorry to hear that, but what about your sister? Didn't she get anything?'

I cleared my throat. 'I pay Crystal six hundred a month for her half of the house, and will probably be doing that for the next hundred years.'

We sat in silence a minute before he asked, 'When did your parents die?'

'When I was in high school.'

'Both at the same time?'

I nodded and cleared my throat again, getting a little choked up as I always do when I think about that night. 'They were in a car accident my junior year.'

'So, the two of you were orphaned?'

I felt my eyes moisten. 'We weren't exactly children,' I said, 'but if you mean *deprived of parents*, then yes – we were orphaned.'

Macaulay leaned forward in his chair. 'Tell me more.'

FIFTY-SIX

C rystal kicked off Cory's old set of sport sandals and left them on the front stoop. Hopefully, it would rain over what little remained of the evening and give them a good soaking. She turned and tossed a hand in the air at Detective Allen Franks, who was already backing his Toyota Camry out of the driveway. Her CPD colleague had been kind enough to extend an already lengthy day another half-hour by dropping her off in Buffalo Grove before heading to his home in Deerfield.

It was quarter to two in the morning. Crystal was exhausted; she'd even nodded off a few minutes in Franks's Camry, while Franks was talking – hopefully, he wasn't too offended, but she'd been too weary to fight it off. She'd be in bed in five minutes; first, though, she was going to have a smoke. Health warnings be damned . . . if a day like this didn't merit a cigarette, she didn't know what would.

Crystal slowly opened the front door and stepped gently on to the floor runner. The last thing she wanted to do was rouse Cory. He'd had a hell of a day, too, and had earned a good night's sleep. Considering her on-again, off-again relationship with Jason Clarke – Jay-C – Crystal had racked up considerable practice sneaking in late at night. She and Jay-C often found themselves slinking about inside the house she shared with her brother after a late night of dinner or drinks, and doing their best to keep from giggling as they slipped off their shoes and snuck up the steps leading to her wing of the castle.

Of course Jay-C was gone – forever this time as it'd ended badly last spring, probably her fault – but Crystal still remembered where to step to avoid blatant creaks in the flooring or egg on any groans of the old house settling at night. Cory lived in the basement – his swinging bachelor pad as they called it – and more than once he'd marched up the steps to register a complaint whenever she'd been fluttering about the kitchen or had the main-level TV on too loud when he'd been trying to catch some shut-eye.

Of course, Cory was more shut-in than swinging bachelor. He'd had that one relationship in high school, around the time of their parents' death, and then a handful of blind dates over the intervening years, most forced upon him by old high school chums who had themselves since faded into the woodwork. None of the blind dates ever amounted to anything, and Crystal worried about her little brother, more so since he'd shared with her the remorse he'd been lugging around since the night Mom and Dad died.

Crystal thought it a good thing Cory was going back to school. He'd be around people his own age.

And, hopefully, there'd be a girl.

And, hopefully, there'd be a spark.

Crystal hit a creak in the floor halfway through her trek to the kitchen. She'd forgotten that spot and stood still, as though she were traipsing a minefield. After a couple seconds of silence she continued on her journey toward the cookie jar on the kitchen countertop. Crystal wasn't interested in eating cookies at this time of night. The jar was where she stashed her box of Newport 100's.

Yes, she'd eventually quit smoking altogether . . . just not tonight.

Cory must have been so exhausted he'd forgotten to turn off the light over the stove. At least it kicked off enough of a soft glow to keep her from bumbling about in the dark. Crystal shook a cigarette out into her hand, grabbed the book of matches, and tiptoed the ten remaining steps to the sliding glass door that led out to the deck. She flipped the lock and slid open the door about three inches – all she needed to blow the smoke into the backyard – when a delicate little hum caught her attention. It was coming from nearby, directly below her in fact, and Crystal recognized the noise.

Alice was outside, and she was softly whining.

FIFTY-SEVEN

Macaulay was good.

It was as if he were lulling me into some kind of trance or spell . . . like a cobra before it struck. Tears had fallen, my face was wet, but the words poured out of me like water through a strainer. I told Macaulay everything about the night my parents died. Everything. And I felt an odd sense of relief wash over me as I confessed my guilt and shame and regret to the homicidal madman perched in the chair before me.

I knew who Macaulay was . . . and I knew how the evening was going to end . . . and, for unexplainable reasons, I no longer cared.

But then I heard a nearly soundless creak from the floor above . . . and I knew my sister was home.

Macaulay hadn't noticed. He continued staring my way, giving me time in case I had anything else to add. Finally, Macaulay said, 'If that's the ice-storm I remember, I slipped on my walkway and damned near put a chip in my thigh.'

'The entire city was an ice-skating rink that night,' I said, engaging Macaulay, wanting his attention focused on me in case Crystal made another sound.

'Well, unless I'm mistaken, you're not in charge of the weather,' he replied. 'Are you in charge of the weather, Cory?'

I shook my head.

'And you're not *secretly* the head of the Illinois Department of Transportation, are you?'

I shook my head again.

Macaulay collected his thoughts and said four words, 'Then that leaves biology.'

'Biology?' I stared at him, truly confused by what he'd just said, but at the same time alert for any movement from the floor above us. If Macaulay overhears my sister scampering about upstairs, I'll scream to warn her, and he'll kill me. If I hear Crystal heading up the steps to go to bed, I'll also scream, as I suspect after he's done with me, Macaulay will be staying here the night and would eventually stumble on to her.

'You were seventeen and you had this plan – a good plan, by the way – to get rid of your parents so you could be alone with your best gal, but then they figured it out.' Macaulay took a breath and continued, 'I don't mean to be crass. Loris Renn – you remember Agent Renn, of course – well, Loris would find a more cultured way to phrase it, but your parents wrecked your night of *amore* with your girlfriend. Of course you were angry – you got cock blocked. What red-blooded seventeen-year-old boy wouldn't get pissed off and spout all sorts of things he didn't mean?'

Another tear streamed down my face.

I'd heard nothing more from upstairs, and began to think my mind had played tricks on me.

'Like I said, Cory, it's biology. And you want to know something else – your parents were young once, they knew exactly what you were up to. I bet they laughed their ass off about it on the way to the movie theater.'

I blinked back more tears. 'It's not that simple.'

Macaulay shrugged. 'Tell me about it. I had a basket case for a mother and, well, you met my *dear old Dad* tonight – the man never wanted anything to do with me.' Macaulay added, 'I'd have *killed* for parents like yours.' Macaulay leaned forward, knife gripped in his right hand. 'Their deaths weren't that long after Christmas, were they, Cory?'

I shook my head.

'Do you remember what they gave you for Christmas that year?'

'A snowboard,' I said, not sure where he was going with this.

'Wow – snowboards are pricy. I bet they loved you,' he said. 'Yet in these dreams of yours, they never say anything, right? They just stare at you?'

I nodded.

'These are your dreams, Cory – *your dreams*; you're the wizard behind the curtain, inserting whatever kind of judgement or condemnation that you've crafted into their eyes.' He thought for another second. 'Can you do me a big favor?'

I nodded again, slowly.

'I think you'll like this exercise. Picture back to that Christmas morning, Cory, OK? Picture yourself unwrapping that big old gift you found under the tree.'

'OK,' I said.

'How did your parents react when you opened the snowboard?'

'They smiled,' I said. 'Happy because I was happy – they were . . . content.'

I got the distinct impression my session with David Macaulay was coming to an end. For some reason my mind flashed to a bird barely escaping from the jaws of a cat, and how happy the bird must feel as it made its way to freedom, not knowing the bacteria it acquired from the cat's mouth is toxic. The bird thinks it's escaped the jaws of death, but, in fact . . . it's not going to live.

'I'd like you to close your eyes now, Cory, and I'd like you to think about that Christmas morning. Picture the scene around the tree. Visualize how content and joyful the family looked that day. Can you do that, Cory?' he said. 'Can you do that for me?'

FIFTY-EIGHT

Crystal turned to shout for Cory to let the pups in when she noticed a plate of hot dogs, a bottle of mustard and a beer sitting near the sink.

So Cory's still up?

She glanced back toward the entryway, from where she'd come. The bathroom door was open, no light was on. She took a few steps and peeked into their mostly forgotten dining room – the place was dark, no one in there. Crystal headed back to the kitchen, looking about the main-level's living room – all dark, no motion, no Cory.

Strange.

She touched Cory's beer. Not as cold as it should be if it'd been recently taken from the fridge. The hot dogs lacked the shriveled-microwaved look to them. Nor had they been doused in mustard, which was Cory's personal preference.

She glanced around again.

What the hell?

On the male tidiness scale from one to ten, Cory ranked a solid six. Sure, her brother may not load the dishwasher as much as she'd have preferred, but at least the dishes made their way into the sink, with the bulk of them rinsed off. There's no way Cory came home, set up a plate of food, grabs himself a beer, then goes downstairs to let the dogs out, and then says, 'Screw it' and goes to bed.

Crystal realized she was tiptoeing, as though she still didn't want to rouse Cory in case he'd fallen asleep, as she made her way across the hardwood floor toward the door leading down to the basement. The door was open a few inches – Cory always shuts it tight at night, so Alice or Rex won't wander upstairs and get into any kind of canine mischief – and she stood off to one side, peeking down. Steps covered in taupe-colored carpeting led down to Cory's dominion. The staircase dead-ended on a bottom stoop, thus forcing you to turn right and take a final step down into the family room.

Lights were on down there, but that wasn't what disturbed Crystal.

What disturbed Crystal were the hushed voices.

Suddenly, she felt as though her own house were haunted as she slowly swung open the basement door another foot, just enough for her to slip through the gap.

'*Happy because I was happy – they were . . . content.*'

That was her brother, a dry monotone, a tenor in which she'd never heard him speak.

'*I'd like you to close your eyes now, Cory, and I'd like you to think about that Christmas morning. Picture the scene around the tree. Visualize how content and joyful the family looked that day.*'

Her blood froze . . . and her hand dropped for her pistol, her holstered Glock now stuffed inside the right-hand pocket of the jean jacket Cory had loaned her at Dr Fienhage's house, a point in time that now seemed eons ago.

Crystal entered the staircase, barefooted, Glock 22 in hand, aimed forward, angled down. She thought of bounding the steps all at once, and hitting the basement like a SWAT team, but she knew if David Macaulay heard her approaching, Cory would be killed.

Instead, Crystal crept down each step, off to the side, near the railing, hoping to avoid any creaks that might give away her presence.

'*Can you do that, Cory?*' She heard Macaulay say to her brother, and she prayed she had five more seconds. '*Can you do that for me?*'

FIFTY-NINE

'Can *you* do me a *favor* first?' I asked.

Macaulay was enjoying himself too much, drawing it out as though savoring the final drops from a bottle of a rare wine. When you stripped everything away, Macaulay preyed on human feelings – he was an emotional vampire – and I needed to drag our warped session out just a few moments longer.

Macaulay leaned back a few inches. 'Of course I can, Cory,' he said with what appeared to be genuine human warmth. 'Name it.'

'Alice and Rex,' I said, nodding toward my two pups, sitting outside the glass door, Alice softly whimpering. 'They don't need to see anymore.' My voice trembled. 'Can you shut the curtains?'

I've spent most of my life in this basement, especially after Mom and Dad died, lying alone in bed, unable to sleep and staring up at the ceiling tiles. And, over time, I became well acquainted with every single sound this old house makes, from when the furnace, water softener or air conditioner kicks on, to someone taking a shower, to a toilet being flushed, to timers going off in the kitchen, to the garage door opening, to Crystal sneaking about with that old boyfriend of hers, doing their best not to wake me.

The reason I needed to string this out a few more moments was what I hoped I'd just heard from the stairwell. The tiniest of groans – the sixth step down, I was certain of it – that no one would ever notice if they'd not gone up and down those very steps a hundred times a week. I've thought about fixing step six, but that would call for ripping up the carpeting in order to screw down the board.

Macaulay looked into my eyes. 'Of course I can do that, Cory,' he said. 'And I'm so grateful you felt comfortable enough to ask.' He stood up from the recliner. 'We've made such progress tonight, haven't we?'

I watched as Macaulay crossed the family room and examined Mom's old drapes as they drooped limply from the curtain rod on faux wood clip rings. He pinched a piece of the blue drape and slid it sideways, covering the entire length of the sliding glass door, blocking my dogs from seeing in.

But I also watched as Crystal stepped out from the stairwell and on to the basement carpeting. She glanced my way, a look of concern spreading across her features, then anger, and finally ice as she set her body into a Weaver shooting stance.

Macaulay turned back to face me, spotted Crystal, jolted as though stung by a bee, and then his eyes returned to mine. 'One of us hasn't been completely honest, have they, Cory?'

'I may have fudged the part about living here alone,' I said.

Crystal cut through the shit. 'Any chance of you dropping the knife, Macaulay, and lying face down on the floor?'

'Hmm,' he replied, his attention on the blade he held vertically in front of him. 'It appears I'm at a crossroads.'

'Drop the goddamned knife.'

'Here's the crazy thing, Crystal, about liver cancer,' he replied, twisting the knife in front of him. 'No signs or symptoms in the early stage . . . but guess what?'

Neither of us replied, and Macaulay continued, 'I've not had the greatest of appetites this past week, and, were I to be honest, there's been a certain pain in my abdomen.'

'I don't give a shit,' Crystal said. 'Put the knife down – right fucking now!'

Macaulay's eyes turned to stone. I saw his fingers stiffen around the handle of his commando knife . . . and I knew there'd be only one way his blade would find its way to the floor.

Macaulay lunged.

Crystal fired four rounds.

Point blank. Center mass.

SIXTY

Two Weeks Later

'He did not.'

'Yes he did,' I insisted. 'Jund was interviewed on the *Today Show* this morning – of course you came out sounding all golden – but he referred to me as your *sniffer dog brother*.'

If you channel-surf, it'd be impossible to have missed CID Director Roland Jund. If you clicked on CNN or NBC, there he'd be, pontificating on all things David Macaulay. If you switched over to CBS or Fox News, there'd be Jund, waxing poetic about ex-FBI Director Mitchell Westbrook.

Crystal chuckled and said, 'I've seen him interviewed and he's been very complimentary about both of us.'

'I keep telling you – the man has no clue what my name is.' I was in front of the TV, roughhousing with Alice and Rex as Crystal and I waited for the oven buzzer to announce the sausage take-and-bake pizza was ready. 'I don't mind being a *sniffer dog*,' I said to my two pups. 'That makes me one of you.'

'What else did Jund have to say?'

I stood up and brushed dog hairs off my pants. 'He believes Westbrook worked to sabotage the original investigation. Jund said he had a guy working the case back then, some agent that specializes in serial killers; he referred to the guy as his *hot knife through cold butter*. Anyway, Jund said Westbrook stiff-armed the investigation, yanked this agent off the case and stuck him on some lesser matter.'

'So Westbrook was pulling strings behind the scenes.'

I nodded. 'Jund said he was *startled* at the time but figured it was due to Westbrook being new in the directorship position, having recently been confirmed by the Senate. He never in a million years thought it was because of something insane like this.' I looked at my sister. After all, she was my main source of gossip. 'Have you heard anything?'

The ex-FBI director was currently out on bond – his case pending, awaiting trial. The ex-director had hired both a dream team of attorneys and PR people. So far he was sticking to the story that he had no idea what in hell his oldest son had been up to until he'd been attacked in the entryway of Dr Fienhage's home. Westbrook swears Crystal and I saved his life that day. He swears Macaulay was on the verge of exacting some kind of twisted vengeance when we arrived.

However, a variety of items discovered at David Macaulay's home in Western Springs begged to differ with Mitchell Westbrook's account.

'I heard his wife left him.' Crystal peeked inside the oven. 'And you already know how Westbrook had been secretly working out of Chicago since before Agent Renn's murder.'

I nodded again. 'What do you think he was doing here?'

'Maybe trying to stop his son . . . maybe trying to kill him.' Crystal shrugged. 'Or maybe he was covering things up.'

'I read they found Westbrook's car parked up the hill from Fienhage's house, so he lied about taking an Uber there.'

'Yeah – his lawyers will be working overtime.'

The buzzer rang and Crystal asked, 'Do you want Tabasco sauce on yours?'

'Goes without saying.' I trekked into the kitchen and washed my hands in the sink while my sister performed surgery with the pizza cutter. 'So,' I said, 'how did it go with Dr Swanson?'

Dr Andrea Swanson, a Chicago-based psychologist, works with CPD officers after they've been involved in fatal shootings. Crystal had attended her second appointment today.

My sister stopped slicing the pizza and said, 'Went well, Cor. She and I just shoot the breeze. And I do feel a little bit better afterward.'

'That's because CPD picks up the bill.'

Crystal resumed slicing. 'You know they'd cover it for you, too. After all, we did catch the freaking Dead Night Killer.'

'Nope.' I shook my head. 'No more *sessions* for me.'

'Dr Swanson only uses duct tape under extreme circumstances.' She pointed toward the fridge. 'Grab the beer.'

We sat at the kitchen table. I lathered Tabasco sauce over my first slice of pizza. Alice and Rex came over – probing our defenses – but I shook my head firmly and they sauntered away.

'Did they finish the carpeting today?'

'Yeah,' I replied. We now have brand-new carpeting in the basement family room. Mom would be pleased. 'The guy went on and on about how it's super stain-resistant. Guess we'll see what the pups make of that.'

Alice and Rex and I had been sleeping in my old upstairs room while the basement had, at first, remained a crime scene – with all sorts of forensic investigators coming and going – and, after that, it'd just been gross.

The old carpeting had proved to be anything but stain-resistant.

We ate in silence for a while. I sipped at my Rolling Rock and then stole another slice of sausage. Though Alice and Rex were in the other room, both stared our way. In all the years of Crystal and me snarfing down pizza, they'd never once gotten even the smallest of pieces, not even the crust.

I guess hope springs eternal.

We had been sitting in the front yard early that next morning, my dogs and I, breathing fresh air and staying out of the way, when several members of the Cook County Medical Examiner's Office hauled David Macaulay out from our house in a post-mortem bag.

I turned away as they loaded him into their van.

'I've been meaning to ask you, Cory,' Crystal said, and put down her fork. 'Have you been having any dreams lately?'

'I had a hell of a doozy starring Macaulay the other night,' I said, but I knew what my sister was driving at and shook my head. 'Nothing with Mom or Dad.'

She glanced from her glass of Rolling Rock to me. 'I know you have these feelings of—'

'It's OK, Crystal,' I interrupted as gently as possible. 'It helped to share those *thoughts* with you rather than keeping them all stuffed inside and buried . . . but it also helps to talk about them. You know, favorite memories, the trips we took as kids, all the joking around, how Dad couldn't cook worth a shit.'

Crystal laughed. 'He really couldn't.'

I took another sip of beer. 'Is it still too early?'

Crystal shook her head. 'It's not too early as much as it's just plain weird, Cor. Coming up with some cheesy James Bond line I'd have said that night,' she nodded toward the door to the basement, 'if I'd had time to think of one.'

'How dare you call James Bond cheesy.'

'You know Macaulay didn't give me time to say anything before he lunged, right?'

'I know, but if he had.'

'OK, in that case,' Crystal got her game face on and continued, 'I'd have said, "You picked the wrong place, Pal. The house always wins."'

I chuckled and said, 'I don't think you'll need any more sessions with Dr Swanson.'

9 781448 314591